A NIGHT AT THE OPERA

A Night at the Opera

A NOVEL BY
RAY SMITH

BIBLIOASIS

RENDITIONS

BIBLIOASIS RENDITIONS

Library and Archives Canada Cataloguing in Publication

Smith, Ray, 1941-
A night at the opera / Ray Smith.

First published: Erin, Ont. : Porcupine's Quill, 1992.
ISBN 978-1-897231-11-1

I. Title.

PS8587.M583N54 2007   C813'.54   C2007-901322-8

COVER IMAGE:
Detail from "Provincetown" by Ken Tolmie

PRINTED AND BOUND IN CANADA

voor lieve

Anja

die het stem gehoord heeft

Part One

THE SMALL CITY of Waltherrott was not heavily damaged in the war, but there was work enough to command the attentions of the citizens for several years. The bomb debris around the Bahnhof and the marshalling yard was cleared away so that the trains ran smoothly and on schedule again. The high peaked roofs and the painted, figured, half-timbered fronts along the winding, climbing streets of the Altstadt were made like new – or like old, as some wags suggested. In its 1958 edition, Baedeker terms this quarter 'unremarkable,' while Frommer's *Germany on Five Dollars a Day* (how long ago that was!) says 'it's cute but you pay for it.' The citizens ignored these slights and continued their restorations. Gradually the shell damage to the precious buildings around the Opernplatz was repaired and the gold leaf restored to the statues, the wreaths, and the inscriptions. To Opernplatz the Michelin Green Guide then as now granted only the one star which betokens 'Interesting.' The stark grey Cathedral Church of St. Adalbert on its hill ('as jejeune as it is dreary' – Fielding) had lost a stained glass window of indifferent virtue; it was replaced by a handsome modern one depicting the saint's gruesome martyrdom. Atop the Böttgerberg, the Waltherburg had been a noble ruin before the war; it was left for later, as was the once fashionable but now derelict spa of St. Irmtraud in the Bergwald.

Then the Economic Miracle brought the new light industrial suburb of Sonnfeld, and in turn new housing estates sprawled away toward the Bergwald and across the meadows down the River Lohbach. By the late sixties, brushed stainless steel shop fronts and smoked glass windows were appearing along fashionable Bahnhofstraße, and it could no longer be doubted: good times had come to Waltherrott. So it was that Herr Bürgermeister Krankheit and the city councillors decided (with some prodding from their wives) that the bus and tram system, which had grown higgledy-piggledy, should be studied, rationalized, brought into line with the other perfections of their city:

anything to get rid of those smelly diesels
too many transfers
too long waiting for
and perhaps pedestrian malls in the Altstadt
vote for an U-Bahn: let's think big
U-Bahn? Hardly practical in a city the size of

But the deliberations, the dreams of such legislative bodies, while they are a necessary part of affairs, do not in themselves get things done. Like the baroque-rococo opera house with its gilding, its frothing plasterwork, its famous ceiling with *The Inspiration of Carl Maria von Stumpf*, so the lives of the citizens are pondered, their aspirations expressed in the vaulting sentiments of these speeches. But just as the opera needs carpenters and electricians, ticket-takers and ushers, stagehands and seamstresses to bring the production to its glory, so the grand visions of the councillors need diligent bureaucrats to translate them into reality. Herr Bürger-meister Krankheit and the Councillors took twenty minutes to wave hands toward the future; after a further twenty minutes of other business, they retired to the Councillors' Library for steins of Renatenbräu and heaping plates of Walthers Versuchung. The next morning the senior officials of the Transportation Board, the Waltherrott Verkehrsverbund, gathered in the director's office and spent several hours deciding who should direct the project of trans-forming the dream into rails, routes, and tramcars.

Herr Bach, Superintendent of Traffic Circulation, thought he was the man for the job. 'I am, after all, in charge of the entire net-work, the many strands radiating out, the relations between all parts of the network,' he argued.

'The major expenditure will be in the purchase of new equip-ment,' Herr Stahlmeister pointed out. 'As Superintendent of Equip-ment, I should be in charge.'

'The point of what you are saying is not equipment, but expenditure,' said Herr Wechsel the Comptroller. 'I should be in charge.'

'The money will be spent in any case,' said Herr Wassertor, Manager of Public Relations and Advertising. 'And we are all confident it will be well spent. What is important is that the councillors, the press, and the public must see that it is well spent, that the work we do fulfils their vision of what is right. That is why I should be in charge.'

They all restated their positions, suggested weaknesses in the arguments of the others. Through it all, the Director of the WVV, Herr Einzelturm, sat immobile. A stolid and austere man, he did not leap to action, but thought things through in an orderly fashion first. He was perhaps unimaginative and a touch too methodical, but when public money and the public good are at stake, it is not wrong to be scrupulous. And if Herr Einzelturm was cautious, he was no coward. Now he drew a deep breath and took courage from the swelling of his broad chest. About the table before him, his staff members were becoming more animated in their attempts to prove their cases.

equipment not primary to the
financial but a part of the
public relations are essential, however routing is more
the overall picture
coordination of the various
a dream of a system, the best
yes, exactly, but
I beg to differ, my dear colleague

Herr Director Einzelturm reached under his spectacles; he rubbed his eyes; he cleared his throat.

The others fell silent.

'Gentlemen, you have all made good points. But the main thing is the dream we have of the city of Waltherrott and the contribution which the WVV makes to that dream. It is because of the importance of this project that it must be carried out with the full weight of authority. Because I am the Director, I must take charge.

9

'It is fitting.'

He glanced sadly, sacrificially at each of them.

'It is proper.'

They nodded assent.

And so the great enterprise was under way. The investigative report alone took the better part of a year. The city was examined from a dozen different aspects: traffic flow current and projected, growth of suburbs, seasonal variations; while the needs of schoolchildren and university students, shoppers, merchants, office and factory workers, opera lovers, football fans, and tourists were all considered. Enquiries were sent to other cities for information and suggestions: Stuttgart, Frankfurt, Düsseldorf, Munich, Vienna, Salzburg, Zürich, Copenhagen, Amsterdam, Milan . . . visits by Herr Einzelturm ('Irmtraud, Liebchen, I *must* go to Essen to see about the relationship between the railway and the municipal transportation; it is my duty.') or by his staff ('Why *again* to Paris, Herr Schmetterling?') while equipment manufacturers were invited to submit estimates. Fräulein Farber of the Design Office collected and compared route maps from near and far, while an advisory group from the university departments of sociology and psychology pondered the more abstruse aspects of honour system fare payment.

Herr Einzelturm's direction was sure and steady; in due course the plan was presented to the City Council and, with some amendments, accepted. In the headquarters of the Waltherrott Verkehrsverbund the lights burned into the night, while the commissionaires on the front door became accustomed to saluting the arrivals on weekends. Gradually the various work groups spread from the headquarters to several hastily rented buildings and office floors in the neighbourhood.

For the next ten years the streets of Waltherrott were torn up and re-surfaced, traffic was diverted, squares were in chaos for months, years at a time, and enough dust raised to raise the ire of every shopkeeper and housewife in the town. But as one after another of the six suburban tram terminuses came 'on stream' (as Herr Wassertor's press releases so proudly put it) and as new bus routes were integrated with the trams, the citizens began to notice improvements:

got to the opera twenty minutes earlier than I expected, so I treated myself to an ice and

almost never have to transfer any more, don't you find?

remember having to get that lazy Hans to dust the shelves and the counters every week

having a beer on the terrace at Die Drei Grafen, and the air was so clean that I says, Hildegard, I says, let's have a skinful tonight!

The air, the famous Waltherrottner Luft, was a matter of particular pride to the citizens. For it signified not just the air, renowned indeed for its sparkle and the scent of pine wafting down from the Bergwald, but the spirit, the liveliness, the gaiety of the citizens themselves. Waltherrott, they assured visitors, was a special place, her situation and climate the most salubrious, her architecture the very finest in Germany, while the Waltherrottners were special people, their food and drink, their humour, their spirit superior to that of all other Germans. These claims, accepted as gospel in Waltherrott, were of course genially rejected in every other town and hamlet in the neighbourhood. 'Waltherrotten!' said the mockers, unfairly making a pun out of English; for the 'rott' has nothing to do with decay but is a dialect rendering from 'Rodeland' which signifies rather 'a clearing in the forest,' testimony to the very ancient origins of the city. However, the Waltherrottners returned mock for mock and scorn for scorn; theirs was a fine city, and getting finer all the time:

about Vienna on the TV and that St. Stephen's is very gaudy, isn't it? Our St. Adalbert's, on the other hand

in Australia I think it was and Renatenbräu beat out not only the Munich beers but

their Vichy water and their Perrier and take a flying

says our new WVV is the best in the whole

So the dream took shape. Not all the changes were universally popular, of course. Some streets were widened at the cost of narrower sidewalks and, in a few cases, buildings were torn down to improve the traffic flow or make room for tram stops. But on the whole things were better. If some sidewalks were narrower, the traffic moved more easily; and in turn a number of streets were made into pedestrian malls. The buildings torn down were none of them beautiful and were soon forgotten. Barely remembered in the new age of sleek, otter-like trams were the great slow herds of buses lowing and butting their ways into the city centre in the morning and out from it at night.

And through planned purchasing, with new equipment introduced gradually, with a carefully modulated financing package, and with generous grants from the Federal and State governments, the financial burden proved easier than had been anticipated. Indeed, the strength of the Deutsche mark during the period worked in Waltherrott's favour.

There would not come a time when the entire system would be complete for ever: it would continue to grow, change, need repairs, replacements, adjustments. But Herr Einzelturm could tell Herr Bürgermeister Krankheit and his Council that by the summer of the fourteenth year, the sixth suburban tram terminus, Niedermark, would be 'on stream', and by early August the Opernplatz would be restored to its former grace. Waltherrott would take its place as a model of good administration.

THE DAY BEFORE the official opening, Herr Einzelturm was doing a final inspection of the heart of the new system, and took along Herr Wetzenstein, Director of the Verkehrsverbund of the nearby city of Schwermund. Schwermund had undertaken a similar modernization and the two directors had frequently compared notes. But in his visits to Waltherrott, Herr Wetzenstein had little opportunity to enjoy the beauties of the city – much of what he was interested in consisting of holes in the ground – so Herr Einzelturm offered to show him around.

'Forgive me if I am only practising on you, my friend. Tomorrow, on the great day, I shall have to give a similar tour to the other guests and a run through with you will help me.'

'Forgive you for honouring me with a private tour? On the contrary. Where shall we start?'

'Why not at Bahnhofplatz, where most visitors arrive?'

'Why not, indeed?'

Although the hankering by some city councillors for a vast U-Bahn had been absurd, the WVV had decided that within the central area the tram lines might indeed run below ground for a stretch which would include five stations. The expense would be great, but the benefits would be enormous: below ground, the trams would be out of the way, swift, unheard. The streets above, in a nod toward the increasing Green constituency, could be reserved for pedestrians, and several of the squares, despite the bustle of trams and shops below ground, would be returned to almost medieval peace and congeniality.

'Bahnhofplatz itself allows for taxis and automobiles, but as soon as we enter Bahnhofstraße, we are in the pedestrian zone. As you can see, Frankfurt's vaunted Zeil has nothing on us . . .'

Here was the new Kaufhof, there the C&A, next a McDonald's, then Benetton, Bally, Burger King, Herti, Mövenpick, Nordzee: national and international companies were showing their confidence in Waltherrott.

Now below ground, now mounting again to the surface, the two directors made their way gradually through the city centre. On this hot summer day, Rathausplatz with its ancient façades and the famous clock of the beer drinkers was already filled with tourists sitting at their tables, sipping their lagers, and checking their cameras as they waited for the great noontime display when the figures of the butcher, the baker, the candlestick maker, and their companions would come out of the body of the clock and flourish their steins.

odds are it's early and you're off in the can
better with the zoom
guidebook says the last guy actually moons us and then farts
a bit skunky or something?
the wrong ASA
gross you out, eh, Harv?

Marktplatz, after a century of increasing traffic, and after six years of hoardings, mud, and noise, had for two years already been restored to its original function, and every day cheerful shoppers thronged about the bustling stalls.

'The valley of the Lohbach produces some of the finest meats and vegetables in Germany,' explained Herr Einzelturm. 'This is a well known fact.'

Herr Wetzenstein nodded his agreement, for Schwermund also got its produce from Lohbach valley.

Appropriately, Alte Borse station was austere and business-like in simulated grey granite, reflecting the character of the square above with its functional mix of newly built and renovated office buildings.

'But in a moment we shall come to our proudest square, Opernplatz. You last saw it in the spring, I believe?'

'In April, yes.'

'In April it was a sea of traffic. Now . . .'

Herr Einzelturm and his friend rounded the corner.

'My, yes, it is very handsome, very elegant. I had no idea . . .'

All traffic banished, Opernplatz was a haven for buskers – here one juggled rings, another mimed his poignant tale, a unicyclist amazed the children. The square was alive with people strolling, sitting, sightseeing, smiling, listening to the small band on the balcony of the Stadtoper playing the tunes of Carl Maria von Stumpf, the melodies adding their final sparkle to the Waltherrotner Luft.

'And one can stand here and read the history of the city laid out like an open book, or a museum display. In the fourteenth century, the original Graf Walther vom Faß had a dream of a great city. He raised the walls of the Waltherburg up there on the Böttgerberg. Today the Tourist Office is restoring it. Already there is a restaurant which you'll see tomorrow, and soon the keep and the stables will be an agreeable hotel.

'Graf Walther's first wife, the tragic Irmtraud von Linnen, is commemorated in this building on the east side of the square. It is today the head office of the Von Linnen Versicherungen, but it was built in the eighteenth century as the Residenz of the Counts vom Faß. The design is by Jäger von Erlach, the great architect of Waltherrott. Alas, not many decades after the Residenz was completed the family was forced for dynastic reasons to move to Teschen, where the line quickly died out. Some people mutter about dark deeds off in the east, but most believe they died for want of that!'

Herr Einzelturm pointed toward the elaborate fountain which dominated the centre of Opernplatz. A fearsome mailed warrior turned to glance back toward the castle upon the hill. At his shoulder floated an allegorical lady holding a wreath over his head. Beside him stood a boar with a cross between his tusks, obviously the heraldic beast of the Counts vom Faß: the warrior's helmet was surmounted by a boar's head. The emblazoning of the shield had the two hills of the city, the Böttgerberg with its fortress and the Brustenberg with its Dom dedicated to St. Adalbert of Waltherrott; springing from a bush below was a stream. Herr Einzelturm pointed to where the warrior's sword point was planted in a rock: from the cleft sprang a sparkling runnel.

'The spring is the Renatenquelle,' explained Herr Einzelturm, 'the very waters of which flow from this fountain, the Renatenbrunnen. The waters have been known for centuries as a protective against the ill effects of excessive alcohol, as a cure for stomach problems, gas, stammering, and falling fits. Women have claimed it is proof against certain feminine ills, while promoting fertility, and especially as a guarantee of beautiful daughters. You may have noticed that the women of Waltherrott are remarkably attractive. Some people claim to discern an exotic southern look, the best of Italian glamour blended with buxom German good health.'

'I hadn't noticed, but now that you mention it . . .'

Herr Wetzenstein's impression had actually been of heavy ankles, broad behinds, and sour faces; now he had to admit (to himself) that sallow skin and mustaches were much in evidence.

'As a result, no Waltherrottner would think of crossing the Opernplatz without stopping to imbibe of the miraculous elixir which has so encouraged the health and pleasure of the citizens down the centuries. Fortunately the same spring provides water to the brewery which produces the famous Renatenbräu lager, Walther Alt, and Bergbock. In a few minutes, if you feel so inclined, you must let me stand you a stein.'

'I've never said no to a beer.'

'In the meantime . . .' and Herr Einzelturm bent to take a sip of water; Herr Wetzenstein followed suit and found the water bland and rather flat.

'And,' continued Herr Einzelturm, 'why not have our beer there, in the bar of the Renatenhof? You always stay there, I believe, Herr Wetzenstein?'

'Yes, and I always get a good night's sleep.' Despite the knocking pipes, heavy food, and surly staff.

'So did Goethe.'

'Goethe? In Waltherrott?'

'Yes, he stopped off on his second trip to Italy, "das Land wo die Zitronen blühn," if I may quote the great man. He stood on that balcony just there and declared Waltherrott to be: "Eine anmutige Stadt."'

'Such a compliment!'

'Yes, it was heard by several people, including the Bürgermeister and Fräulein Puppel, the prima donna of the opera.'

'I hadn't realized . . .'

'Unfortunately the remark was not recorded by Goethe's secretary in that he, Eckermann, was apparently attending to a call of nature when it was made.'

'Ah, so . . .' Herr Wetzenstein was, of course, not a scholar, but he rather thought there might be another reason – that Goethe had not in fact been here at all. Surely he had only made one trip to Italy? Waltherrottners were well aware of this scepticism, but they pointed out that if Goethe had made the second trip – and they had no reason to doubt he had – what more logical place to have stopped than here, and what more likely remark to have made than 'Eine anmutige Stadt'?

'And just as the insurance company is named for Graf Walther's first wife, so the hotel is named for his second wife, the fabled beauty, Renate Schönbruster.'

'So one might say the whole of the original family is here.'

'Yes, and even the children, in a sense, for on the third side is the original university building.'

Herr Einzelturm pointed toward the university's columned façade, then turned toward the fourth side of the square.

'And finally, the building which gives the square its name: the Waltherrottner Stadtoper, formerly the Hofoper. Tomorrow evening the entire official party will have the pleasure of attending a gala performance of the masterwork of the city's immortal composer, Carl Maria von Stumpf.'

'I have been looking forward to the occasion.'

'I should think so, for it will be a night to remember: Waltherrottner Luft at its sparkling best! But I promised you a taste of our beer. We can go to the Renatenhof as I suggested, or perhaps you would prefer one of these other places?'

In a charming attempt to make the square more inviting, more gemütlich, each of the four institutions had tables out front and offered a variety of meals or snacks according to inclination and kitchen facilities. The opera offered coffee and bar service, but its specialities were its fantastic ices: Sorbet von Stumpf, Plum Puppel, and the lurid red and orange Ice Waltherrotterdämmerung. The Von Linnen Insurance Company offered substantial if rather boring meals from its staff kitchen, an uninspired but safe choice. The tables in front of the Alte Universität were served from the administration lounge and everything was tasteless, over-priced, and late.

'As I don't know what to expect of these others,' said Herr Wetzenstein, 'I'll leave the choice to you.'

'Then the Renatenhof it shall be.'

Accordingly they took their places on the terrace under the welcoming shade of one of the great oak trees.

'Yes, here we can sit at leisure, drink the finest beer in Germany, sip the delicious wines of Sonnfeld – or even Oberdorfer Sekt, if you have a mind – or drink the richest coffee. We may eat a hearty meal, a light salad, or pick at a bowl of almonds. And talk of the niceties of municipal transport.'

'Now that's living!'

In the event they both ordered hearty plates of Walthers Versuchung, Walther's Temptation, the local speciality consisting of suet sausage with boiled potatoes, red cabbage, and brown beans.

'And all the arrangements for the grand opening are complete?' asked Herr Wetzenstein.

'So far as careful planning is able to make them, yes. Even the weather forecast is good. And Herr Wurmlein, the Intendant, assures us the opera company has never been better.'

The climax of the festivities was to be a gala performance of Carl Maria von Stumpf's masterwork, *Der Hosenkavalier*. It is a comic confection of gently bittersweet romance, mistaken identities, and a pair of miraculous trousers, set in eighteenth century Waltherrott. Never quite accepted into the international repertoire despite successes in a number of far-flung venues (Oulu 1877, Cluj 1881, Saratov 1891, to name but a few) it has always appealed to the people of Waltherrott for its charm and good humour. Its melodies are known and loved throughout the region. It would be a fitting conclusion to the great day, a triumph.

THE WEATHER was indeed warm and sunny. By ten in the morning, the score of dignitaries had gathered in the Rathausplatz where Herr Bürgermeister Krankheit and various officials delivered a number of speeches of unexpected and admirable brevity. All then entered Rathhausplatz station and took the A-Tram out to Niedermark terminus. Two polished new buses transported them up to the Waltherburg for a fine panorama of the city spread out below. WVV personnel pointed out the six terminuses and everywhere the garnet and gold trams and buses could be seen sparkling in the sun as they wended their busy ways across the city. Presently Herr Bürgermeister Krankheit suggested that a feast for the stomach was now in order, 'Although from the windows of the restaurant, we shall be able to continue this feast for the eyes!' When at last they pushed back their chairs, a fleet of limousines was waiting to take the political guests and most of the spouses back to the city centre for shopping or naps as desire dictated. Herr Einzelturm and his staff took charge of those who remained, transportation officials who had been particularly helpful in advising the WVV on its new system. These gentlemen, plus one disconcertingly frank lady from Amsterdam, were taken on a tour of all five underground stations, four of the six tram terminuses, the repair barns, the computerized driver training school, and the central control room or 'centre of nerves', as Herr Einzelturm so amusingly put it.

These intensely professional visits lasted until after four o'clock, and it was a thankful, if fascinated group which climbed the steps of the Renatenhof for a restful two hours before the evening's festivities. Along with admiration for the WVV's sense of overall rationale, its elegant solutions to a number of vexing problems, and its exemplary attention to detail throughout the system (Fräulein Farber's route maps and signs were a shoo-in for an award at the Dortmund Transportation Expo that fall, everyone agreed) the guests were bothered by one tiny anomaly. Mevrouw de Jordaan from Amsterdam put it this way to her husband:

'Interesting? Well, yes, I admit it was, despite the elephantine explanations of Herr Einzelturm. It's not quite the dream scheme he claims it is, although they have done a solid job of it. But how they ever allowed him to make such a spectacle of himself over the station announcements, I'll never know. I suppose the old fool simply insisted.'

Actually, he had not insisted; rather, faced with a seemingly insoluble dilemma, he had shouldered his responsibility. It was an unfortunate choice, but certain aspects of the problem related to matters of civic pride, and this muddied the reasoning. The problem in question was the voice to be used on the sound system which, on trams and buses, announced the next stop, along with transfer options:

Bahnhofplatz. Umsteigen zum Linien B, C, D, 2, 3, 5, 6, 7, und 10. Deutsche Bundesbahn.

Alte Borse. Umsteigen zum Linien B, C, D.

The question of whether or not even to have the announcements was easily answered: given the financial incentives scheme, the equipment was virtually a gift; and every other city of consequence offered its passengers the same courtesy. Next, there was the question of when to bring the recordings 'on stream'. So long as the system was being built, there were changes in routing every month or two, and the recordings would have to be done over and over again. So it was decided that the recordings would first be used when the system was complete, on the day of the grand opening of Opernplatz station. There remained only the question of the voice.

Herr Bach, in charge of traffic circulation, argued that he was the man for the job: 'I am, after all, in charge of the entire network. Who knows better than I do the exact stresses which should be given to each station, each transfer?'

He was tempted but properly reluctant to mention that a certain Fräulein with the Hamburg VV had remarked upon the appealing flow of his voice, the sensuousness of it.

'But your accent, Herr Bach,' objected Herr Stahlmeister. 'The people of Waltherrott would be up in arms if we used your Freie und Hansestadt Hamburg accent. No, I am in charge of equipment; I should be responsible.'

But Herr Stahlmeister's voice, it was carefully agreed, while authentically Waltherrottner, was rather too harsh. In contrast, the voice of Herr Wechsel, the comptroller, was too thin, too tight. Herr Schmetterling's voice was too fluttery, and Herr Wassertor, the director of public relations, was a Mannheimer Bloomäuler, a loud-mouth, and clearly impossible. However, Herr Wassertor had several trenchant suggestions:

'Have we considered a woman's voice? The Frankfurt system uses a woman, and if you go by the voice, she must be built like the coat of arms,' referring to the two mountains of Waltherrott's emblem.

'Yes, of course,' piped up Herr Schmetterling, 'And I know just the woman for the job.'

If the others in his long line of flirtations were anything to go by, she would likely be a pliably drugged art student from the university and incapable of speaking a coherent sentence.

Herr Wassertor made a diplomatic diversion.

'I've been on the Frankfurt system, and the first problem is she has a real bedroom voice: all the men on the trams would be drooling and all the women would be jealous. Second, Frankfurt hired an actress, and it seems clear that . . .'

Consternation. An actress? A professional who, no matter how well trained, would not have the true Waltherrottner Luft in her voice? Herr Wassertor argued with some force – he had in fact promised the job to a certain young woman in return for favours already received – but he could make no headway against his colleagues' reluctance toward the recent fashion for equality of the sexes.

Herr Director Einzelturm reached under his spectacles to rub his eyes; he cleared his throat.

'No. What we want is a voice which is confident but pleasant. Firm but friendly. A fatherly voice.'

'Why not a motherly voice?' muttered Herr Wassertor. 'A sisterly voice?'

'A fatherly voice, exactly,' exclaimed Herr Wechsel. 'But who shall play Papa?'

'Perhaps we should ask the father of the city, in effect,' suggested Herr Bach. 'Surely Herr Bürgermeister Krankheit's voice has all the proper attributes?'

The suggestion had merit, and the others seemed about to adopt it when Herr Einzelturm again slipped his fingers beneath his spectacles. Gradually the others fell silent.

'No, gentlemen, it will not do. While it is true our esteemed Bürgermeister has a fine voice and I am sure would do the job if asked, we may not ask him. It is beneath the dignity of the Bürgermeister to be heard calling out tram stops. That is why, reluctantly, I must do the job myself.'

The others sat silent in shock.

'I am the father of the Waltherrott Verkehrsverbund. I must shoulder my responsibility.

'It is fitting.

'It is proper.'

It was precisely because he was the father of the WVV that the others could think of no way to deflect the formidable, honourable, fatherly Herr Einzelturm from his course. For the fact was that Herr Einzelturm's voice, no matter how he thought it sounded, was ridiculous.

'Thin and reedy,' said Herr Bach in the men's toilet after the meeting.

'Fräulein Farber's voice is more manly,' sneered Herr Stahlmeister as he levered himself back into his trousers.

'And yet,' said Herr Wassertor, 'It also has a sort of hectoring quality which immediately irritates everyone who does not know him well.'

Herr Wechsel scratched his chin.

'The sad truth, gentlemen, is that we are looking for the voice of a kindly father who will put an arm over our shoulders and point out the way; we are going to get the voice of a nagging, quibbling mother-in-law who wags a finger in front of our noses and asks why we don't already know where we're going.'

Although his colleagues were depressed by the accuracy of his description they all managed a smile at his well-turned jest: here was Waltherrottner Luft in action.

Over the next months there were discreet attempts to dissuade Herr Einzelturm. Herr Wassertor surreptitiously encouraged press speculation about a possible public contest to find a speaker. Herr Wechsel, who as Comptroller always had the ear of city council, tried to interest various members of that body in the problem but retreated quickly when councillors began nominating themselves, their wives, children, grandchildren, nephews, nieces, courtesans, and catamites. Herr Stahlmeister, with more subtlety than one might have expected of him, attempted to work through his wife to

Frau Direktor Einzelturm, but Frau Stahlmeister replied, 'Try to persuade Irmtraud Einzelturm? I'd rather wrestle a bear . . . a python.'

Thus it was that on the day of the grand celebration, passengers all over the system were introduced to the voice of Herr Einzelturm from the speakers above their heads. They listened with a good deal of surprise.

Rathhausplatz. Umsteigen zum Linien B und D . . .

Sonnfeld Terminus. Technische Universität. Umsteigen zum Linien 24, 25, 26 und 27.

Passengers hearing the voice for the first time shook their heads in disbelief.

What in . . . ?

A voice, Mother, a voice announcing something

What?

announcing the next stop, isn't it?

and we'd better get off or else, from the sound of it

By the second or third stop they were frequently irritated and, if ill-tempered by nature, enraged. But after twenty stops or so, as they alighted for their offices or their shopping, people found that Waltherrottner Luft had asserted itself and all but the most surly were chuckling: the voice was absurd.

sounds like my Uncle Otto, so stupid he got his nose caught in a door

me of those yappy little dogs

Why are they laughing, Gretl?

and what he caught in the WC, don't ask

sure it's that old Herr Bohnsack who lives at our corner. An officious windbag – wind from both ends!

I'll explain later, Mother.

Scotties?

like a toilet that's not working properly

both pompous and effeminate

a schoolteacher who sounded like that: Herr Knurrhahn, the terror of the second grade, but his wife beat him regularly with her broom, her rolling pin, anything.

23

All through the day, merry passengers laughed their way back and forth across Waltherrott speculating on the identity behind the voice, making up stories about him, claiming to know him.

Herr Einzelturm went in splendid ignorance of the laughter. His colleagues had already heard the tapes and had their own worries: anything could go wrong, and several small things did. The honoured guests had frequently heard Herr Einzelturm's voice before, so were simply stunned into silence when they boarded the A-Tram at Rathhausplatz and heard their first announcement. In the discretion of the Renatenhof bar after their tour they could afford to admit their host had made a mistake.

'I had no idea he was so vain,' said Herr Neckar from Stuttgart. 'Does he have dreams of a career on the stage? Or do you suppose he doesn't know how ridiculous he sounds?'

'Ridiculous isn't the word for it,' said Herr Weser from Bremen. 'Poor old Einzelturm and Waltherrott will be the laughing stock of the transportation world.'

'Ach,' scoffed Herr Isar from Munich, 'What's a good laugh now and then? The Waltherrottners are always bragging about their sense of humour.' He raised his glass to the light. 'Too bad about their beer.'

With this glum suggestion, the honoured guests tipped their reluctant glasses back, then went to their rooms to change for the evening.

THE CATERING COMMITTEE had sensibly and perhaps uniquely solved the problem of food on theatre night by offering a hot buffet between six and seven, then a banquet beginning when the opera ended and continuing as long as the guests could endure. With the security of a pleasant meal behind them and the promise of another later if they felt peckish, the guests were in an expansive mood as they strolled across from the Renatenhof to the Stadtoper. A similar mood animated the crowds of Waltherrottners who were now milling about the Opernplatz, chattering with pride about the simulated marble halls of the tram station below, the brisk escalators, the chandeliers.

They say the Moscow Metro has stations like palaces: ha!
They say taxes aren't going up this year: ha!
I'm glad I don't have to do the dusting in here.
Give it a rest, Irmtraud, you don't even dust your

Dressed in their finery, the cream of Waltherrott society emerged into the Opernplatz and gazed with pride from the restrained elegance of the Residenz to the pillared confidence of the university, to the glittering windows of the dining room and lounges in the beloved Renatenhof, and at last to the grandeur, the spectacle, the vivacity of the opera house, deep gold and ivory. Beautiful women and handsome men waved from the balcony, while the vaulting arches invited, the open doors beckoned, holding out the promise of gaiety, taste, occasion.

What a dream of a night it would be!

Yeah, where's your Vienna now?

Or Munich? Frankfurt?

Same place they've always been!

But you wouldn't be able to hear Der Hosenkavalier *there!*

Vienna's loss is Waltherrott's gain!

Ah, that noble soul, Carl Maria von Stumpf!

Long live Carl Maria!

He's been dead a century and more.

It's a figure of speech, Lisl.

Long may his melodies brighten the Waltherrottner Luft!

Baedeker's *Germany* calls the Waltherrottner Stadtoper 'a naive blend of late baroque and early rococo with jarring elements of the neoclassical on the façade.' The *Blue Guide* says much the same, but in greater detail, adding some unnecessarily sarcastic remarks about the murals and sculptures. The Michelin Green Guide is also accurate about the architectural elements, but rather more forgiving, calling the Stadtoper 'unorthodox but charming.' Fielding's *Germany* briskly dismisses the building (and indeed all of Waltherrott) but admits that after a day shopping for the local rock crystal ('an acquired taste; overpriced') a night at the opera is preferable to 'customary local entertainments,' apparently meaning drunkenness and fornication. Frommer's *Dollarwise Germany* says the ice creams are cheaper and just as good at Luigi's in the student quarter. But what all the guidebooks have missed is the unspoilt exuberance of an evening at the Waltherrottner Stadtoper, especially for a production of one of the works of the city's own Carl Maria von Stumpf. All the operas he wrote during his tragically short career are still regularly mounted in Waltherrott, and everyone who knows them well agrees it is a shame that they are not given a wider currency.

Der Fliegende Waltherrottner perhaps suffers from certain longueurs in the plot, and the melodies are not up to the later work, but the motival elements were praised by Schumann in a letter written in his final year. The deeply symbolic significance of *Die Zauberfaß* has attracted the attention of a number of scholars, and a suite of its melodies was a staple in the repertoire of certain Polish and Finnish brass bands in the nineties. *Die Freieschürze* is as delightful a light comic opera as anything by Offenbach, and it is a matter of regret that much of the magic is only accessible to those fluent in the rather obscure dialect of the Bergwald and the upper reaches of the Lohbachertal. While the historical drama, *Waltherrotterdämmerung*, is admittedly heavy going, cognoscenti agree the spectacle rivals anything in Meyerbeer.

But it is undoubtedly the bittersweet romance, *Der Hosenkavalier*, which has secured for von Stumpf his niche, however obscure, in the annals of opera. And if the work has usually been received with indifference or hostility beyond the stage of its first home (closed early in Biel 1859, Kirkaldy 1864, Küstrin 1882) this does not lessen its appeal to the people of Waltherrott. Everyone hums along with the beloved Holzschuhtanz in the second act. No one with a heart could be immune to the touching love duet between Sonia Schönbruster (noble scion of the same family as the original Renate) and Walther Faßbinder, the supposedly illegitimate hero. And when the climax is reached as the closet doors are flung open to reveal the loutish Baron Lachs wearing the missing trousers, the laughter cascades from the balconies.

But it is the character of the Feldwebelin which raises the stature of the work above the common. Clearly une femme d'un certain âge, she has been taken for granted, deserted, betrayed by the men she has so generously loved and served. Her dream of winning the young Faßbinder with the gift of the trousers is, we all know, doomed to failure. But it is her calm and dignified acceptance of the truth, the blessing she bestows on the young lovers, and her revelation about the missing letter from Walther's real father which show the Feldwebelin's touching humanity. She is regarded as the paragon of Waltherrottner women, even as a symbol of the town itself, of its spirit, its Waltherrottner Luft.

It was *Der Hosenkavalier* which was to crown the celebrations for the completion of the new and improved Waltherrott Verkehrsverbund. No choice could have been more appropriate, for the opera perfectly expresses the Waltherrottner character with its simple joy in the good things of life, coupled with the melancholic acceptance that they'll cost more next year.

Herr Wurmlein, the Intendant, peeped through the spy hole and watched as the audience took their seats.

'I *told* you, Gunther, they're coming in *fast* tonight. Get that great *sot* of a tenor to *shift* his behind or they'll be *stamping* their *feet* and calling for my *head* on a *platter*.'

Backstage everyone moved with the controlled hysteria characteristic of theatres the world over; the audience buzzed and fidgeted as audiences always do on special evenings; and the musicians in the pit lounged about, gossiped, and speculated on the morals of the girls in the chorus until Herr Platt came striding toward the podium. Nonchalantly they butted their cigarettes, licked their mouthpieces, tightened their bows; the arm of Herr Platt rose; the arm of Herr Platt descended.

In the great central box of the Counts vom Faß sat Herr Bürgermeister Krankheit and Frau Bürgermeister Krankheit along with their special guests, Herr Direktor Einzelturm and Frau Direktor Einzelturm. Herr Einzelturm turned to his Irmtraud with a smile and touched her hand in the dim privacy. Gold-tasselled garnet velvet hung beside them and the chairs on which they sat were gilded and covered in garnet velvet. Small tables stood about bearing plates of chocolate truffles from Süßmayer in the Bahnhofstraße and glasses of Oberdorfer Sekt ('curious' – André Simon; 'best taken extremely cold' – Hugh Johnson). What an honour! And what a glow of pride and satisfaction coloured Herr Einzelturm's cheeks that evening!

As the curtain rose, Herr Krankheit leaned over to Herr Einzelturm:

'Enjoy it, my friend: it's in your honour and you deserve it.'

Herr Einzelturm turned a moist eye toward the stage to enjoy the familiar and lively opening to Act I. Yes, a burst of applause greeted the bedroom set with the great four-poster and the Feldwebelin obscured within, save for one enticing leg dangling to the floor, while there, caught in the act, as it were, is young Walther Faßbinder pulling on the worn-out old trousers. 'Ihr wurst,' sings the Feldwebelin, 'Ihr nudeln,' he replies. The conclusion to this touching duet is interrupted by a knock on the door, and Walther (showing obvious experience) climbs to the window ledge, wafts a kiss to his beloved, and disappears. They are assuming it is the Feldwebel himself, but instead the naughty maids Mariette and Mariandel burst into the room and rush about, pretending to dust. They join the Feldwebelin in the trio, 'Wo ist meinen Schlüpfer, du Schlumpen?' and are just finishing when they are interrupted by another knock. Everyone in the audience leans forward in anticipation of the entrance of Baron Lachs, recognized the world over by anyone who knows opera (and the Waltherrott area) as the very type of the minor nobleman of Waldental an der Lohbach. His bellows of lust and frustration which close the first act never fail to rouse the audience to cheers, whistles, applause, and stomping feet.

'Wonderful, as usual,' said Frau Krankheit to Frau Einzelturm. 'What a comfort it is to know that this masterpiece is here year after year for us to enjoy; don't you agree, Frau Direktor Einzelturm?'

Frau Einzelturm didn't like Renate Krankheit with her Milanese fashions (a flashy red number tonight with one bare shoulder), her health club figure, and her face lifts. Word was she picked holiday spots with topless beaches. And what was the name of that perfume she was wearing? *Putain? Salope?* Frau Einzelturm didn't much like opera either and would have preferred being at home with a crossword or a good mystery novel, but she appreciated an honour as well as the next person.

'I most certainly do agree, Frau Bürgermeister Krankheit,' she replied, and took the offered arm; together they led the way to the Grand Salon where an ice mountain covered with bottles of Oberdorfer Sekt awaited them. Smiling waiters and waitresses came forward with plates of sausages on sticks, celery stuffed with cheese, toasted triangles of cheese and bacon, and asparagus spears rolled in ham.

better make it two glasses for each of us
starving
three
never can figure out how to eat and
middle of the act and I'm dreaming about a foaming
why not just park that plate here, Mädel
always make such a pig of

Besides the honoured visitors, all the members of the city council were there, along with the department heads of the WVV and their wives or, in the case of Fräulein Farber, her gentleman friend. In between bouts with glasses and vorspeisen, a number of people found time to press their compliments upon Herr Einzelturm and he thanked everyone with ponderous grace and sincerity.

'Such an evening!' Herr Einzelturm enthused. 'The greatest evening of my life.' Then, with a glance at his Irmtraud he corrected himself: 'The *second* greatest!'

Frau Einzelturm blushed to the roots of her blonde hair.

But the lights dimmed soon enough and nothing could hold the Waltherrottners from rushing back to their seats for the lively second act. The overture gives tantalizing snatches of the famous Holzschuhtanz but the melody in many forms suffuses the act as all the lovers get a chance to kick up their heels: Mariette and the butcher's boy open the action, followed by Baron Lachs and

Mariandel. After she has run screaming from the stage with her dirndl in tatters and the Baron in hot pursuit, it is the turn of the Feldwebelin and Walther. But the Feldwebelin soon relinquishes her place to Trudi, the horse trader's helper (in reality, of course, she is Sophie, daughter of the mysterious stranger, Count 'X'), while the Feldwebelin dances in turn with the postmaster, the poetaster, and the last ostler. The Holzschuhtanz gives way for a time to the raucous drinking song from the chorus of soldiers and swineherdesses, the audience invariably joining in with verve. But the more sober if not necessarily more dignified air of the dance is restored with the entry of the actress and the bishop, and the act rapidly builds to its climax with the return of the Baron pursued by the hunters and the milkmaids. Soon everyone is swirling and bouncing to the intoxicating thunder of the Holzschuhtanz . . . everyone but the Feldwebelin, who pauses at the mouth of the cave, holds her finger to her lips, then with more resignation than enthusiasm mounts the camel and is gone.

'How touching it is,' said Frau Bürgermeister Krankheit. 'How true to life. I'm always amazed, as I'm sure you are, Frau Direktor Einzelturm, at the stubbornness of other opera companies: they continue to slight our native genius.'

Frau Einzelturm was actually of the opinion that Carl Maria von Stumpf, if he was a typical Waltherrottner male, had probably been childish, lecherous, dim, and drunk a good part of the time. Not all local men were entirely so – her husband, for example, was neither lecherous nor drunken – but in her experience these were their common qualities.

'I entirely agree with you,' she replied, and together they led the way to the Sekt.

When everyone had a bumper of bubbly, Herr Bürgermeister Krankheit called for attention.

'Ladies and gentlemen,' he began, 'We are here this evening to celebrate a dream come true . . .'

And briefly, eloquently, he alluded to the great achievement of the new WVV, of the city, of everyone here assembled. 'But one man especially . . .' and he put his arm across Herr Einzelturm's shoulder.

Not everyone in the room could hear, but the mayor's voice carried well beyond the immediate circle of WVV staff, city councillors, and dignitaries:

'Thus . . . pleasure . . . to you the architect . . . father . . . wonderful new system which . . . fair city . . . Director . . . Waltherrott . . . Herr . . .'

Gradually a hush fell on that half of the Grand Salon, and when Herr Einzelturm stammered out his thanks to the mayor, the city council, his colleagues, his voice was heard by as many as fifty people:

'. . . and also mention the generous help . . . representatives . . . Stuttgart, Hannover, Göttingen . . .' and went on with rather more confidence and volume, '. . . a few of whom we are fortunate . . .'

He spoke for barely a minute, but in that time his voice was heard by enough people that he was revealed as the man of the announcements on the trams and buses.

Who did you say?
someone named Sturm
from Stuttgart, it seems
definitely a Waltherrottner accent
on City Council, she told me
No, I thought it was Saganthurm
the same voice, that's certain
looks like someone I went to school with . . . Einzelturm?
in front of the one in red with the big
It is, I'm sure of it!
sounds like a Klotsack
the oaf in the rented soup-and-fish . . . just beside the Bürgermeister.

No, I heard it quite clearly. He is Herr Einzelturm, and he is the director of the WVV.

As the Salon lights dimmed and the bell chimed, the news of the identity of the announcer seeped back into the hall.

31

During the overture, as Walther and Mariette direct the waiters in the setting of the trap doors and false windows, Herr Wurmlein noticed the buzz from the audience.

'Gunther, what the *hell* is *happening* out there? Has that *ponce* left his *fly* down again? Is the tart's *knocker* on the loose? Lieber *Gott*, why didn't I go into the *fish* business with Uncle Heinie? What *is* going on? If the wretched *band* gets us into *another* rape scandal, I'll just *scream*, I *swear* it . . .'

The third act is a prodigy of plot complications and psychological nuance: the audience must pay attention. Tonight, a susurrus of whispers moved over the surface of their concentration. Heads bowed, leaned toward one another, faces turned to search out further hints, sources. Most of those seated in the stalls had used the ground floor lounge, but a few rubberneckers had ascended to the Grand Salon and had picked up scraps of the news.

A Herr Eigengarten, it seems
lives in Solothurn . . . that's in Switzerland
Wow, Otto, I didn't know
I'd hide in Switzerland too, if I had a voice like that.
Herr who?
enough of the sarcasm, Irmtraud, just for
Eisenklotz . . . from Rottweil
Klotzweil . . . from Eisenach
Eisenrott . . . from Bachrach
ridiculous, he's a composer . . . in America . . . 'Feelings.'
and stuff it up your royal
No, I heard it quite distinctly: Herr Einzelturm from Waltherrott.

On the circle and balcony levels, more people had heard, but such is the magnificence of the gilded pillars and garnet velvet hangings (as a precaution, in earlier times, against assassination), that very few could see into the Grafinical box. Thus, gradually the fuss died down, eyes returned expectantly to the orchestra and the curtain, ears were tuned once more to the glories of von Stumpf's music, the niceties of his libretto. Herr Wurmlein relaxed as much as he ever did during a performance.

32

'Gunther, are the *bladders* ready for the Furzkampf? Make *sure* the valves are *well moistened* or there'll be nothing but a *limp hiss* of wind. Where the *hell* is Second Juggler? . . . Then *mop up* the blood and get her *out* here!'

It is the fate of intendants to worry, but somehow the show does go on, the trap doors do finally open, the trapeze makes its several passes without hurling the mezzo-soprano into the Stumpfstraße, the tenor en travestie in the further travestie of playing a boy finally remembers the missing parts of his costume. The moon rises, the bed collapses, and the cannon fires, all more or less punctually. The soprano manages to swallow her repulsion for the tenor, and they embrace convincingly in the alcove, fully within so that the little curtain closes in front of them. With that cue, the peasants and the trolls return bearing Lachs and Mariette (now in triple travestie) and the lively ensemble Holzschuhtanz follows. All the trap doors mercifully hold, so that Third Gypsy does not, as she did in the tragic performance of January 1912, fall through and impale herself on the truncheon of the bailiff waiting below. With the return of the Feldwebelin, of course, the action becomes more calm, as she clears the stage of the dragoons, the woodchoppers, and the gravediggers; First and Second Bear successfully navigate their unicycles onto the swan boat and sail off, while the giants fall asleep within the ring of fire. The Feldwebelin turns to the Baron:

'Is eine wienerische Maskerad' und weiter nichts.'

To the thunderous applause of the Waltherrottners, Lachs is soon scampering off, pursued by the Police Commissioner, the Nubians, and the Three Graces. Mariette, in her fifth travestie evolution is revealed in her true self as an hermaphrodite already married to the one-legged major who returns unexpectedly from the wars to claim her and, not incidentally, his pension. They exit, she with eyes sparkling, he twirling his mustaches and singing the suggestive 'Nimst einige Madeira, mein Schatz!' There is not a dry eye in the house because, touching though this reunion may be, it is only a foreshadowing of the great trio which follows, beginning with Walther's famous:

33

'Auch Marie, auch Marie . . . wie gut sie ist.'

The action moves poignantly to its conclusion. The notary digs the letter from his dossier and is taken away in chains, the Feldwebelin produces the locket with the portraits, the young lovers trade skirt for trousers, trousers for skirt, and steal away, leaving the Feldwebelin alone with her broken dreams. She eyes the beer kegs reflectively, then fills a stein for herself.

She muses on mutability and the passage of time, ('Heut' oder morgen . . .') until the hunchbacked dwarf scampers in to grab an extra keg. He helps the Feldwebelin into the wicker gondola, not neglecting the chance to slip a hand up her skirt as he winks to the audience. 'Ja, ja,' she sighs, and strokes the dwarf's hump; as the curtain falls, the inn collapses into rubble, but the balloon rises, the very essence of Waltherrottner Luft, the gay and buoyant spirit of the city rising above the turmoil and disappointment of life.

The applause is always thunderous.

The curtain calls over at last, Herr Intendant Wurmlein slumps in his seat. 'It is *done*, Gunther, and *so* am *I*.'

It should have been done. Every member of the audience was standing. As happens in every opera house when the lights go up, all looked about to reassure themselves that they have not been sitting alone, or dreaming it all, or transported to a faraway land; all were reassured that everyone else was there and clapping in accord, that Herr Dickbauch the auto salesman was not with his wife but with his tart, Fräulein Strudel, and that snooty Frau Silberhaar had obviously laced her corset too tightly tonight.

But after Fräulein Puppel, our Feldwebelin, had received her bouquets from the ushers, and the cast had taken its seventh curtain call, the focus of attention gradually shifted back to the Grafinical box where stood Herr Bürgermeister Krankheit and his wife, along with a frumpy woman and a burly man in ill-fitting evening dress.

Is that the yodelling yokel?

A Swiss?

How his bald dome shines in the light!

No, no, he's from Eisenach
where she ever got that dye job
of the hooters on the Frau Bürgermeister, eh?
reflection from his spectacles
Stuttgart
can't see him clearly
but quite large
Shh, the Bürgermeister is saying something
Why don't they shut up?
The accent on the tram is as Waltherrottner as Uncle August breaking wind.
   Shh . . .
says the performance tonight is for the new tram system, the underground stations
   obviously thinks we couldn't read the programme
her once or twice round the track, by God
can't hear
the Director of the WVV, I think
didn't catch the name
Eisentor?
Look . . . Krankheit's going to make him speak, I think

Herr Bürgermeister Krankheit put a comradely arm around Herr Einzelturm's shoulders and pulled him gently to the front of the box from which hung the great garnet and gold banner bearing the coat of arms of the city. Herr Einzelturm gripped the railing nervously, then raised his hand to cover his mouth in a cough. From the stalls, all faces were raised toward him, while around the circle and up in the gods people craned forward, smiling, expectant.

Herr Bürgermeister Krankheit concluded in loud, clear tones:

'And so I present to you the father of the Waltherrott Verkehrsverbund . . . Herr Direktor Einzelturm!'

Ha, didn't I tell you so!
Shh!
The hell you did, you said Herr Klotzgard.

Herr Einzelturm gripped the railing more tightly.

'Meine Damen und Herren . . .' he began, and again, 'Meine Damen und Herren . . . am diesem Opernhaus . . .'

The name of the owner of the next voice is lost in the mists of time, claimed, inconclusively, to be known to dozens of Waltherrottners; but his words are known to all. Delivered in a brilliantly accurate but nightmarishly exaggerated imitation, the mimic concluded Herr Einzelturm's sentence:

Umsteigen zum Linien A, B, C, D . . .

The laughter burst into the great well of the opera house, washing the walls and splashing, vaulting to the ceiling with its *Inspiration of Carl Maria von Stumpf,* then showered down on all those cheerful folk, and all were awash in that laughter, that Waltherrottner Luft.

Part Two

THE BERGWALD in all its glories is not, perhaps, as well known as it deserves to be. Neither the *Blue Guide* nor Fielding mentions the Bergwald at all, while Frommer merely suggests that southbound Eurailpassers have a better view from the right-hand side of the train. One might have expected that Baedeker, a German publication, could have taken a more informed and generous view, but it dismisses the Bergwald as 'locally popular.' The Michelin Green Guide devotes a subordinate clause to the Bergwald, praising its 'unspoiled and undeveloped charms,' but it unaccountably neglects to bestow even the single star denoting 'Interesting.' Herr Reiser of the Waltherrott Tourist Office has written to Michelin suggesting the omission is a typographical error which ought to be corrected in subsequent editions, and that the newly restored spa of St. Irmtraud ought to be designated one of the most salubrious on the continent. Michelin replied with a form letter declining to enter into substantive correspondence. Herr Reiser is not the only one in Waltherrott who believes the Bergwald deserves not just one star, but two – 'Worth a detour' – while a few enthusiasts would have nothing less than three stars – 'Worth a journey.'

However, if the rest of the world ignores the Bergwald, the Waltherrottners esteem it all the more. Some, indeed, are pleased that it remains a private playground, free from the incursions of brusque Rhinelanders or insincerely smiling Bavarians, never mind boorish foreigners.

'It's a well known fact,' people remarked, 'that the English and the French never wash. Imagine that sort of pollution in the Bergwald: compared with a Parisian's armpit, who's complaining about acid rain?'

The Bergwald in springtime has been immortalized in Carl Maria von Stumpf's ever popular lied, 'Frülingstraum im Bergwald.' The forest's cooling summer shade is treasured by all, and the snow-clad silence of winter is frequently enlivened by the puffing and yelping of cross-country skiers. But it is in the autumn that the Bergwald is at its loveliest. On fresh, crisp days of gentle sun, the air takes on a radiance and a sparkle not to be found anywhere else on earth, according to the Waltherrott Tourist Office brochure entitled *Wanderung in Wahrheit* (Eng. ver.: *Hiking to Heaven*). On such a day in September, if you take a stroll around the peaceful Spiegelsee, or hike one of the hill paths from Oberdorf to Waldental, why, you'll arrive more rested than when you started, your body invigorated, your mood softened, your spirit uplifted and refreshed, and your palate tingling for a litre or ten of Renatenbräu.

On such a September day, Herr Einzelturm, in leather and loden, stepped briskly along the path which follows the cliff edge some ten meters above the Lohbach. The merry stream gurgled and sparkled down there through the pines and oaks. Above the path vaulted more trees, and through the sunbeams slanting down to the forest floor the fall warblers flickered and chirped. In the distance, a woodpecker tap-tapped, the rhythms echoing through the scented naves and choirs of this bosky cathedral.

Herr Einzelturm was making for a notable spot, the crag overlooking an elbow bend of the stream just where the smaller Keilerbach comes tumbling down the gully on the far side. A stone wall stands at the edge of the drop and a seat provides a comfortable rest stop with a superb panorama up and down the noble Lohbach, and across to where the dramatic rock face of the Adlerspitze soars a majestic fifty or sixty meters above the rushing waters.

This Keilerfelsen, or Boar's Crag, came upon its name in an exceptional fashion. For to this very spot, *Wanderung in Wahrheit* tells us, had come the first Graf Walther vom Faß, that chevalier sans peur et sans reproche, in a time of trouble and doubt. Should he stay in Waltherrott, the town he had founded, the town whose protector he was, or should he follow the urgings of wily Father Adalbert and undertake a crusade to the Holy Land? As he knelt in prayer for guidance, he heard a rustling and snuffling from the river bank below. Like all of his family, Walther was a mighty hunter, a very Nimrod, and immediately divined that a wild boar was rooting about. How to get to the beast, that was the question. Upstream or down, both directions for some distance offered only precipitous drops. The boar himself answered the question by heading downstream, so Graf Walther untied his horse's reins and was about to follow when the snuffling took an unexpected turn: against all possibility, the beast seemed to be mounting the embankment. And indeed, a few moments served to confirm this, for the noises, increasing in volume and ferociousness, were approaching the path. Graf Walther stood, intrigued and curious, for this was surely a remarkable boar, a worthy trophy. The noises ceased and he sensed the boar had reached the top; he could hear it breathing now in the first flush of undergrowth, yes, and now a rustling as the beast advanced. Graf Walther stuck a foot into the stirrup and stroked his restive steed.

But when the bushes parted and the great boar, the largest Walther had ever seen, a behemoth among boars, stepped onto the path, the brave knight's ardour for the kill was quelled. Not from fear, but rather because, miracle of miracles, between the boar's tusks there glowed a cross, radiated a rood, eerily in the green shade of the great pines. 'Im hoch Siegnus,' murmured Walther, rendering the Latin as best he could, and prostrated himself in reverence. The boar regarded him for what seemed an age, and Walther, his face to the earth, seemed to hear a choir of angels singing just overhead. Gradually the singing became more distant; as it died away, Walther essayed a look and found the miraculous boar was gone. He arose and returned to the city to make his peace with Father Adalbert, to make his plans for the crusade.

Herr Einzelturm did not expect divine intervention. The knights, the Grafen vom Faß on their caparisoned steeds, had passed from Waltherrott, and the age of chivalry, of great deeds, of sagas, of miracles was past.

'We live,' he would to say to his wife Irmtraud, to his colleagues, to anyone he thought needed the truth, 'in an age of administration. We look at the problems of the world with a calm gaze, we consider solutions, we plan and test, we carry out the steps necessary to solve our problems. We don't ask for miracles, but for self-discipline and hard work. Look about you.'

This last he would say with a wave of his hand, pointing out that the Wirtschaftswunder, the Economic Miracle, had come about because of discipline and hard work. During the years of the great project of the Waltherrott Verkehrsverbund he made these observations frequently. But now that the project was complete, the man who had worked the hardest, who had shown the most self-discipline was now seeking, if not a miracle, perhaps some solace.

As he paced out the last familiar windings of the path and came into the sparkle of the open air, Herr Einzelturm walked more and more slowly, as one does in the Church of St. Adalbert, stepping forward to the railing where the light glows in through the choir and the south transept, and there one stands, one kneels in the presence of something greater than oneself. It may be as the builders meant, a sense of divine presence, or simply a sense of the dedication which inspired the builders themselves. At the Keilerfelsen, it may be a transcendent vision of the glory of the natural world expressed in the pines, the oaks, and the sunlight, or it may be simple enjoyment of a beautiful view. For the unfortunate Herr Einzelturm in his confusion and doubt, it was perhaps a mixture of all these impulses which brought him to his knees at the stone wall, which filled his eyes with tears, his heart with a confusing, overpowering throb.

Certainly he had been ridiculous in the matter of the announcements, but it is a wise man who can see all of his own faults, especially when it is such an unexpected one. Herr Einzelturm well knew how to test himself in self-discipline, in hard work. He could not have been expected to have a sense of the fitness of his own voice.

'You are not an actor, my friend,' remarked Herr Bürgermeister

Krankheit when at last the laughter had ended, the mob had dispersed, and the great servants of Waltherrott were sitting alone in the Grafinical box at the Stadtoper. 'They should not have expected a voice like honey . . . a voice from a beer advertisement.'

'I thought . . . I thought the purpose of the announcements was to provide information. I thought I had done that.'

'You did, my friend, you did, and very admirably. You did the best you could.'

'That is the most anyone can ask of us, isn't it? That we follow orders and do our best?'

'Indeed it is. And Waltherrott thanks you for that. As you can see . . .'

He gestured toward the stage, deserted now, the curtain up and the crew stowing the last of the set.

'The performance was for you and your achievement. We'll have someone else do the recordings, perhaps someone from the opera, or from the Stadtheater, or maybe from the drama department at the University. New announcements . . . and in a few weeks all will be forgotten and we'll go on as before.'

'Is it possible?' asked Herr Einzelturm.

'Of course! How can you doubt?'

But Herr Krankheit was being less than honest, for he sensed that the incident of the announcements and of the laughter would become part of Waltherrottner legend; more poignantly, it would be exalted and cited as an example of Waltherrottner humour, zest for life, Waltherrottner Luft.

'But I'll tell you what we shall do. The great job is done, you are exhausted from ten years of overwork and too few holidays – no, don't deny it – and this unfortunate incident simply adds to the debt owed you by all of us. Therefore, you are going to take a long holiday, as long as you like. As you may know, Frau Krankheit and I have a little chalet in the Bergwald, a nice drive past Oberdorf. It's private, there's a pleasant view, it's not far from the spa of St. Irmtraud, there's the famous air of the Bergwald, what do you say? It's yours for as long as you want it. Until the snow flies, at least – it's

41

not warm enough for winter, but there's a fine fireplace to take the chill out of the autumn evenings. It's really quite cosy . . .'

Seeing that he was getting the point across, the Bürgermeister pressed home his advantage with a grip on Herr Einzelturm's forearm.

'Tell me you'll accept!'

'But you and Frau Krankheit?'

'She has been talking – in a theoretical way only, you under-stand, as women are fond of doing – about the delights of Mauritius and the Seychelles, so I shall be a good husband and surprise her. You take Frau Einzelturm with you, forget about work, and you'll be back soon enough, fit as a fiddle and with all this silliness forgotten.'

'I'm not sure . . .'

The persuasion took another half hour, and Frau Einzelturm had to be consulted, if only out of politeness, but it was soon enough agreed upon. On Monday of the following week, Herr and Frau Einzelturm closed up their own flat, and loaded the car with blankets, outdoor clothes, crossword puzzles, and food.

'All this?' he demanded when he saw what he was to pack.

'You won't sleep on any sheets but your own. And the Bergwald gets chilly, even in September, I know, because my Uncle Georg . . .'

'I know all about your Uncle Georg. What about all this food? We're only going five kilometres toward Waldental, not to Siberia . . . to Canada.'

Frau Einzelturm explained about coffee and mustard, about politeness in the matter of replacements, about prices in villages like Waldental. And so they mumbled and grumbled along the road to the chalet. Like all arguments between spouses, it was just one of the repertoire which they played through like favourite cassettes. But as they at last got clear of the suburbs and wound their way through the hills, Frau Einzelturm sensed something different this time: her husband was not really trying, was confusing things somehow. Indeed, this script (*Why all the hoarding when rationing ended years ago?*) was about organization and was used during any change of

42

household routine. Her husband was confusing it with a similar, but quite different one (*I should have married Ilse Taubenegg, the chicken farmer's daughter; it would have been a simple life, but a healthy one*) which was used during house repairs or the purchase of major appliances. After nearly three decades of editing, these scripts are supposed to be reassuring, no matter how dramatic the mise-en-scene. For just as no one leaves the opera house dry-eyed after a performance of *Der Fliegende Waltherrottner* (though everyone has seen the work twenty times) yet all are at the same time calmed and reassured, so also the playing of familiar domestic scripts keeps the ship of marriage on a steady course. This confusion, then, this dislocation made Frau Einzelturm uneasy, concerned, vaguely apprehensive. She let the argument slip away and over the next week was careful not to renew it. The incident in the opera house she had thought of as something trivial, a joke of her husband's which someone misunderstood – God knows that happened often enough – but discreet enquiries and a short tram ride quickly corrected her error. Time indeed to keep out of his way, or perhaps to keep him out of hers. She therefore took to sitting on the sunny balcony with a cup of coffee and her crossword puzzles.

'More of those silly things? What do you see in them?'

'I'm on holiday. The featherbeds are airing over there, the dishes are done, the soup is simmering, and the sun is warm here. Why don't you try one?'

Herr Einzelturm snorted, shook his head, retreated.

'At least I shall go for a walk,' he called from within. 'To benefit from the exercise.'

'Stop off at the spa of St. Irmtraud; the waters will do you good.'

'If I want to breathe sulpher fumes, I can have them for nothing over by the Waldental pulp mill.'

'Enjoy your walk.'

Frau Einzelturm smiled to herself. From the time of the original Irmtraud von Linnen, it has been the duty of the wise wives of Waltherrott to bear the foolishness of their husbands, to watch their absurd posturings, to listen to their wild rantings, and finally to direct them back to their duties. Thus Frau Einzelturm was able to peek, with some satisfaction, around the corner of her balcony at the bulk of her man as he stomped away into the forest, his green stockinged legs pumping, his gnarled stick marking the pace.

Yes, she told herself, As long as I keep him out and about, he'll be his old self again in a few weeks. And however disagreeable that old self might be, he was a sight better than this eccentric she was now closeted with.

For the first week or so, Herr Einzelturm also thought it was just a matter of rest, exercise, and fresh air. He really had been working too hard for too many years, his body had got slack, while his mind had become a machine at the service of the Waltherrott Verkehrsverbund. Now his muscles stretched and toughened as he strode the forest trails, and his mind gradually let slip the myriad details of the WVV system, attending instead to the sound of birdsong, of pine boughs sighing in the breeze, of silence.

But peace did not come.

More and more, Herr Einzelturm found himself drawn to the Keilerfelsen, to that lofty promontory where, it has so often seemed to souls in turmoil, the forces of the universe are somehow concentrated, at least such forces of the universe as may be considered to have found in Waltherrott and the Bergwald a suitable focus of cosmic convergence. To Herr Einzelturm, it increasingly seemed that this gathering of forces was considerable.

Thus it was that he came here, and when he came he contemplated his life and his doings more deeply than ever he had before.
What did his life mean?
What was he?
Where was he to go?
But especially: why the laughter?
Indeed, apart from his eminence as director of the WVV, Herr Einzelturm's life had not been remarkable. Born in 1931, he managed to spend the war playing with the lead soldiers and electric trains he inherited from his brother Karl. The war was fairly peaceful in Waltherrott. The bombers took occasional interest in the

marshalling yard, and sometimes when primary and secondary targets were blanketed in cloud a few squadrons dumped their loads in the general direction of the town. In 1942 it was attacked with moderate damage when it was mistaken for Schwermund forty kilometres away. The worst night came in the fall of 1943, when three streets of apartment blocks were destroyed, but they were far from the Einzelturm home. Most of the time, Waltherrott's farmers had their fields churned up. In the final winter of the war, the fighter bombers destroyed the Lohbach bridges and kept the railway out of service for the duration, but they ignored the town. When the western Allies swept into Germany in the spring of '45, Waltherrott had been briefly lost on a seam between elements of the First and Ninth U.S. Armies. Consequently, the surrender had already been declared (and a good many embarrassing uniforms and papers destroyed) before the first G.I.s appeared with their cigarettes, chewing gum, and nylons.

Of course, the Waltherrottners had contributed their share to the ranks of the dead – Herr's Einzelturm's brother Karl had died near Orel in 1943 – and had suffered from shortages of food and fuel. But with rich farmlands nearby, a city nearly undamaged, the Bergwald to scavenge, and a native talent for the black market, these shortages had not been unbearable. With the occupation had come some pointed questions about the fate of Schmucker the jeweller, Pelzer the furrier, and other Jews, and the answers were about as forthcoming as they were elsewhere in the former Reich. In any case, Dummkopf Einzelturm really hadn't noticed anything. Even the abrupt closing, in 1938, of Herr Spielmann's toyshop had been but a brief inconvenience. 'Don't worry,' his father had said, 'I expect it will open again soon.' Sure enough, the following week Herr Schakal was having the sign repainted. But there were no new lead soldiers or model trains anyway. Herr Schakal himself disappeared abruptly in the early months of 1945, but by that time Herr Einzelturm was fourteen and facing the fact that with his brother dead he was heir to the family name. The prospect of this future responsibility, along with a general glumness in the air, told young

Herr Einzelturm that it was time to put away childish things and start thinking about a career.

What he most wanted was a job with the railway, but he encountered problems. In the immediate postwar years, he was too young. In any case, although there was more than enough work to be done, the surviving railway workers and demobilized soldiers got all the jobs. When Marshall Plan aid began to arrive and expansion took off in a big way, Herr Einzelturm applied again, but was told he was not properly qualified for any but menial jobs. He enrolled in extra engineering courses at night, but when he was at last acceptable, he was told the only posts were far from home. It is a rare Waltherrottner who willingly leaves the city of his birth.

'Well, if Duisburg doesn't appeal to you, young man, what about Kiel? Bracing sea breezes and lots of lively mermaids . . .'

Reluctantly, Herr Einzelturm joined the WVV. But he soon found his affections shifting from trains to trams: it was an affair of the heart.

'Tramlines,' he explained to smiling young Irmtraud Rodegast, 'are like the veins and arteries of the city. The central garage is like the heart, sending the tramcars all through the city and the suburbs, and then back to the centre. People are like oxygen, you see, while a derailment temporarily upsets the system like a wound. Special events, such as football matches or performances at the opera, are like blood clots, and . . .'

They were walking in the Volkspark by the river, and Irmtraud gazed soulfully at the waters of the Lohbach flowing swiftly past: how like her young life was the river, slipping, rushing away, disappearing into a hazy distance. She was five years older than Einzelturm the Dummkopf. There had been other young men who had admired her ample figure, her ready smile. Where were they now? Beneath the wheat fields of Russia, several of them; not a few buried in France, Italy, Greece, Yugoslavia, North Africa; others under the waves of the Atlantic or Arctic Oceans. And so many young women who would now never have a man to keep them warm at night.

'. . . while a power failure is like a heart attack, of course, and . . .'

'Hush a moment,' she murmured, and squeezed his arm. 'Listen to the warm breeze of springtime. How does the song go, "Frülingstraum im Bergwald"?' And she murmured,

> When April comes, I'll blithely wander,
> The flowering oaks and pine trees under . . .

'He is a great poet, our von Stumpf.'

'Springtime: and soon the summer will be here . . .'

'The breeze is very pleasant, yes. It is our renowned Waltherrottner Luft.'

'I never want to be cold again.'

Herr Einzelturm understood this young woman but dimly. He had seen an article in the *Waltherrottner Tagesblatt* which had explained the facts clearly enough: a generation of women had lost their husbands and sweethearts and there would be no replacements. 'So, young Hans and Fritz,' the article had concluded, 'If she's waiting for you under Herr Bieber's clock in the Bahnhofstraße, have another stein and read the sports pages. She'll still be waiting for you in half an hour.' A typical example of the famed Waltherrottner sense of humour.

But Herr Einzelturm never kept her waiting, and they were married before the spring was gone. As the country found its feet, so the Einzelturms established themselves – first in her parents' flat, then in their own little flat, then in several larger ones as the children arrived, as the city grew. At the same time, Herr Einzelturm moved up through the series of positions which brought him to the directorship at the young age of forty-five. The society had lost a generation of men: between the outgoing director, seventy-four years old, and young Einzelturm, there was simply no suitable man.

Yet, as he had shown himself a capable, loyal, hard-working husband, so he came to earn the respect, if not the affection, of his employees. He played no favourites, backed them up when they made mistakes, had a solid grasp of all branches of the service, and worked longer hours than any of them. The city councillors would perhaps have preferred a more genial director, one who was more pliant in his interpretation of the conflict of interest guidelines for the awarding of contracts. But they gradually came to see that he had one overriding virtue: he kept the WVV working without undue tax rises, without mounting debts, and without scandals; without, that is, embarrassment to the city councillors.

It was this life he had built that was the subject of his contemplations when he came each day to sit at the Keilerfelsen. A life is like a building, a house, he thought. I have not built for myself a palace, nor a manor, nor a grand city residence designed by Jäger von Erlach, Waltherrott's famous architect. Nor have I made a hovel, a slum, nor an old farmhouse added to willy-nilly over the years. No, I have built solidly, sensibly, within my means, according to my needs.

'I have built an exemplary life,' he intoned.

An exemplary, a vorbildlich life.

And much as he poked into the niches and corners of that structure, much as he cast an inquisitive light into the darkness where dry rot might be lurking, he could see no flaws of consequence.

'An exemplary life,' with conviction.

The Einzelturm children had turned out well, although all had taken the extraordinary step of moving away from Waltherrott. Karl was with a sparkasse in Hannover, Anneliese was a teacher and married to a teacher in Munich, and young Dieter was at university in Bonn. Even while the children were still at home, the Einzelturm's had a social life. They had their friends, they went to parties, and like everyone else of their means in Waltherrott, they had subscription seats to the opera, the chamber orchestra, the theatre, and even attended performances of the university theatre. Irmtraud no longer played tennis at the health club, but she enjoyed the swimming, it seemed, and joined group trips to other cities, sometimes to Switzerland, Austria, or France. It was true that in the last few years the two of them hadn't taken many holidays together – that week in

Benidorm two years ago April had not been a success, a week among English lager louts and typists with hormonal imbalances – but he could make that up to her now that the great project was done. Why, they might go away somewhere next week if that was what she wanted.

In the meantime they were both enjoying the chalet – Herr Einzelturm had toyed with some costing estimates for a chalet of their own – and both were finding the soft weather, the air, the peace soothing to the soul. Irmtraud had her crossword puzzles. Should he perhaps sneak back to town for the video cassette player? No, it was enough, it all fitted together as it was, it made perfect sense, this holiday. It was exemplary, vorbildlich.

Herr Einzelturm stood solid at the wall atop the beetling Keilerfelsen.

Exemplary . . . vorbildlich.

Far below, the waters gurgled; the pines clinging to the slopes, towering above, sighed in the breeze; the sunlight hung in the air, effervescent, like bubbles in champagne, bubbles rising in his brain, clouds of bubbles filling the valley, floating through the pines and the oaks, bubbles enough to intoxicate the very Waltherrottner Luft itself!

Herr Einzelturm felt dizzy, swayed, staggered, clutched at the railing.

Exemplary! . . . Vorbildlich!

And yet . . .

And yet he had stood that night, the night of his triumph, that horrible night, he had stood at the railing of the box and had gazed with surprise, confusion, shock at the swirling pool of upturned faces contorted with raucous laughter, the eyes shut in laughter, popping open briefly, shutting again, mouths gaping, throats open with the cawing, guffawing roars of the laughter, he had stood that night before those faces, that laughter, that roar.

Now Herr Einzelturm cried aloud to the sky:

'Vorbildlich!'

And the echo came back:

. . . bildlich . . .
. . . bildlich . . .
How to understand that horrible night at the opera?
How to explain an exemplary life made absurd?

HIS FIRST VISIT to the Stadtbibliothek was not a success. Herr
Einzelturm was not a sensitive man; he kept his attention
directed toward its proper object and was little aware of extraneous goings-on about him. But he could not help noticing, as he
stood before the information counter, that an unusual number of
eyes seemed directed toward him. There two women leaned together whispering as they glanced at him, here a pudgy man
snorted abruptly and covered his mouth with his hands, while a
young blonde woman gaped at him from an office doorway, then
disappeared in an explosion of giggles. The older lady who turned
from her filing cabinet and approached him did a better job of
controlling herself, but the corners of her mouth twitched when
he spoke.

'Yes, please,' he said. 'Do you have information about the opera
Der Hosenkavalier? The words of the songs, perhaps, or some writ-
ing about the opera, or about the composer, Carl Maria von
Stumpf?'

The woman covered the biting of her lip by putting her hand
up to adjust the half-spectacles on her nose.

'The libretto? I doubt we have that, but let me just check, sir,'
she murmured as turned to a computer terminal. As she hunched
over the keyboard, her shoulders shook in gentle, suppressed
merriment.

'Thank you,' replied Herr Einzelturm, and stared at a portrait
which hung below the clock. It seemed to be of a nineteenth century librarian or perhaps a benefactor. The mouth was obscured by
a large droopy mustache.

'As I suspected, we do not have a printed libretto of *Der
Hosenkavalier,* but someone at the Stadtoper might be able to help
you. On von Stumpf himself, you could begin with the *Brockhaus*

and we have *Meyers Grosses Konversations-Lexikon* which is often helpful with out-of-the-way information. Over there,' and she pointed toward a section of the reading room, 'You will also find several encyclopædias and dictionaries of music: Mendel and Reissmann, Riemann, or Moser should all have something on von Stumpf although probably not separate entries on *Der Hosen-kavalier*. There will also be references to the composer in general works on nineteenth century opera, especially on German opera of the romantic period.'

The computer's printer ran off a few lines; the librarian tore off the sheet and considered it. 'There are references to scholarly articles on the composer, but they seem to be in French, and we do not take the journals.'

'In any case, I doubt my French would suffice.'

'There is one recent critical monograph in German solely on von Stumpf; I believe it is by a professor in the music department of the university here. The only other work is also in German – a biography. It was written shortly after von Stumpf's death and was published here in the city.'

He took the proffered sheet.

'I shall borrow these two books as I leave, but I shall take your advice and consult the encyclopædias and the musical dictionaries first.'

The Frau Bibliothekarin was not the first to note that Herr Einzelturm's speech was ever so slightly over-formal; she turned away to stifle a sudden outburst of snickers.

Herr Einzelturm found the general and specialist encyclopædias readily enough. Information on von Stumpf was harder to come by and unsatisfactory when he did find it. It was universally agreed that the man had been a composer of little talent, his operas of local interest, his short life quite as long as his competence merited. All the entries stressed the fact that he had made a living as a pianist in a tavern. This irritated Herr Einzelturm. 'Did not Schumann get his start playing in brothels?' he mused, 'Or was it Brahms? One of the great composers. I wonder if he is criticized for that.' The entry in

51

Riemann's *Musik-Lexikon* (12th ed., 1959-67, ed. Gurlitt) was the most comprehensive and the most insulting:

STUMPF, CARL MARIA VON (*b* Waltherrott, 1813(?); *d* Waltherrott, 19 Dec. 1848). Composer and pianist. Birth and life obscure, but he never left his home city. Only known teacher, Geza Tzigano (*qv*), seems to have stopped in Waltherrott for only a few months as itinerant tavern pianist and teacher but his baleful influence was decisive: Stumpf was never better than a composer of bar ditties and it is for these that he will be remembered, if at all; the best known is 'Frülingstraum im Bergwald,' rec. Lale Andersen (1943) and still, reportedly, sung in Waltherrottner drinking holes. His operas [a list which leaves out *Der Fliegende Waltherrottner*] are of purely local interest. Naive and derivative, they exhibit all the excesses of extreme romanticism and none of its virtues. His so-called masterpiece, *Der Hosenkavalier*, is merely vulgar. Suggestions by Pintadeau [*Nouvelle revue musico*LOGIC*ale*, II, 3, Oct 78, pp. 1423-32] that Stumpf may have influenced Wagner, R. Strauss, etc., are revisionist deconstructionist absurdities.

BIBLIOGRAPHY: *Der Waltherrottner Tagesstern*, SARDONIKUS, Waltherrott, 1849. SCORES, LIBRETTI: none published. DISCOGRAPHY: Andersen, *op. cit.*; of the operas, none known.

Herr Einzelturm closed the volume in some confusion and not a little disgust. This would not do; he consulted the computer print-out. The books listed were:

Sardonikus [Meyerhofer, Franz]. *Der Waltherrottner Tagesstern*. Waltherrott: im Selbstverlag, o.J. [1849].

Dunstler, H. '*É/cr(i/ea)ture*,' '*Texte*,' '*Mus(ch)ik:*' *Waltherrotterdämmerung/damen-erinnerung zum Mar(x)ks und Frauenrechtlertum*. Waltherrott: Universitäts-Verlag, 1981.

He returned to the counter and, while hints of giggles drifted through the air like snow flurries, waited patiently until the Frau Bibliothekarin came to his aid. She directed him toward the correct section and in a few minutes Herr Einzelturm was walking out of the library with the books in his hands, while behind him the giggles and snickers exploded like a crystal chandelier dashing itself into bits upon a marble floor: it was the night of his humiliation all over again.

O N THE TRAM to Oberdorf, Herr Einzelturm examined his finds. The older book was dusty, smelly, and printed in gothic script which he could read only with some trouble and irritation. The other had a shiny cover and a full-colour illustration obviously done by computer; like something on a brochure from a manufacturer of automated signalling systems. At least the type was readable; the content was another matter:

> This reading of *Waltherrotterdämmerung*, clearly authorized by von Stumpf himself, is a traditional one encased in approved incrustations. Against it, however, can be set an entirely different one, I shall argue, a 'Buchstäbliches' reading bristling with heterogenous indeterminacies, and leading to irreducible incompatibilities: the ontological self stalked by its iterating, semiotic, subversive doppelgänger.

A man of my age and accomplishment, thought Herr Einzelturm, does not have to read books which use the word 'ontological.' He flipped over a few dozen pages:

> Standing precariously between the suzerainties of imperialist confidence and the insouciance of revolutionary modernism, *Der Hosekavalier* was forced to defend itself against the coercive codifications of a late feudal Todeskampf with a retreat to the already derelict redoubt of that bourgeois capitalist apologia, liberal humanism. On

the defensive in this period of Winterfeld and Ambros, the text is perfunctorily exposed by the lambent inversions of Sardonikus, and is to be seen 'pinnacled dim in the intense inane'.

What in God's name was this about? Were Professors at the University drawing salaries for producing this, shovelling it? Herr Einzelturm consulted the index entries for *Der Hosenkavalier*, selecting at random one of the pages listed, he turned to:

The Socratic imperative, whether engaged in by a person or by a libretto, may well open an interpretive discourse in orthodox schematologies, but ignored or unnoticed 'others' will inevitably throw the achieved paradigm askew. The parerga of *Der Hosenkavalier* are but one of the skewing factors which can be 'un-read' as self-reflective textual folds. This folded construct is best visualized as what Derrida, in a happy phrase, terms an 'invaginated pocket'. Useful in its concept, this pocket can be turned inside-out to yield up a forceful fecundity of self-presence in another emanation of s'entendre parler, a gush of, as it were, Xanthippean counter-dialogue.

Did 'invaginated' have to do with what he thought it did and if it did what did it have to do with opera? And what was so lacking in the German language that this man needed French? And what was 'parerga'?

This delicious unreadability emerges thematically for characters, linguistically, allegorically, and harmonically for listeners and 'composers/librettists'. The Feldwebelin's Act II aria, 'Ach, du, du, du,' is a poignant example of a text in which a denotative structure – the Baron's scato-logical excursus – is lucidly exposed by her in the first two verses as she unwittingly adopts the terminology offered by the Baron, and which has only just been denounced by herself as erroneous: the Feldwebelin is unable to 'read' her own text. So also is von Stumpf helpless when he discovers that the lucidity of his libretto is unable to dispel the error of redoubtable darkness which is its inevitable concomitant.

Herr Einzelturm had in mind a few errors he would like to dispel. In desperation, he flipped to the last chapter; surely he would find something clear, direct in the conclusion:

In 'Entrées' Athalie Homais points out the contrast between von Stumpf's neurotic and phallocentric monosexuality and the Feldwebelin's embracing bisexuality which, she argues, gives her a privileged relation to the libretto and the score. Male sexuality insists on 'monolithic' resistence to the 'other', while female bisexuality encloses the 'other' as does the act of composition. Léocadie Rollet sees in Sister Irmtraud a powerful coalitional goddess she terms 'la terre-mère-nature (ré)productrice'. Galsuinde Lestiboudois privileges the figure of Sister Renate, the orgasmic nun ('la mère qui jouit') and sees opera as the language of la jouissance maternelle, for the feminine is the space not only of music and of writing, but also of truth, 'la vréel' [the 'trureal' or 'she-truth' (vrai-elle)]: the unrepresentable truth that lies beyond and subverts the male orders of logic, mastery and verisimilitude. Yseult Binet finds Freudian 'science' and Nietzschean raptorality in the attribution throughout von Stumpf's works of a dangerous self-sufficiency in woman; Binet deciphers these images to find the Feldwebelin as affirmative woman asserting her own double, unafraid of castration.

Herr Einzelturm lifted his eyes from the page and sighed. The book reminded him of a certain Herr Kauderwelsch who, in the early years of the great expansion, had been hired by the technical department of the WVV. Kauderwelsch's vocabulary was so intimidating that everyone assumed he was a brilliant engineer. But after a number of irritating blunders surfaced, Herr Einzelturm asked the personnel department to initiate discreet enquiries. Herr Kauderwelsch was soon unmasked as a fraud, his diplomas faked, his expertise bogus, his discourse hot air. Before the WVV could take action, however, the police arrived with a warrant for his arrest on charges of gross utterance in, appropriately, inevitably, Mannheim.

Herr Einzelturm closed the book and returned it to his briefcase as the tram slid into the Niedermark terminus where Frau Einzelturm sat waiting in the car.

A PRACTICAL MAN accustomed to crunching his way through 'Monthly Vehicle Maintenance Record,' 'Staffing Projections 1978-79,' or *Wheels: The Monthly Journal of the Municipal Transport Association of the Federal Republic* – a man accustomed to thirty years of this sort of reading material may be excused if he feels a certain anxiety about travelling in such realms of gold as are offered by *The Waltherrottner Day-Star.* Such a man may well leave the volume lying in a dark corner until his wife arises from her chair on the balcony and withdraws to the kitchen to prepare the evening meal. Perhaps he now retrieves the volume under a noisy pretence of selecting another magazine, and then sits at the far end of the balcony ('To enjoy the last of the sun,' he is prepared to say) and cautiously opens the creaking covers, sniffs in disapproval at the rising dust, frowns at the antiquated typeface, and then begins, in his methodical way, at the beginning.

Poetry?

A terrified flip through the rest of the book reassured Herr Einzelturm that it was indeed in prose, and that, apart from what were obviously quotations from the operas, poetry did not much figure in the work. He returned to the beginning:

A Most Humble Dedication to
Alexander Ivanovich Herzen:
European, Writer, Revolutionary.

Herr Einzelturm had taken his political views from Adenauer; he knew little about revolutionaries except that they started riots, and rioters frequently damaged tramcars.

> Shades of Parnassus, ancient groves of sacred oak,
> Beneath which, in dappled light of bronze, stroll folk
> Whose noble miens . . .

Surely one could skip this sort of thing? With an inadvertent glance over his shoulder, Herr Einzelturm turned the page.

Invocation To the Muses

> Inspired by the gift of your benisons nine,
> What chance of failure for this book of mine?
> And certain I am of your kindness to me,
> When I consider how generous you've been to he
> Who forms the subject of my . . .

And skip this as well; surely the man's prose would be a cut above his poetry? On the next page, he found an engraving of the well known – because the only – portrait of von Stumpf, the portrait by Eisel which hangs in the Stadtmuseum, the composer looking pensive, haunted, melancholy. Past the Table of Contents and other business, the text proper began.

The Waltherrottner Day-Star
Chapter the First
Portrait of the Man

READER! thou here beholdest the Eidolon of Carl Maria von Stumpf. So looked and lived, unto his thirty-fifth year, here in the bright little friendly circle of Waltherrott, 'the clearest, most universal man of his time,' save perhaps Goethe. Strange enough is the cunning that resides in the ten fingers, especially what they bring to pass by pencil and pen! Him who never saw aught of the World save his small home town, the World now sees: from the Frontispiece he looks forth here, wondering, doubtless, how *he* came into such a 'Lichtstraße,' yet with kind recognition of all neighbours, even as the moon looks kindly on lesser lights, and, were they but fish-oil cressets, or terrestrial Lustgarten stars (of clipped tin), forbids not their shining. – NAY, THE VERY SOUL OF THE MAN THOU CANST LIKEWISE BEHOLD. Do but look well in those twelve volumes of 'musical wisdom,' which, under the title of *Von Stumpfs Werke*, from Cotta of Waltherrott, we can confidently expect within the twelve-month, – once offer them a trifle of drink money, – will cheerfully hand thee: greater sight, or more profitable, thou wilt not meet with in this generation.

Good Grief! What was it about von Stumpf that attracted lunatic commentators? Herr Einzelturm began to skim:

The Writer of this Volume is not without decision of character, and can believe what he knows. He declares that here is the finest of all living heads; blended passion and repose; serene depths of eyes; the brow, the temples, royally arched, a very palace of thought; – and so forth. It is no wonder the head should be royal and a palace; for a most royal work was appointed to be done therein.

Reader! within that head the whole world lies mirrored, in such clear ethereal harmony as it has done in none since Beethoven left us: even *this* rag-fair of a world, wherein thou painfully strugglest, and (as is like) stumblest, – all lies transfigured here, and revealed authentically to be still holy, still divine. What alchemy was that: to find a mad universe

58

full of scepticism, discord, desperation; and *transmute* it into a wise universe of belief, of melody, of reverence! Was not *there* an *opus magnum*, if one ever was? This, then, is he who, heroically doing and enduring, has accomplished it.

Reader! to thee thyself, even now, he has one counsel to give, the secret of his whole poetic alchemy: GEDENKE ZU LEBEN. Yes, 'think of living'! Thy life, wert thou 'pitifulest of all the sons of earth,' is not idle dream, but a solemn reality. It is thy own; it is all thou hast to front eternity with. Work, then, even as he has done, – 'LIKE A STAR, UN-HASTING, YET UNRESTING.' – *Sic valeas.*

Well! This Meyerhofer certainly did not suffer from the sour cynicism of the encyclopædists; he might have been writing of Goethe or Schiller, the way he was going on. But while it was fine to see von Stumpf receiving the praise which every Waltherrottner knew was his due, it was going to be heavy going if the rest of the book was in this style.

'Are you coming to eat or are you going to sit out there all night?'

'In a minute.'

Herr Einzelturm riffled through the remaining pages: no, this was definitely not going to be an easy read. From the look of it, much of the early part of the book was given over to Stumpf's political education. This came as a nasty surprise, in that his operas suggested that Stumpf had never had any more interest in politics than had Herr Einzelturm himself. Certainly when his life story was studied in school, his impoverished beginnings were impressed upon the students, but nothing was said about politics, so far as Herr Einzelturm recalled. Much as it galled him to weaken before a challenge, he began to admit that perhaps he should skip forward to the operas.

'Your meal is getting cold.'

'Put more mustard on it.'

WHEN THE MEAL was done, Herr Einzelturm steeled himself to the possibility of sarcasm, settled into his reading chair, and blatantly opened the covers of *The Waltherrottner Day-Star*. But by nothing more than a raised eyebrow did Frau Einzelturm betray her interest in her husband's extraordinary activity. Gaining confidence, he turned to the Table of Contents and ran his finger down the list of chapter titles until he found:

This should get past the dreary politics and to the meat of the business; he turned to page 143 and again skimmed.

Chapter the Ninth
The Grand Opening of
Der Hosenkavalier

The last rehearsal done, the last costume altered to the last unexpectedly plump body, the last note for the piccolo or trombone properly sharpened or flattened despite the copyist's efforts to untune harmony, the grand opening could commence. Let us, however, reverse the natural order of affairs (opera being a topsy-turvy world) and reprint here the account of the event as it appeared to the notice of a distinguished visitor to our Milan (as it were) of the North: *viz.* one Professor Bohnmehl, distinguished lecturer in Sacred Musical History at the University of Schwermund, our neighbouring city, and a notably humourless place as will become evident.

Grand Opening in an Historical Perspective

by our Special Correspondent

Music is well said to be the speech of angels; in fact, nothing among the utterances allowed to man is felt to be so divine. It brings us near to the Infinite; we look for moments, across the cloudy elements, into the eternal Sea of Light, when song leads and inspires us. Serious nations, all nations that can still listen to the mandate of nature, have prized song and music as the highest; as a vehicle for worship, for prophesy, and for whatsoever in them was divine. Their singer was a vates, admitted to the council of the universe, friend of the gods, and choicest benefactor to man.

Reader, it was actually so in Greek, in Roman, in Moslem, Christian, most of all in Old-Hebrew times: and if you look how it is now, you will find a change that should astonish you. Good Heavens, from a Psalm of Asaph to a seat at the Hofoper in Waltherrott, what a road men have travelled! The waste that is made in music is probably among the saddest of all our squanderings of God's gifts.

Music has, for a long time past, been avowedly mad, divorced from sense and the reality of things; and runs about now as an open Tollhäusler, for a good many generations back, bragging that she has nothing to do with sense and reality, but with fiction and delirium only; and stares with unaffected amazement, not able to suppress an elegant burst of witty laughter, at my suggesting the old fact to her.

Fact nevertheless it is, forgotten, and fallen ridiculous as it may be. Tyrtæus, who had a little music, did not sing Barber of Seville, but the need of beating back one's country's enemies; a most *true* song, to which the hearts of men did burst responsive into fiery melody, followed by fiery strokes before long. Sophocles also sang, and showed in grand dramatic rhythm and melody, not a fable but a fact, the best he could interpret it; the judgements of Eternal Destiny upon the erring sons of men. Æschylus, Sophocles, all noble poets were priests as well;

and sang the *truest* (which was also the divinest) they had been privileged to discover here below.

David, king of Judah, a soul inspired by divine music and much other heroism, was wont to pour himself into song; he, with seer's eye and heart, discerned the Godlike amid the Human; struck tones that were an echo of the sphere-harmonies, and are still felt to be such. Reader, art thou one of a thousand, able still to read a Psalm of David, and catch some echo of it through the old dim centuries; feeling far off, in thy own heart, what it once was to other hearts made as thine? To sing it attempt not, for it is impossible in this late time; only know that it once was sung. Then go to the Opera, and hear, with unspeakable reflections, what things men now sing!

Herr Einzelturm found his eyelids drooping; when he focussed his mind on the book, he was reminded of some particularly nasty dental work he had suffered through just after the war. But the threat of a little pain could not stop him. He plowed on:

Of the Waltherrottner Hofoper my account, in fine, is this: Lustres, candelabras, painting, gilding at discretion; a hall as of the Caliph Alraschid, or him that commanded the slaves of the Lamp; a hall as if fitted up by the genii, regardless of expense. Upholstery, and the outlay of human capital, could do no more. Artists, too, as they have been called, have been got together from the ends of the world (or at least of the county), regardless likewise of expense, to do dancing and singing, some of them even geniuses in their craft. The very ballet-girls, with their muslin saucers round them, were perhaps little short of miraculous; whirling and spinning there in strange mad vortexes, and then suddenly fixing themselves motionless, each upon her left or right great toe, with the other leg stretched out at an angle of ninety degrees, – as if you had suddenly pricked into the floor, by one of their points, a pair, or rather a multitudinous cohort, of mad restlessly jumping and clipping scissors, and so bidden them rest, with opened blades, and stand still, in the Devil's name! A truly notable motion; marvellous, almost miraculous, were not the people there so used to it. Motion peculiar to the Opera; perhaps the ugliest, and surely one of the most difficult, ever taught a female creature in this world. Nature abhors it; but Art does at least admit it to border on the impossible. One little Kirschen, or Taglioni the Second, that night when I was there, went bounding from the floor as if she had been made of India-rubber, or filled with hydrogen gas, and inclined by positive levity to bolt through the ceiling; perhaps neither Semiramis nor Catherine the Second had bred herself so carefully.

Such talent, and such martyrdom of training, gathered from the four winds, was now here, to do its feat and be paid for it. Regardless of expense, indeed! The purse of Fortunatus seemed to have opened itself, and the divine art of Musical Sound and Rhythmic Motion was welcomed with an explosion of all the magnificences which the other arts, fine and coarse, could achieve. For you are to think of some Rossini or Bellini in the rear of it, too: to say nothing of hosts of scene-painters, machinists, engineers, enterprisers; – fit to have drained the Red Sea, levelled Mount Sinai, or taught the beasts of the field to talk in the tongues of men, had they so set their minds to it!

Alas, and of all these notable or noticeable human talents, and excellent perseverances and energies, backed by mountains of wealth, and led by the divine art of Music and Rhythm vouchsafed by Heaven to them and us, what was to be the issue here this evening? A few hours' amusement, not amusing either, but wearisome and dreary, to a highly-dizened select populace of male and female persons, who seemed to me not much worth amusing! Could any one have pealed into their hearts once, one true thought, and glimpse of Self-vision: 'High-dizened, most expensive persons, Aristocracy so called, or *Best* of the World, beware, beware what proofs you are giving here of betterness and bestness!' And then the salutary pang of conscience in reply: 'A select populace, with money in its purse, and drilled a little by the posture-master: good Heavens! if that were what, here and everywhere in God's Creation, I *am*? And a world all dying because I am, and show myself to be, and to have long been, even that? 'Johann, the carriage, swift, swift! Let me go home in silence, to reflection, perhaps to sackcloth and ashes!' This, and not amusement, would have profited those high-dizened persons.

Amusement, at any rate, they did not get from Euterpe and Melpomene. These two Muses, sent for regardless of expense, I could see, were by the vehicle of a kind of service which I judged to be Paphian rather. Young beauties of both sexes used their opera-glasses, you could notice, not entirely for looking at the stage. And, it must be owned, the light, in this explosion of upholsteries, and the human fine arts and coarse, was magical; and made your fair one an Armida, – if you liked her better so. Nay, certain old Improper Females (of quality), in their rouge and jewels, even these looked some *reminiscence* of enchantment; and I saw this and the other lean domestic Dandy, with icy smile on his old worn face; this and the other Marquis Chatabagues, Prince Mahogany, or the like foreign Dignitary, tripping into the boxes of said females, grinning here awhile, with dyed moustachios and macassar-oil graciosity, and then tripping out again; – and, in fact, I perceived that Schnitzel and Kirschen and the Rhythmic Arts were a mere accompaniment here.

Wonderful to see; and sad, if you had eyes! Do but

64

think of it. Cleopatra threw pearls into her drink in mere waste; which was reckoned foolish of her. O Stumpf, you whose inborn melody, once of kindred, as I judged, to 'the Melodies Eternal,' might have valiantly weeded out this and the other false thing from the ways of men, and made a bit of God's Creation more melodious, – they have purchased you away from that; chained you to the wheel of Prince Mahogany's chariot, and here you make sport for a macassar Chatabagues and his improper females past the prime of life! I lament for you beyond all other expenses. Other expenses are light; you, Stumpf, are the Cleopatra's pearl that should not have been fluid into Mahogany's claret-cup. And Rossini, too, and Mozart and Bellini – O Heaven! when I think that Music too is condemned to be mad, and to burn herself, to this end, on such a funeral pile, – your celestial Hofoper grows dark and infernal to me! Behind its glitter stalks the shadow of Eternal Death; through it too, I look not 'up into the divine eye,' as Richter has it, 'but down into the bottomless eye-socket' – not up towards God, Heaven, and the Throne of Truth, but too truly down towards Falsity, Vacuity, and the dwellingplace of Everlasting Despair.

'I don't mind if you sleep in your chair, but you'll have a stiff neck all day tomorrow, so you'd better come to bed.'

He shook himself, shivered, muttered something about resting his eyes, stared with blank incomprehension at the book on his lap. He had read perhaps half a page: only a fool would have read more.

'I'll make you a cup of hot chocolate, if you'd like.'

'What time is it?'

'Just coming on ten o'clock.'

'Yes, hot chocolate, please.'

A snooze after dinner should be one of the finest of the gentler delights of life. For Herr Einzelturm tonight, this had not been so.

He had been dreaming of stretching machines.

B UT THE MAN who had masterminded the modernization of the WVV was not to be daunted by a book, however out-of-date, digressive, irrelevant, or florid it might be. The next morning he took a brisk walk (going nowhere near the Keilerfelsen), returned for coffee and rolls, then sat himself on the balcony to subject this book to the light of day. He would skip about as he wished, he would disagree when so inclined, he would draw judgements.

Frau Einzelturm peeked over her spectacles; the determination she saw in his face, in the set of his body reassured her: he was on the mend. She returned to her crossword.

Herr Einzelturm opened the book at random, riffled through some pages, began to read at the first chapter beginning he encountered:

Chapter the Seventeenth
Some Interpretations

WE DEFY the most careless or prejudiced reader to witness these works without an impression of something splendid, wonderful and daring. But they require to be studied as well as listened to, and this with no ordinary patience, if the listener, especially the foreign listener, wishes to comprehend rightly either their truth or their want of truth. Tried by many an accepted standard, von Stumpf would be speedily enough disposed of; pronounced a mystic, a German dreamer, a rash and presumptuous innovator; and so consigned, with equanimity, perhaps with a certain jubilee, to the Limbo appointed for all such wind-bags and deceptions. There are few composers with whom deliberation and careful distrust of first impressions are more necessary than with Stumpf. He is a phenomenon from the very surface; he presents himself with a professed and determined singularity: his harmony itself is a stone of stumbling to the critic; to critics of the harmonic species, an unpardonable, often an insuperable, rock of offence. Not that he is ignorant of harmonics, or disdains consonance or tonality; but he exercises both in a certain latitudinarian spirit; deals with astonishing liberality in dissonance and chromaticism; invents new tonal progressions, alters old accepted ones, or chains and pairs and packs them together into most jarring combination; in short, produces melodic lines of the most heterogenous, lumbering, interminable kind. No opera proceeds without the most erratic digressions, and voluminous ragtags rolling after it in many a snaky twine. Ever and anon there occurs some 'Extraleaf,' with its satirical petition, program, or other wonderful intercalation, no mortal can foresee on what. It is indeed, a mighty maze; and often the panting listener toils after him in vain; or, baffled and spent, indignantly stops short, retires, perhaps to the saloon bar, perhaps forever . . .

Oh, good heavens, what gas! If I can't find something with more meat to it . . . let's just skip on here . . .

The secret of the matter is . . .

That sounds as if he's coming to the point:

The secret of the matter is, that Stumpf requires more study than most readers and listeners care to give him.

I can well understand that, especially if this is the study required.

As we approach more closely, many things grow clearer.

By page 293, I should think so.

Stumpf has been called an intellectual Colossus; and in truth it is somewhat in this light that we view him. That, in the point of humour, Stumpf in his libretti excels all

German authors, is saying much for him, and may be said truly. Lessing has humour, – of a sharp, rigid, substantial, and, on the whole, genial sort; yet the ruling bias of his mind is to logic. So likewise has Wieland, though much diluted by the general *loquacity* of his nature, and impoverished still further by the influences of a cold, meagre, French scepticism. Among the Ramlers, Gellerts, Hagedorns, of Frederick the Second's time we find abundance, and delicate in kind too, of that light matter which the French call pleasantry; but little or nothing that deserves the name of humour. In the present age, however, there is Goethe, with a rich true vein; and this sublimated, as it were, to an essence, and blended in still union with his whole mind. Tieck also . . . But of all these men, there is none that, in depth, copiousness and intensity of humour, can be compared with Carl Maria. He alone exists in humour; lives, moves and has his being in it. With him it is not so much united to his other qualities, of intellect, fancy, imagination, moral feeling, as these are united to it . . . Not without reason have his Waltherrottner panegyrists named him '*Carl Maria der Einzige*, CARL MARIA THE UNIQUE.'

Impossible; the Waltherrottner Luft which should have produced an airy, buoyant, and lucid writer had instead produced a windbag. Grotesque, absurd man.

Another chapter:

Chapter the Twentieth
Judgement

OF STUMPF's individual Works, of his opinions, his general philosophy of life, we have no room left us to speak.

What in God's name was the book about if not these very things?!

Regarding his Operas, we may say, that, except in several instances, they are not what, in strict language, we can term unities: with much callida junctura of parts, it is rare that any of them leaves on us the impression of a perfect, homogeneous, indivisible whole. A true work of art requires to be *fused* in the mind of its creator, and, as it were, poured forth (from his imagination, though not from his pen) at one simultaneous gush. Stumpf's works do not always bear sufficient marks of having been in *fusion*; yet neither are they merely *riveted* together; to say the least, they have been *welded*.

In character, however, he is at home; a true poet; a maker; his Walther, Adalbert, Max, the Waltherrottner are living figures. With his heroines again he is even more successful; they are often true heroines, though perhaps with too much variety of character; while the opera stage cries out for a few high-minded ideal figures, he gives us bustling, buxom wives and wenches, with all the caprices, perversities, and warm generous helpfulness of women: in Irmtraud, Renate, Senta, and especially Gisela, he exhibits an imagination of a singularity, nay on the whole, of a truth and grandeur, unexampled elsewhere.

Stumpf's Philosophy, a matter of no ordinary interest both as it agrees with the common philosophy of Germany and disagrees with it, must not be touched on for the present. . . .

Good. Over the page.

Of writings which, though with many reservations, we have praised so much, our hesitating readers may demand some specimen. It is a summer night, and Carl Maria has taken leave of myself and several other of such of his friends as met regularly round our Stammtisch at the charming inn named Die Drei Grafen; it had been an evening of laughter and of tears; like us, he is sad to part: –

'We were all deeply moved. We tore ourselves apart and, while my friends retired, I was left alone with the night.'

Now this was interesting: it seemed to be from von Stumpf's journal.

'And I walked aimlessly through woods, through valleys, and over brooks, and through sleeping villages, to enjoy the great Night, like a Day. I walked, and still looked, like a compass needle, toward the polestar, to strengthen my heart at the gleaming twilight, at this upstretching aurora of a morning beneath my feet. White night-butterflies flitted, white blossoms fluttered, white stars fell, and the white snow-powder of clouds hung silvery in the high Shadow of the Earth, which reaches beyond the Moon, and which is our Night. Then began the Æolian Harp of the Creation to tremble and to sound, blown on from above; and my immortal Soul was a string in the Harp. – The heart of a brother, everlasting Man, swelled under the everlasting heaven, as the seas swell under the sun and under the moon. – The distant village clocks struck midnight, mingling, as it were, with the everpealing tone of ancient Eternity. – I walked silently through little hamlets, and close by their outer churchyards, where crumbled upcast coffin-boards were glimmering, while the once-bright eyes that had lain in them were mouldered into grey ashes. Cold thought! clutch not like a cold spectre at my heart: I look up to the starry sky, and an everlasting chain stretches thither, and over, and below; and all is Life, and Warmth, and Light, and all is Godlike or God. . . .

'Towards morning, from the prominence behind the Oberdorf churchyard, I descried the late lights, little city of my dwelling, which I belong to on this side of the grave (and that deep bed soon enough arrived at, I fear); I returned to the Earth; and in thy steeples, behind the great

70

midnight, it struck half-past two: about this hour, in 1848, Mars went down in the west, and the Moon glowed in the zenith; and my soul desired in grief for the noble warlike blood which is still, in Act III, streaming on the blossoms of Spring: "Ah, retire not, noble Revolution, like red Mars; and when the struggle is o'er, thou, still Peace, come forth like the mild divided Moon." The very subject for Walther's aria; and so homeward, "Fleet beyond imagination" through "scenes of celestial light;" first the words, then the music: – a cornucopia of Revolution onto the page, fingers racing to keep abreast! Ahh, Art! Ahh Life!'

Yes, this was a taste of the true von Stumpf! A sensitive being, a poet writing out of the depths of his soul! How amazed he would be were he to return today: from that prominence above the church-yard he would have been privileged to see spread out before him the Oberdorf tram terminal in all its splendour! And he was an artist; he would understand the beauty of it, certainly!

And what a contrast to his biographer! One last chance: what is Meyerhofer's conclusion? Herr Einzelturm turned to the last page, leafed back to a space break:

AS A COMPOSER, Carl Maria von Stumpf's character will oc-casion little difficulty. A richly gifted nature; but never wisely guided, or resolutely applied; a loving heart; an intel-lect subtle and inquisitive, if not always clear and strong; a gorgeous, deep and bold imagination; a true, nay keen and burning sympathy with all high, all tender and holy things: here lay the main elements of no common poet and com-poser; save only those two still wanting, – the force to culti-vate them, and mould them into pure union; and the higher duty to mould them into exempla of the political life of his fellow man. But they have remained uncultivated, disunited, too often struggling in wild disorder: his music, like his life, is still not so much an edifice as a quarry.

71

Stumpf had cast a look into perhaps the very deepest region of the Wonderful; but he had not learned to live there: he was yet no denizen of that mysterious land; and, in his visions, its splendour is strangely mingled and overclouded with the flame or smoke of mere earthly fire. Of his 'Gesamtkunstwerke,' – music dramas – we have already spoken; and with much to praise, found always more to censure. In his shorter, orchestral works we are better satisfied: here in the rude, jolting vehicle of Bergwald peasant dance metres we often find a strain of true pathos, and a deep, though quaint significance. But his 'music dramas,' are among the worst operas known to us; each a misshapen, lumbering, complected coil, well-nigh inexplicable in its entanglements, and seldom worth the trouble of unravelling.

As a man, the ill-fated Stumpf can still less content us. His feverish, inconstant and wasted life we have already looked at. Schober, his determined well-wisher, admits that in practice he was selfish, wearying out his best friends by the most barefaced importunities; a man of no dignity; avaricious, greedy, sensual, at times obscene, and IN HIS TREATMENT OF ONE DELICATE FLOWER FROM THE CHORUS OF THE OPERA, AN UNFEELING BRUTE; in discourse, with all his humour and heartiness, apt to be intolerably long-winded; which exposed him to incessant ridicule and manifold mystifications from people of the world. On his sordid dereliction of responsibility to his fellow citizens, fellow men, in the Great Year of 1848, we have already ventilated our arguments; and we can only wonder what might have been the state of political life in Waltherrott – in all of Germany! – today had only Stumpf, as has Herr Wagner recently in Dresden, pronounced himself against tyranny; with whatever consequences. The truth is, his defects as a composer were also his defects as a man: he was feeble, and without volition; in life, as in music, his endowments fell into confusion; his character relaxed itself on all sides into incoherent expansion; his activity became gigantic endeavour, followed by most dwarfish performance.

Unfortunate von Stumpf, that he had ever met this odious Meyerhofer, obviously consumed by jealousy behind his fawning praise; away with him, this posturing, puffed-up jackanapes, this coxcomb, this 'hound of poodle breed!' What a wretched life the man must have had with this windy tormentor as his only commentator and biographer. It was widely known among the people of Waltherrott that the composer had suffered noble despair:

Yet, every morn I tremble when I wake . . .

But who would have suspected that while he was wrestling with the angels of creation, this snake was at work in his garden?

Herr Einzelturm closed the book upon his lap and turned his face to a shaft of golden light which fell though the pines.

And yet . . . and yet there was something curious about the book. In the early chapters Stumpf was being praised as the light of German theatrical literature, a poet for the century, and a composer without equal; in the later ones he is being reviled as a moral degenerate, a political coward, an incompetent composer.

Very strange.

It was as if this Meyerhofer had undergone a change of attitude halfway through the writing and had not bothered to resolve the inconsistencies.

Herr Einzelturm would have been the first to admit he knew nothing about the arts, but he could understand a written report. When you were trying to make your case, you had to plan your argument with great care, lay out your facts clearly, anticipate objections and problems, and summarize your main points, driving home your conclusion with force, but with all apparent reasonableness. This Meyerhofer would have benefitted from a term or two of the University's evening course, 'Functional Writing for Effective Communication.'

Yes, it certainly had the smell, and Herr Einzelturm had seen enough such, of a report which changed course in the middle of the journey. Think of the logic behind the writing: if the subject was as irritating or nasty *when he began to write* as Meyerhofer seemed to think *by the time he was finished*, then how could the man have begun to write a biography, have struggled through several hundred pages, and then have published it at his own expense? Was this likely? No, it was not. It seemed likely Meyerhofer had begun writing about a close friend whom he loved and admired, and had finished with a diatribe against a man he considered a traitor to some political cause or other, some obscure local faction which flourished during the revolution of 1848; and as a seducer of women. This latter was likely true, if what little Herr Einzelturm had heard about artists was anything to go by, but the political business was more complicated.

What hidden conflicts had sparked the change?

Herr Einzelturm had plunged into waters over his head, but was beginning to learn to swim. If he was going to find out the truth about Carl Maria von Stumpf, he was not going to find it in *The Waltherrottner Day-Star.*

H E MEANT to return the two books then drop the subject, there being nothing left to investigate. But in the Niedermark tram terminus (where his wife again dropped him while she did her shopping) he opened the Meyerhofer book again and was reminded of von Stumpf's journal. The few footnotes, when he began to understand their abbreviated form, seemed to point to this source. But where would it be? Long lost, no doubt. Then, in the short acknowledgements, he found:

> I could not have written this work without the invaluable and generous help of Herr Staubig, the Director of the Waltherrott Stadtbibliothek, and his knowledgeable and hard-working staff . . .

'Giggling staff' would have been more like it for most of them . . .

> who were kind enough to guide me through the treasures of the Manuscript Room, and to help me locate the von Stumpf papers . . .

Well, he was not to meet his wife until five, so he might as well try to find the journal. If the staff could help the wretched Meyerhofer, they could also help Herr Einzelturm, for it seemed clear the von Stumpf papers had been in the library and there seemed no reason they should not still be there. The first step was to question the librarian he had spoken to the other day. But in the vestibule of the library, as he slipped the books into the return slot, he glanced at the directory on the wall. The final item was:

Manuscript Room

> Not open to the public. Access is restricted to bona fide scholars with letters of reference from universities and other recognized centres of research.

The Waltherrott Verkehrsverbund, however august in its own field, could hardly be called a centre of scholarly research. Would Herr Einzelturm be deflected from his purpose? No one who knew him could be in any doubt about the answer.

But the task was not the sort he was used to. He returned to his flat to get a few things for his wife and pick up the mail. From the envelope containing a professional journal he took the germ of an idea. The problem was to transform into a musical scholar the man who had been the laughing stock of the library a week earlier.

From a stationery shop, he bought several sheets of press-on letters with which he constructed a letterhead for the Institut für Musikwissenschaft und Forschung, Meiringen. As he anticipated, the letters seemed a bit stark, a bit unconvincing alone on the page, so he added the seal of the *Journal of German Mechanical and*

Electrical Engineering, a smudgy engraving of a nineteenth century device of forgotten origin and use, resting on a plinth and encircled by leaves of a sort unknown in the neighbourhood of Waltherrott. This master, photocopied half a dozen times, gave him a safe supply on which to type the letter To Whom It May Concern, introducing Herr Professor Doktor Gräber and signed with an illegible flourish by Herr Professor Doktor Doktor Direktor Zwingli, all most satisfactory and impressive. But there was another detail . . .

A T THE TOP end of the Geflügelstraße, the end closest to the side entrance of the Hauptbahnhof, one finds several cheap hotels, questionable bars, sex shops; down nearer the river, one finds shops for used appliances, inferior fishing tackle, and, to Herr Einzelturm's satisfaction, 'H. Schnabernack – Novelties, Tricks, Costumes.' He was not known here and would not be expected to rent a full costume, as he might from the toney costumiers in the streets near the opera house where the bonton of Waltherrott reserved their costumes for Carnival. Here in the shop of H. Schnabernack, Herr Einzelturm guessed one could claim one wanted something with which to amuse the grandchildren when it was perfectly obvious one planned to rob a bank, kidnap the Chancellor of the Federal Republic, or blow up a nuclear power station to protest fur coats. Here no questions were asked, no eyes raised.

'Perhaps this red clown's nose, mein Herr.'

'I wish to be disguised as a professor, not a clown.'

Herr Schnabernack raised an eyebrow to suggest that professors and clowns were not all that easily distinguishable.

'So then, perhaps these buck teeth? No? Of course not. Well, why not a beard? The perfect thing!'

'That sounds promising.'

'I have beards in a number of styles. Would you wish to glue it on, or would it be sufficient to use elastic?'

'What is the difference?'

After a discussion of the merits of each, Herr Einzelturm reluctantly decided to adopt the glue method, and Herr Schnabernack brought from the back room a cardboard box overflowing with undergrowth.

'Now then, mein Herr, as to style . . .'

Herr Schnabernack laid them out on the counter, a luxuriant display: a braided *postiche* from ancient Egypt, a full beard of an Old Testament prophet, a trimmed beard of a Roman patrician, a forked Moorish beard, a natty Van Dyke, a dashing moustachio-and-beardlet of *The Laughing Cavalier*, a spiky Imperial, a pair of bushy mutton chops, a limp Abe Lincoln chin curtain, and . . .

'This looks familiar, but . . .'

'You will know it as soon as it is on, mein Herr: the Franz Josef, a very popular model. And a fine choice if disguise is desired, because the side whiskers and large mustache give ample coverage while leaving the chin free, an advantage when one wants to eat or drink. It is also not too hot for summer wear or for those who plan to dance the night away.'

'I do not plan to dance the night away.'

'As you wish. In any case, with your strong chin to enhance the effect, it will be quite . . . distinguished.'

Frau Einzelturm had frequently spoken, in the early years of their marriage, of her pride in his manly chin; more recently she had been calling him Lump-Jaw.

'I'll take it.'

'A wise choice, mein Herr. Now, as to the glue . . .'

FOR THE FIRST few blocks, it seemed to Herr Einzelturm that passers-by were gawking at him. But accustomed as he was to the loneliness of power, he strode stolidly on towards the library, trusting his virtues to announce his dignity. In addition to his own natural consequence, innate, matured these many years, he also walked with the bearded dignity of his assumed character. At the Stadtbibliothek, he strode up the steps, through the vestibule, and over to the information desk where he flourished his letter, the very figure of the distinguished Herr Professor Doktor Gräber of the distinguished if not very well-known Institut für Musikwissenschaft und Forschung, Meiringen.

Whether because she was impressed by the letter, by the distinguished personage before her, or by Herr Einzelturm's request to visit the Manuscript Room, the young blonde woman was struck dumb. She backed away, mouth agape, and disappeared into the office. Presently the older lady came out, patting her hair and peering over her reading specs.

'Good afternoon, Herr Professor Doktor,' she murmured, placing the letter upon the counter. 'I understand you wish to visit the Manuscript Room.'

'That is so, Frau Bibliothekarin.'

'Well, the letter seems . . . to be in order. Is there something specific you are seeking? The Manuscript Room is not as fully catalogued as the general collections. It will be easier for me to help you if I know what you wish to see.'

Herr Einzelturm had hoped to avoid mentioning his subject: the repetition of interest in von Stumpf from two visitors, however different in appearance, over several days was liable to arouse suspicion. But he could think of no other composer whose papers might be found there, so there was nothing for it but to proceed with confidence and trust that his dignity would see him through.

'Yes, I wish to examine any papers you may have relating to the great Waltherrottner composer, Carl Maria von Stumpf.'

The Frau Bibliothekarin eyed him doubtfully.

'I'm not at all sure there are any such papers here, but we can certainly look.'

She murmured a few words to the younger woman, found a ring of ancient keys in a drawer under the counter, and motioned Herr Einzelturm to follow her along a corridor to the rear of the building.

'The manuscript catalogue is not in the computer, nor even on microfiche. We get so few scholars,' she remarked as they descended a bleak iron staircase. 'There is, it seems, little interest in the lives of long dead Waltherrottners.'

78

'A failure, Frau Bibliothekarin, which, perhaps, in my small way, I can rectify.'

'It will be much appreciated.'

He thought she was showing a more than polite interest in his beard.

'Here we are,' she said as they arrived at the bottom, a sub-basement level. A sign which had clearly been affixed in a bygone era announced that the steel door guarded the Manuscript Room.

'It is meant to be fireproof,' she remarked. 'Let us hope it is not proof against this key. As I say, it has been years since . . . Ahh . . . and if I can find the light switch . . .'

The room would have been as bleak and claustrophobic as an air raid bunker save for the reading desk and the bookcases; like the sign by the door, they were relics of an age when labour was cheap and civic pride expressed itself in ornate decoration. The cabinets were of mahogany with carved mouldings, pilasters, and pediments. Behind glass doors the books, boxes, dossiers, and portfolios were shelved in embossed and uniform ranks, in crenellations, in jumbled and chaotic piles. Brass fittings held slips of card stock inscribed with characters faded to sepia.

'Finding anything here is a problem because it is consulted so rarely. I doubt I can even remember how the holdings are arranged. However . . .'

Herr Einzelturm watched with trusting wonder as the Frau Bibliothekarin pushed her reading glasses up her nose and sat before a large ledger which lay upon the desk. She turned the pages slowly at first, then more quickly back and forth until she skewered an entry with her finger.

'Possibly . . . if I can find the section . . .'

She went to the bookcases and began scanning the labels. She moved from case to case, peering high and low and muttering to herself until after a minute she said, 'I think perhaps we . . . if I can just find the right key . . .'

After half a dozen tries she swung open the door and began examining the items on the shelf. She pulled several from the row and placed them on the reading desk: a handsome volume bound in morocco, a dogeared notebook, and a black folder with untidy sheets puffing from its open ends.

Thus so easily confronted by the objects of his desire, Herr Einzelturm gazed at them with some dismay. If he was to find the answer to his questions, it might well be here before him: but was there an answer? And would he recognize it?

The Frau Bibliothekarin gave a peremptory cough which Herr Einzelturm's experience told him meant a change of tone, and indeed she went on to list the rules for the use of the room: protection of manuscripts; how to turn pages; marking or crimping of pages verboten; locking of door even during visits to the WC; food, drink, and smoking materials strengste verboten; search of briefcases upon leaving, and, in extremis, possibility of strip searches, arrest, incarceration.

'I understand exactly.'

'It's not that I suspect distinguished visiting scholars, but orders . . .'

'Are orders. Of course.'

He clicked his heels very slightly, came to a shambling sort of attention, and nodded his head.

'Of course.'

In a few moments he found himself alone in the room, seated at the great oak desk with its leather surface. He glanced at the portfolio and saw the musical lines on the pages which protruded. There would be no truth for him there. The morocco volume was handsomely printed, but seemed to be about church matters, so perhaps the Frau Bibliothekarin had included it by accident. The notebook with its marbled covers must be the journal.

Following the Frau Bibliothekarin's directions, he lifted the cover and with the palm of his hand smoothed it gently back.

Part Three

The Journal of
Carl Maria von Stumpf
Genius.
Failure.
Volume IV

20 APRIL 1848: I shall blow my brains out. *If I can get my hands on a pistol* I shall blow my brains out, splatter them upon the ceiling of this wretched room. How to get the pistol, I haven't the money for a stein of beer, never mind a pistol, I could steal one, but from whom? How load it, how hold it, how fire it? Blow off my left cheek and live, more wretched than I am now? Is it possible?

No, it is not possible!

Not possible.

Failure I am, wretched failure, hopeless, impossible, useless. I look in the shard of mirror in the morning (at noon, at night come to that) and I see nothing there, an absence of a person, of a creature, of flesh, of soul.

Yet there is something there, here: not me, not Stumpf the pianist, the composer of operas and, alas, wretched soul, worm, composer of ditties, Stumpf the lover, drunk, once little boy, happy little boy until Papa ran off and Mama died and he went to live with Uncle Heinie, *not this Stumpf,* some other creature taking over my brain, my soul, some demon creature, doppelgänger set to enslave me, drive me mad, taking over the country of my soul, burning towns, burning bridges, fertile (*sometimes* fertile) fields, hamlets, farms, devilish, skeletal captain out of Dürer leading his faceless marauding troops, rabble, they're burning, looting, raping, leaving all behind them in ruins, scorched earth, wisps of smoke drifting across the horizon, dying sun red above a blackened horizon, lurid red through the smoke.

The Black Death, Great Peasant War, Thirty Year's War, inside this skull.

Oh, God in Heaven, I swear I have not wanted this, I would have lived the quiet life of a grub content to see, to investigate, to disturb nothing beyond the succulent leaf on which I munch, had I but known what tortures await the ambitious.

No, not true.

I am ambitious for Truth and Beauty, ambitious to embody the passion of my immortal Soul in operas which blaze out like comets from the stage and the pit and sear the souls of the audience so completely that the dross of boredom and stupidity and envy is purged from them and they can become clear and joyful, radiant as angels, as seraphim, as the music of the spheres.

Yes, I admit to ambition.

But there is another sort of ambition, ambition for wealth, power, fame – jealous, spiteful ambition, ambition to win not with Truth and Beauty, but with lies, cunning, slander, conspiracy, ambition which seeks to conquer all about, to eat the hearts and souls of friend and enemy alike and, worse, *to break the innocent, break, humiliate, enslave, destroy all humanity . . . to deny hope!*

To . . .

To force him to slouch nightly to Die Drei Grafen and sit at the piano playing 'Frülingstraum am Bergwald,' 'Die Mädchen mit dem rote Hut,' 'Ein hübsch Husar was gekommen.'

Oh, dear God, why did you give me the talent to write trash?

'Hey, piano player, d'youse know, "Ein Rose im Winter?"'

How about 'A Rose up your Nose' you drunken churl?

'My Arse in Winter'?

I cannot stand it, I cannot live with my soul eaten by these vermin.

And the solution is simple enough, for I have an appointment in three days' time with the famous, the notorious Herr Wurmlein, the Intendant, the Field Marshall, the Pope of the Waltherrott opera house, well known to me, I, unfortunately, well known to him. To this Wurmlein I wrote two weeks ago dangling a little bait:

> Beg leave to present idea for new opera . . . very special to city and to opera company . . . prefer not to commit myself to paper . . . would be willing . . . in confidence . . . verbal proposal for work . . . highest seriousness, but box office success . . .

All very well and just like half a dozen other letters I have sent to Herr Wurmlein since my *Fliegende Waltherrottner* was so heinously, cruelly, viciously, criminally *assassinated* three years ago; just like the other letters except that this one brought an answer: Herr Wurmlein invited me to visit him and present my proposal. Which means my chance has come, the wheel of fortune has borne me to the top again and all I need to do is convince Herr Wurmlein that my proposal is worthy.

And then he will loosen the purse strings;

And I can stop noodling 'Frülingstraum am Bergwald' and get on with writing my opera.

Except:

There is no opera.

There is no idea.

Nothing.

And I have only promised *The Marriage of Figaro* crossed with *Fidelio*.

I shall go leap into the Lohbach.

I shall throw myself before a train.

I shall take poison. I promise I shall.

Throw myself from the Waltherburg.

Definitely. For Certain. Beyond any doubt.

This time I have decided: I shall end it all.

But first I shall go around to Die Drei Grafen to see if I can raise enough of an advance on next month's wages to drink myself into a state of divine inspiration or devilish oblivion.

Then, in three days, I shall either be scaling the heights or plumbing the depths.

And I have only too solid a premonition which it shall be.

Farewell World, you'll not much miss this wretched failure.

I vomit in your face.

Oh, my beautiful soul!

21 APRIL: At Die Drei Grafen, at our Stammtisch, everyone was helpful, generous, *insistent* with ideas, not so generous with subsidies for drink (to be fair, none have much to be generous with); but I managed to while away the evening with enough lager to loosen the tongue, although not so much as to loosen the brain. Of course, they had only one subject: the revolution. Well, yes, I can see the appeal. I suppose I ought to rush off to Frankfurt, drink down the atmosphere as if it were Renatenbräu, stir up my spirit with the Spirit of the Times, New Age which is upon us, caught up in the whirlwind, knock out an opera filled with patriotic melodies – there can be money in them if you get a good enforceable contract with a moderately honest publisher. I expect Haydn was well enough paid for the Emperor Hymn but what did Rouget de Lisle ever make from 'La Marseillaise'? Or perhaps he got a pension or something, Legion of Honour, whatever. Anyway, the Spirit of the Times is in Frankfurt-am-Main, while I – need I belabour the point? – am stuck here in Waltherrott without enough money for train fare to Schwermund, never mind Frankfurt.

'But you should be the poet, the composer of the Revolution!'

'And you, my dear Senn, should be the assistant fishmonger to the Revolution.'

'Don't be insulting!'

'I am most certainly not being insulting. Revolutions need fish as much as they need flats and sharps. And they certainly need clerks,' I added, pointing a finger at Schober, 'and typesetters, Spaun, and even maltsters, Wayss, perhaps *especially* maltsters . . .'

'Point granted,' conceded Meyerhofer. 'We should all go to Frankfurt to join the Revolution, but we can none of us afford the trip, never mind the room and board once we get there. Not now, at least. In the meantime, my friends, the question is how do we help advance the revolution from where we are?'

'Or perhaps,' said Steinsberg, sotto voce, 'We should just start it here?'

'Sweep Waltzing Walther, Twenty-third (Four-hundred-and-fiftieth?) Graf vom Faß out of town? Waltzing, drinking, philandering, useless Walther right out of town, declare a republic, Free City of Waltherrott, marching into the bright dawn, noon? of Liberté, Égalité, Fraternité, Truth, Beauty, free cakes for all, free beer, barmaids (but keep Fat Sophie for yourself, thank you), milkmaids' bosoms suddenly accessible for a quick squeeze on a whim, all this with exit of Waltzing Walther, I'm all for it, show me the barricades.'

'Scoff if you wish, Carl, but the world is changing, a fresh wind is sweeping across the land.'

'And not just this one. In France, Italy, Austria, Prussia, Hungary, things are changing, Metternich is out, the old order is everywhere in disarray, in retreat. This time mankind shall rise up and throw down the shackles of tyranny. And if we are not part of it, we are no better than traitors to the German people, the German nation, mankind!'

They all nodded vigorously, fists thumping on table, 'Ja, ja!' Nonetheless they kept their voices low and their eyes alert. Die Drei Grafen is reasonably safe, but one never knows, despite pious claims in the *Zeitung* that censorship has been abolished, and the Rights of Man everywhere declared. You never know: Fat Sophie might be writing it all down, if the lazy slut could write. People in power have a way of proving that their plots are free speech and ours are sedition. Although who is in power hereabouts, I don't know. Official head of state is Waltzing Walther, but he is more evident in his absence than otherwise. Does he even live here any more? Seems to me the vom Faß box at the opera (when I deign to climb to the gods to view the competition) is always occupied by the bürgermeister or other civic or graffinical official. Walther waltzed away? Prussian agents behind the scenes? Who knows?

We pulled our heads closer together and talked over the possibilities of overthrowing the powers that be, whoever they might be. Frankly, the possibilities were very tenuous. Although I admit they must have seemed even worse in Vienna, not to mention Berlin: rebelling against Habsburgs is serious enough, but those Hohenzollerns can get very nasty and the Berliners are trained to show an Ausweis before they fart. Still, they've pulled it off, haven't they? So far.

So the heads all drawn together talked of occupying the Rathaus or the Dom or the Waltherburg or the Bahnhof, and gradually I sat back and listened with less than complete attention, and began doodling with some melodies.

First I jotted down old Haydn's effort[1]:

FIG. 1: 'Gott erhalte Franz den Kaiser,' Haydn, 1797.

Too churchy for me – and he did call it the 'Emperor *Hymn*' didn't he.

The French one is certainly more lively:

---

[1] All musical illustrations are facsimiles of the von Stumpf autograph notes in the *Journal* and appear courtesy of the Waltherrott Stadtbibliothek.

86

FIG. 2: 'La Marseillaise,' Rouget de Lisle, 1792.

But with that kind of activity, the Revolution would dissolve in frenzied Gallic argument and vituperation:

Kindly remove your elbow from my eye while I try to aim zees rifle, you species of camel!

Sacré bleu, did ze cook pees in ze café pot?

Allons enfants de la Patrie!

Allons your behind on a splintery broom handle, sale cochon!

On the principle that this is all serious business, I tried a serious theme of my own:

FIG. 3: Unidentified theme.

Too boring: 'Brothers and sisters of the Revolution, choose your pillows and let's go fall asleep on the barricades.'

No, it had to be a noble melody, not too slow, not too fast, a catchy tune that stirs the heart and is easy to remember. After a bit I came up with this (as best I recall it):

FIG. 4: Unidentified theme.

Which seemed to hit just the right note of starry-eyed optimism and wide-awake activity.

But you need more than altruism and smiles to win a Revolution; you also have to thump the enemy from time to time, so I cast about for a good thumping theme and came up with this one (again, as best I recall it):

FIG. 5: Unidentified theme.

Put some stirring words to that, teach it to a gang of beer swilling louts, and in no time you'd have all the thumping you care to see.

When I recopied these two onto neater paper, I handed the sheets to Meyerhofer: 'Here you are, two revolutionary marches, perfect ditties to rouse the populace, throw down Bastilles, release political prisoners, overthrow tyrants, cudgel enemies into submission, promise great future, march we all together in glowing sunrise, etc.'

He was suspicious, can't read music, thought I'd just re-cobbled 'Frülingstraum am Bergwald' or something, so I played them on the piano and everyone was most impressed.

'Thank you, Carli,' he said. 'Your cynical attitude suggests the music you offer might be more fit for a tavern or brothel, but these are just the sort of thing we need.'

'Oh yes, proper marches, get the troops swinging along in step, left, right . . .'

'I'm determined to go to Frankfurt, and if I do, I'll try to pass them on to someone who can make use of them.'

And that is the last we'll hear of those tunes. About the best I can do, I expect: with my cough and sunken chest, with my shakes and stumbles, I don't think I'm cut out for the barricades. But this Revolution really does give Waltherrottners – and all Germans – the first chance in centuries to change the world. Freedom, dignity, democracy at last? Wonderful: just the subject for an opera; I'd be pleased to do it, if someone would vouchsafe me a vision of exactly where the Revolution is going. No, I'm not being silly: I know that if someone could tell me where it was going it wouldn't be a revolution: that's the whole point about revolutions. And, in truth, I suppose where it's going is better than here. But a political composer needs more information than is on offer. I try to get into Die Drei Grafen every day to glance through the papers as I sip my lunch, and there seems to be a certain confusion. Well, it's only natural, isn't it? I'm not complaining. But an opera takes at least two months to write, twice that for a really good job, and if I had started two months ago on an opera about the Revolution, I'd have one large stack of wasted paper by now. Following events is a job for reporters, not composers.

Imagine it's 1792, whatever, and you're slogging through an opera which extols the received wisdom of the French Revolution *to this point*: a constitutional monarchy. Then Louis and Marie Antoinette decamp for Koblenz: two months' work up in flames. No, with my luck, I'd sit down to rewrite the thing. Take out hero-king who was merely born to job of leader, accident of history, disgraceful perversion of political truth, whatever, recast scenes, rearrange arias, replace king with leader who earns the job through virtue: Citizen Robespierre, say. Can't recall the exact chronology here, but with my luck the opera would actually make it on stage just in time for fall of Robespierre, his arrest and mine, *La Patrie en danger! Off with their heads!*

No, anyone embarking on such a project in the middle of the events needs a lot of luck, and I have never been noted for an excess of luck.

But.

But there might be a way around the problem, I found myself musing: *Why not an historical subject?* Pick one of the great German heroes of the past, and write about him. First there would be the choice of subject, but with a reasonable hero there would be ways of bringing up this aspect or the other so that the subject would fit any number of situations the Revolution might throw up in the coming months. That way I would have freedom to draw parallels, to comment, but I could shift emphasis fairly quickly according to the progress of events.

Yes, I think I have it now. The question is just one of finding a suitable subject; but I can do that tomorrow.

If my brain will be kind enough to let me sleep.

22 APRIL: A German Hero
(Name to be Substituted)
A New Opera on An Historical Subject
by Carl Maria von Stumpf

Possible subjects:

Ariovistus, Ambiorix, Gundahar, or one of those characters from ancient Roman times. Could be fictional.

(Advantage: No one would be able to argue with anything I was saying. Disadvantage: No one would have the remotest idea what I was saying. Truth to tell: neither would I.)

Widukind. (Meyerhofer introduced us to this forefather.)

(Advantage: His rebellion should make for lots of neat parallels with current Revolution. Disadvantage: He lost.)

Frederick Barbarossa.

(Advantages: long enough ago and not so far away; strong characters – Henry the Lion, Albert the Bear, Hubert the Stag, Walther the Boar, whoever, some pope or other, etc. Disadvantages: not a revolutionary; besides, audience sound asleep when bar opens at first intermission.)

Perhaps a minor crusader or Teutonic knight?

(I am getting impatient; I must calm down; must stop being silly.)

The Great Peasant War.

(Advantages: obviously, this is the area where I should be looking for my subject; cast of thousands, very popular with chorus of Hofoper. Disadvantages: why am I fooling myself? – I know next to nothing about the period and haven't the time to find out enough; and cast of thousands singing the minutiae of protestant theology will not, let us face it, make for an evening of first class operatic entertainment. Some of the livelier passages of Luther's *Freedom of a Christian Man* set to a mazurka, perhaps, ländler at least; set his *Against the Murderous and Thieving Hordes of Peasants* to a lilting waltz, swing of rebels on the gibbets in three-quarter time, sway of moral backbone of aristocrats.)

I give up.

Hopeless.

Perhaps try it from the other direction: focus on the opposition.

Frederick the Great.

(Advantages: sucking up to Prussian arrogance, popular with their toadies. Disadvantages: I would lose all my friends, gain some very dreary new ones; then, not a sniff of an allegory of revolution; besides which, no drama in hours of debate with Voltaire, sixty-three identical battle scenes; love interest restricted to buggery of cadet corps if rumours are right.)

Why not go all the way:

Fictional medieval hero but with supernatural goings-on? Witch's Sabbath? Ride of Witches? Haunted Valleys?

(Advantages: good musical possibilities, popular subject, interesting sets and staging. Disadvantages: Impossibly silly; waste of time.)

Love story: Romeo and Juliet, Heloïse and Abelard, Antony and Cleopatra, Tristan and Isolde.

(Advantage: love story. Disadvantage: love story.)

This is ridiculous. I'll never find a subject this way. Steal something from Goethe or Schiller? Beaumarchais or Shakespeare? Dante? Do the *Divine Comedy*, take only twenty years to write, Herr Wurmlein paying my rent and food the whole time, I don't think. *Don Quixote. The Bible.*

I must think of something! Nearly midnight, candle nearly gone, composer nearly frozen, bed awaits.

I'll come up with something in the morning.

23 APRIL: Today Waltherrott, tomorrow the world! Vienna Hofoper, Munich, Berlin, Paris! Lady Glory, though she little knows it as she flies languidly over the green hills of this gentle land, is about to descend upon this lovely *genial* old city, and place the laurel wreath upon my brow. Not immediately, perhaps, but in October, certainly. When the great night arrives, when the audience is at last seated (so impatient to hear it begin!) and the conductor – not Herr Platt, we must get von Klar from Duisburg – the conductor raises his baton, and the curtain goes up on the first act of my new opera. Waltzing Walther, ninety-fifth Graf vom Faß will nod, smile, make a small flourish of welcome from the Grafinical box (before collapsing in a drunken stupor during the overture) while Herr Wurmlein, sitting beside me in the Intendant's box, will take a glimpse at the set

to see that all is well, then he will lean over to me, grasp my hand in his and say: 'Confidence, my dear von Stumpf, confidence is justified: do you not know it is a masterpiece?' Between acts, I shall stand modestly in the grand salon and allow minions to force Oberdorfer Sekt upon me, and avert my eyes when the great, the rich, the powerful gaze at me, shaking their heads with wonder and pride. And when the lovely ladies of Waltherrott, surely the loveliest ladies in Germany, in Europe, when they glance shyly from under their eyelashes or over their fans, I shall blush becomingly; and when one, upon a dare from her friends, is brazen enough to approach and ask me to autograph her fan, I shall decline with shock: 'I can't imagine, my dear, why you could want my insignificant . . . in any case, I have nothing to write with . . . but perhaps I may plant an invisible mark upon your glove with . . . my lips?' And she will rush, proud and giggling, back to her silly, giggling, chattering friends and like lightning the story of my gracious modesty will spread far and wide. But the greatest example of my modesty, of my innate nobility of soul will come when the final curtain falls and the applause rolls like waves of the great Ocean and crashes before me, vaulting in the air, falling only to rise again even higher, and I shall stand mute at the rail, head bowed in modesty and the waves of applause thunder up toward me, and at last I shall raise my head and open my arms in a moving gesture of acceptance and thanks. And from the flowers thrown to me by the admiring throng, I shall pluck a single red rose – no, a single white rose for purity, for modesty, for the innocence of my joy – and a single tear will course down my cheek at the overwhelming power of this emotion: so unexpected. My decorum will be so gallant, so noble that . . . that I shall be forced to make a speech, which I should write at once, no, better it be ex tempore, or at least written closer to the time, more natural that way . . . If Waltzing Walther sobers up enough to think of it, perhaps he'll invite me to the Residenz or up to the Waltherburg which I'd gladly do if the evening isn't too chilly, very draughty up there, I hear; or perhaps the bon ton, or the sporting crowd (this is getting ridiculous: I'd rather have the pit musicians vomit on me than mix with those rich louts), recognizing a new star in the firmament, will burst into the box and carry me on their shoulders jubilantly over to the Renatenhof, and there the champagne will flow until dawn, the band will play selections from the opera, and the ladies . . . will not be so coy . . . Or perhaps after an hour or two of caviar I'll slip away to Die Drei Grafen, loyal to my humbler friends, yes, no snob that von Stumpf, good fellow, stout fellow, and I shall slip some money to Dieter and tell him the drinks are on me, don't tell anyone, but the word will get out, always does, someone will guess, but the result will be the same: foaming tankards of lager, the praise of friends, the sweet kisses of laughing ladies. I may even consent to sit down at that wretched, out-of-tune piano and play some of the themes from the opera – but *not* 'Frülingstraum im Bergwald!' But why not go immediately? Because with this hundred thalers from Herr Wurmlein for my advance I can bring the rent out of arrears, put some aside to see me through until I get the instalment for the first draught, and . . . sensibly?

Sensibly! Sensibly, rubbish! I am an artist, not a clerk with the insurance company. If I were to act sensibly, I would sit down to write the opera, but that can wait.

Sensibly? I spit on your sensibly. All, the entire hundred thalers for wine, women, and song, and we'll see what tomorrow brings!

Away!

26 APRIL: When I was young and just getting my first piano jobs in the bars out Niedermark way, I remember an old fellow telling me that, when I got to be his age, the drinking would be easier and the hangovers harder. Right, of course.

But 'The beat of life returns, in throbbing pulse/ Muted to the dawn.' Yes, I found my subject and even after the scrutiny and sarcasm of Herr Wurmlein, and the cold trout eye of a hangover to make it look particularly rancid, I still think it can work: I shall immortalize the founder of our fair city, the original Graf Walther vom Faß.

I got the idea while drinking coffee. An expensive treat I don't often allow myself, but as the condemned man prepared for his walk to the executioner he had a last meal, last wish: bread and coffee in the Alte Markt. Standing there watching bustle of life, river at bottom of street, new railway station, palace to the dawning of a new age, while behind, on the Böttgerberg, the Waltherburg, reminder of past: began to think of town, unity of it, continuity, amazing thing that people cleave together like this, despite Waltzing Walther and most of his ancestors: suddenly, there it was, suitable subject. Jotted it down, walked to Hofoper, almost running toward end, strode into Wurmlein's office not like whipped dog, failure I have felt myself these three years and more, but content, sunshine in my smile, young birch tree in my step, flowing river in my speech . . . Laid out my proposal on one page, talked it through, talked him into it, amazed him, I think, amazed myself, walked out after twenty minutes with 100 thalers!

The more I look at it, the more I realize I could do a lot worse. The story has everything:

How the *original* Walther

of mysterious origins, possibly not earthly,

gathers together a few companions, how they wander about from hill to valley in quest of noble deeds to perform, damsels to save, dragons to slay,

how they appear in the upper slopes of the Bergwald as if set miraculously upon this earth, come wandering down the Lohbachertal and find a miserable little settlement menaced by barbarians,

drive them off,

Walther takes village under his protection, it prospers,

he erects castle atop the Böttgerberg,

marries Irmtraud von Linnen, weaver's daughter, together they encourage industry,

love duet to peace and prosperity on castle ramparts – I already have the theme – domestic bliss, children, etc., but:

tragic death of Irmtraud in childbirth,

Walther distraught,

famous vision at Keilerfelsen, known to every Waltherrottner schoolchild, inspires Walther to:

join crusade (must check which one; must get it right),
Walther returns, sadder, wiser,
sets up convent to memory of Blessed Irmtraud,
falls in love with Renate Schönbruster, devout but cultured young lady,
prosperity now crowned with the arts encouraged by Walther and new wife,
city a Garden of the Renaissance in the North, Golden Age,
but:
various problems, conspiracies, trouble with scheming priest Adalbert, distant bishops, obscure anathemas or whatever, the great Walther with aid of noble wife holds head up, rallies one last time, trounces foes, dies happy in wife's arms.

Title: *Waltherrotterdämmerung*

Good ring to it: sunrise of Waltherrott. Morning-twilight of Civilization hereabouts.

Marvellous, can't fail idea, music, characters, sets, colour, action all built in, could perhaps sharpen the drama, the conflict, but that'll come with the selection and blocking. Could be love story wife-death-wife, could be contrast of life-of-action, life-of-contemplation, could be symbolical-allegorical: history of Germany, history of European civilization: primitive struggle with forests, rise of towns, reaching outward (thump the barbarians, crusade, whatever) then increasing civilization, arts, lute music, delicate airs in garden or something; in any case, all works on personal, civic, European, cosmic scales: great chances for orchestration of effects, meanings here, struggles between brass and winds, the whole thing almost more a symphony, holding together, show these Italians, musical revolution.

Not, it must be noted, intimately related to Frankfurt and political Revolution, but I can do that later. I admit Herr Wurmlein remarked after I had told him the idea, 'Well, it's on a subject which is partly political and people are talking politics these days, but at least it won't have anything to do with the Frankfurt Assembly.' As long as he is happy.

96

Waltzing Walther, if he is sober for the occasion, or if he hasn't been drawn and quartered by his not-so-loyal subjects, ought to love it.

Convincing Meyerhofer and the others may take a bit more doing. But I think it is very much about Frankfurt: genesis of German civilization, seeds of later problems, Walther on deathbed warns of betrayals, need for human dignity, etc. Something there, I'm sure of it; enough to satisfy them, as long as I argue that there's a deeper symbolism to things, you must understand the significance of the sunlight in Act II, the role played by the honest bürgers, etc., etc. And if they don't like it, it won't matter. Even if I don't get rich from it (Wurmlein is, of course, buying it outright) at least it will make me famous, so that my *next* one will earn me a fortune.

But enough of this wasting of time: to work!

2 MAY: Opera would be much improved if it could do without singers. It would also be much improved if it could do without intendants, without stage managers, without drunken musicians who begin the evening sharp and end it flat, without conductors who follow the beat about as well as a cow's tail, without stagehands who drop a prop on someone's foot during any pianissimo passage and nail shut the doors which are supposed to open, leave unnailed doors which should stay shut.

But most of all, opera would be much improved without singers.

Especially female singers.

Especially large-busted, narrow-waisted, big-eyed, small-brained, blonde-haired, ever-so-slightly-off-key, fluff-headed, gossiping, frothy little tarts named Fräulein Sängerin Gisela Klatschmeyer of the chorus of the Waltherrottner Hofoper who has the room across the hall here at The Sign of the Pig's Trotter, the rooming house of Frau Schweinehaxe and which I call home; especially such a singer who has, for some months now, been sharing my bed when it suits her to be warmer than she would be alone.

On her particular flaws, irritating habits, I maintain a polite, a discreet, a diplomatic silence. I am a gentleman, I should hope, gentleman of the soul, though not, obviously, of class. Composer: class is beside the point for artists. But not for singers. I do not go into detail, but let me register this alone: it is the job of the artist to make art; it is not the job of the artist to get a regular job so that he can afford to marry another person who claims to be an artist but who is entirely governed by the instincts of her vulgar petty bourgeois acquisitiveness.

When she is not governed by her urge to sleep with the entire wind section, brass in particular if I'm not mistaken.

Enough. I hold my tongue.

6 MAY: I have twelve themes, twelve. Only twelve. Seven of them the first day (the second day, actually, after I recovered from my hangover – God in Heaven, how people take advantage of one: Friends!) seven themes with my pen flashing and spitting across the paper, then three more a few days later (after a small and *deserved* celebration of the seven and some elaboration thereof) then one *inspired by, not stolen from* Stammitz the elder (well, the Mannheim orchestra is long gone, as is old Stammitz himself, so who's to tell the difference?) and one borrowed, no, *adapted* from my string quartet (and for certain no one is going to be able to identify *that one!*) and one more two days ago.

No, I shall blow my brains out.

Or wander off into the Bergwald, there to be torn apart by wild dogs. Wild boars. Carcass picked clean by the crows.

Seen von Stumpf around lately?

Von Who?

Stumpf. Scrawny, half-crazed fellow, thought he was a composer.

Oh, Stumpf with the alcoholic twitch? Stumpf the half-starved, the consumptive, the tottering scarecrow? Stumpf with the venereal drip from his wurst? (I know damned well that's what it is, the pox ridden bitch, I'm sure of it, what else could it be?) *The von*

Stumpf who used to tinkle the piano down at Die Drei Grafen and drank more than they paid him, ran up a bill as long as my wife's arm.

As long as my wife's nose.

As fat as my wife's arse.

Dear God, what is to become of me? Why didn't I get into the feed grain trade with Uncle Heinie when he offered it? (No, lucky I missed that job, all blown to hell by East Prussian competition when we joined the Zollverein.)

Perhaps I'll blow myself to hell.

Gunpowder.

Steam power?

Where is the nearest active volcano? *And* I have to write the libretto myself. The *whole* work: music, words, sets, costumes, all under the direction of von Stumpf, genius. Under my control nominally, so Herr Intendant Wurmlein will have someone to blame if anything goes wrong. Not *actually* under my control, of course. He'll have them change my words, music, action, anything, my very soul if it suits his purposes.

Von Stumpf, scapegoat.

O, Inspiration! O, Muses! Come breathe life into my sawdust soul, lift my hand, my eyes to the glories of Art.

Please.

Inspiration in one minute, I give you one minute or I'm off to Die Drei Grafen and you know what that means.

I'm waiting.

You have ten seconds.

10 MAY: Draft outline of *Waltherrotterdämmerung*,
Opera in Three Acts
by Carl Maria von Stumpf, Genius.

Prologue (fades into ACT 1):   Aubade over virgin forests of the Bergwald, basic theme standing for the idyllic peace possible for the people of the valley if they can live in harmony with the forests and streams, and it is the morning of civilization, the morning of the world:

FIG. 6: Theme: 'The Morning of Civilization'.

this theme interrupted by:

the discordant arrival of the barbarians, marauders from the East, the theme and orchestration against the expectations of audience, because played on flute, I think, not trumpets, (write it tomorrow), quietly, impersonally menacing, not all sturm und drang, done against the grain, snare drums, even tabors, not tympani, primitive; interrupted by, fading under curtain rising and beginning of:

ACT I, *Scene I:*   We discover young Walther and companions asleep under the great oaks of the Bergwald, waking in the morning of his first day, the first day of the new world, an innocent, full recapitulation of prologue themes, development, then disturbed by drums and flutes coming nearer;

arrival of barbarians, battle, slaughter, Walther bloody but triumphant, disgusted by gore, by bloodlust coursing through his veins swears to dedicate himself to arts of peace, of industry, to raise the peasants from the degradation of their poverty;

missing a few scenes here, may leave them out altogether except for Walther's arrival in the village, or perhaps have peasants rush onto stage, acclamation of their hero, etc.; skip on to:

100

Scene 2:   Duet on battlements of partly built Waltherburg, perhaps with belvedere – no, that would be anachronistic, must be historically accurate, set it on parapet – and not duet as such, but *The Great Vision of Graf Walther of Domestic Peace for Himself, for His Wife, His City, All of Civilization* duet between Graf Walther and wife Irmtraud, she great with child to get sympathy of ladies in audience, always suckers for Irmtraud, later sainted mother of city;

> Behold, I sweep my arms from horizon to horizon,
> And all I see bows to these walls,
> The trees, the very wind more gentle than e'er before
> The trees retreat, the fields advance, the earth smiles
> And the swords are made ploughshares . . .

Well, perhaps that's going a bit too far; old Walther was no doubt a Christian, but they were well armed for Christ in those days of Huns and Visigoths and Mongols and Vandals or whoever they were; and perhaps swords to ploughshares is not entirely politic these days, either; swords made into bigger and better swords – for Christ, of course – but in any case, a vision of the Good World, Peaceable Kingdom, Good Husbandry; lots of Beaming Children, Paradise on Earth, Love and Amity Abounding . . . (Scene needs some dramatic tension. Later.)

Scene 3:   Graf Walther on his throne or something, dignity of virtuous ruler dealing with matters of state, dispensing wisdom and justice to grateful peasants, perhaps doing a dance, capering like clumsy horse; arrival of monk Adalbert, priest Adalbert, whatever he was. The history books speak of a simple man, martyred into sainthood by barbarians or neighbouring warlord, but I see him as sleek, well-fed, Papal snake, stooge of French faction or something (Burgundian faction? it begins to look as if I may need to do some research, damn it, perhaps some other local baron or whatever, Albrecht the Boar, Bear? Name remembered from schoolbook? Sounds right. Whatever: for dramatic tension, thug, contrast to virtuous Walther) anyway: arrival of priest Adalbert preaching crusade.

Walther:
Begone, varlet, stooge of corrupt Romish popes with their plots, poisons, concubines, harlots, perfumed boys (they'll really eat that up when they hear it, though perhaps leave out perfumed boys, Herr Wurmlein's inclinations being considered), what quarrel have I with distant infidels when I have local thugs menacing my poor children whom you see gathered about their father's coattails, feet, knees, what-ever? Squabbles in distant lands of no interest to me, charity begins at home, etc, etc.

Debate on politics and theology possible here, with sections to cut if it runs too long, but I'll leave it in to prove I'm Serious Thinker will-ing to bow to Dramatic Necessity. Debate comes to precipitate end as minion rushes in:

Minion:
Oh, Graf Walther, terrible news, your beloved wife, Irmtraud von Linnen, has died in childbirth, taken from us in our hour of need, the child lives, a girlchild, boychild, whatever! Tragedy! Horrors! What are we to do?' Anguished cries and weeping, exeunt all. (C$\sharp$min?)

Scene 4: Keilerfelsen, encounter with the boar, etc., all well known to locals, but perhaps can be elaborated for foreigners. Graf Walther in brown study, dark mood, night thoughts, night scene, overhang-ing trees, pale moon glimmers, etc., mystical atmosphere suffuses all, Graf Walther mourns loss of beloved Irmtraud, curses fate, fists toward night darkness – no, toward moon, pull out all stops on an-guish, got to have great melody, unified musical development all very well, but I have to have a few saleable excerpts if I'm to make something extra from this thing, provide for future – at any rate: the arrival of miraculous boar with glowing cross, etc., Walther amazed, falls to ground, vows to go on crusade after all, etc., etc., modulate to E Maj. or some other resolute key, triumphant end of Act I, audience goes to bar in cheerful mood, buys gallons of drink, see if I can get cut of concessions (no hope, there!) and return drowsy from Oberdorf's finest, but I have Act II to wake them up.

ACT II, *Scene 1:* (this is getting good! Begins to look like the real thing.) Triumphant return of Waltherrottner crusaders, led by great Kreuzritter Walther himself, write a real rouser here, something like this:

FIG. 7: 'Solemn Processional for Returning Knights'.

Perhaps it'll get picked up by some army which will pay me some royalties (usual army practice, ho-ho), scene adaptable for great throng including horses if it gets mounted in larger opera house, lions and camels, etc., as trophy animals for really elaborate production, Paris, Berlin, Vienna, whatever (beasts brought back to start Waltherrottner Tiergarten, famous throughout north in late Middle Ages, why not?) anyway, good mob scene with grateful local maidens in low-cut dirndls, surely they had them then? *But:*

Crusaders, maidens, bubbling bumpkins all rush off to stube, bed, whatever, and Graf Walther pauses by gate to Waltherburg: it hasn't been the enjoyable lark for him that it was for the others, muses on life and death, mutability, life empty despite Smiting of Infidel Hordes, memory of other Triumphal Entry – Jerusalem, Acre, Baghdad, whatever – despite visions of Miraculous Hogs, memory of virtuous Irmtraud, sweet breath of Beloved Wife now safely in Heaven due to his efforts . . . or is she sainted yet? More needed: founding of convent in her sainted memory. Turns to priest lurking in shadows, Adalbert, still snuffling about, recognizes him, calls:

Walther:
Ho, priest, go you to your masters in Rome with tale of virtuous Irmtraud, get her sainted; succeed and I vow to endow finest convent ever seen in these parts, cash, lands, a hundred pure virgins, girls of decent family I'll furnish with funds sufficient, etc.'

Adalbert:
(Aside, 'How can I turn this to my credit with my Abbot or whatever?') Yea, Graf Walther, your wish is my command, grovel, grovel, shoe me a horse and I'll hie me off to Castel Gondolfo, whatever, Avignon, but best to get convent going first, then try for translation to exalted state, so you get going on one, I'll work on other, a deal, say you?

Walther:
Yea, verily, forsooth and all.

Exeunt.

Scene 2: In chapel of Convent of Blessed (a little poetic licence here, story as far as I recall is W. didn't get together sufficient bribe money for another few years, although the school histories put it rather more delicately) of Blessed Irmtraud on the day of the consecration of the chapel, convent, whatever, big day, Te Deum for sure, set it really well, no money in it, but won't do my reputation any harm. Procession of novices, Walther notices devout one, her eyes cast down – but very large eyes, whatever – anyway, sings declaration of love in harmony with Te Deum, whole Te Deum becomes rousing anthem to love, Protestants won't mind, but may have to adapt for Catholic opera houses, must be willing to adapt to circumstances, Truth and Beauty all very well but pointless if Light Hidden Under Bushel, etc.

Serious trio with Mother Superior, Walther, novice arguing out best way to serve God, Walther settles it with point that he is giving establishment small fortune, one hundred of his healthiest peasant milkmaids less one is still ninety-nine, what the hell, find another one somewhere, throw her in to round it up to promised century, whatever, not to mention memory of wife, trip to crusades, etc., and doesn't he deserve at least one of the young ladies, not that he has any intention save to make honest woman of her, nay, more than honest woman, Gräfin vom Faß, chance to be active in all church charities, mother to the whole district, etc., etc., whatever. And that about settles that, and he leads Renate, erstwhile potential Bride of Christ, to altar for vows of marriage (future marriage?) altogether different from one she expected when she entered chapel that morning, evening going to be different too, but not for opera stage, a pity. Chorus of novices to Hymen instead of St. Cecilia or whatever, another rouser, sell a few copies of this one. Exeunt in jubilate. Exeunt audience humming final melody, charge to bar for more schnapps, sekt, why not have sheet music of best tunes of the evening on sale for piano playing daughters?

(Scene 3: Their Wedding? poss., lay on rouser of wedding march, so much for you, Mendelssohn, beloved and mandatory wedding march

for every bourgeois little virgin north of Italy! No, ridiculous: combine marriage with Scene 2.)

ACT III, *Scene 1:*   Springtime morning in the garden of the Waltherburg, Renate lounging in an arbour, surrounded by musicians, lutenists, harpers, whatever they played back then, flute, other artists, perhaps painter doing portrait, sculptor. All vying for her attention, but she only has eyes for her husband who stands on high parapet musing upon garden scene, turning from time to time to gaze out over his domains. Perhaps a few children if we can find some that can be trusted not to try to steal the scene; no, probably distracting; perhaps one son with Walther; father points out extent of dominions. (How many kids did he have, what kind? Etc. *More damned research!*) But: real point of scene is songs of mature love, romantic and all that, love between mature serious ruler and wise, sensitive young woman who is patron of arts: Not just Civilization is come to Waltherrott, but the Arts, Culture, Polish. Where's your Versailles now? No, Florence, Siena, I suppose. The Renaissance comes early to Germany, hitherto unrecognized historical trend, no objection to that notion hereabouts.

Scene 2:   (A problem here: dramatic tension required, no drama in old Walther drifting peacefully off to deserved restful sleep of ancestors. Tensions with young wife? No: audience burns down opera house (though not such a bad idea if Herr Wurmlein and a certain soprano included!) How did he die? Does anyone know? Wasn't there a final battle? More research! Think! He has fought barbarians locally, fought infidels in Holy Land, who else can he vanquish? Demons of his own soul? Great dramatic possibilities there, I don't think! Ahh, got it) –

Scene 2:   Crypt of Dom, monastery, some other local nobleman's castle or whatever, gloomy, underground, *contrast to Sc. 1,* torchlight flickering behind pillars, spooky in the gloom, hooded conspirators come slinking in to minor key with dissonances, none of

106

your pizzicato for tiptoes, no clichés (oh why not, they'll expect it.)

FIG. 8: 'In the Crypt' theme.

Leader of group sniffs, peeks into corners, 'We're alone,' menacing baritone growls near bottom of his range, throws off hood, it's crafty Adalbert as if we didn't know:

Adalbert:
Take we now our places round this table,
Let us thus form an unbreakable ring of steel
Ring of resolution to be done with this interloper
Who has come betwixt your noble selves and
Your willing subjects, your children, your very soil

(Meaning their incomes, not to mention Rome's (Avignon's?) own income, erstwhile so graspingly gathered, wrung from the peasants' hides, *mulcted*, by my own sanctimonious self for uses not always entirely approved of even by Whore of Apocalypse, otherwise known as Romish church, but meaning not Rome's income, not one groat of it to cross the Bergwald, never mind the distant Alps, income for priest Adalbert himself for drink, women, luxe, *not mentioning any of this but audience understands, plant it elsewhere, perhaps a solo, perhaps have Adalbert arrive before the others?*) Anyway:

107

What say you, noble sirs, are we as one?

Omnes:
All: Yea and verily, crush the viper,
Expunge him from our midst,
Rightful hands on golden thalers again,
Rightful whips on peasant hides again,
Rightful harvesting of fields, trees, rivers,
Rightful hunting of stags, boars, virgins
Bringing in the sheaves, loot, antlers, bosoms, etc.

Should have some argument, no honour among thieves, Adalbert oozes out oily words, placating hand on shoulder, quick knife in ribs (poisoned cup?) and dissenter is swiftly dispatched, body thrown in alcove, bottle dungeon, whatever.

Conclusion: sinister handshake of conspirators. *Possibly*: Adalbert calls for paraphernalia, announces:

Now will we of the body and blood of our Lord and Master,
In sacrament of our own choosing!
(Holds high crucifix, slowly, deliberately inverts it in rictus of grin, all becomes clear! Sinister low trill on oboe, dissonant crash of trumpets(?), curtain. *Possibly.*)

But: Obvious now must insert scene in Act II, if not also Act I – at least hints in Act I – to establish this major sub plot.

Having looked: Idiot that I am, can't have Act I ending with mass exit of entire cast from full stage, *then* Act II beginning with return march of crusaders filling stage again! Obvious answer, begin Act II with conspirators, Adalbert dropping hints to Graf . . . Albrecht didn't I say? Whatever:

Like you, my lord, the adulation granted this Walther?

Albrecht:
Nay, verily, forsooth, and not just the adulation,
Cold cash I am missing as well,
Fleece of these sheep was once mine . . .

Adalbert:
You speak metaphorically my friend. But say,
Wouldst not like having fleece in hand again?

Albrecht:
Yea, and all, fleece of various sorts. (leering) Etc, etc.

Adalbert:
Know you aught of like-minded men?

Albrecht:
Yea, verily, forsooth, stout men and true . . .
Etc. etc., obvious continuation.

(Poss. problem: Graf Walther was away to crusades several years, surely? Why didn't conspirators take over, had lots of time, why the delay? On the other hand, it's an opera: what are set designers for if not to make audience forget the petty details?)

Anyway, that is beginning of Act II, and I can insert other developments: somewhere in chapel scene (at the end for surprise?): Adalbert in chat with Mother Superior, turns out he knows her well, old bawd from Hamburg, whatever, plans to run convent as brothel, whatever, *dark hints only, must keep this on an elevated level, hints at corrupt liturgy (but dissonant chords, twisting of love motif will give it away to cognoscenti)*

Getting back to Act III:

Scene 1: Renaissance garden, all brightness love and future;

109

Scene 2:   Conspirators in cellar, darkness, hatred, black mass;
Scene 3:   Battle scene? Gathering of bürgers in Altemarkt:

Young Hotblood:
Make we now our choice: go like sheep to be fleeced again
as once we were, or take up arms at the side of Graf Walther,
Kreuzritter, father of this town, etc., etc.

Foregone conclusion, exeunt all to another glorious march, threat-
ening trombones, battle of the Lohbacherfurt rendered by orchestra
rending the air to shreds, wake up the audience during change of
scene to:

Scene 4:   Corner of battlefield, perhaps, more likely throne room
or whatever in Waltherburg: begin with noble Renate at window,
no, lady-in-waiting at window, reports progress of battle, what she
can descry, whilst noble Renate sits, stands, paces, slumps in chair,
whatever director wants, not my business: mainly she sings of her
terror, beloved husband will leave her children without a father, etc.,
(perhaps calls children to her, child: fourteen year-old Walther II
(soprano en travestie? I can think of just the soprano who wants solo
part, give her three dreary lines, music off key: 'But Gisela, my dear,
we're trying to indicate the lad's voice is breaking!'), anyway, young
Walther II declares he is ready to stand and fight: 'I am a man, worthy successor, etc.'), screw up the anticipation until lady-in-waiting
screams, covers eyes, faints. Renate rushes to window, but can see
nothing 'They've already gone round the corner, whatever!' and indeed messenger arrives, herald, whatever, 'What news, herald? Do
not spare me, I pray you!' Herald tongue-tied, points to door, retainers enter in ascending rank until noblest companions, alte
kameraden (have to establish a few from outset; another baritone? is
Adalbert a bass?) bearing litter with wounded Walther.

Graf Walther:
Sweetest wife, fear not, the battle is won,

Sweetest victory is peace and prosperity
My subjects free from threatened yoke of tyrants,
Hairy Albrecht the Bear
(That's the name! Education pays off!)
                              spitted on my lance,
Ready for roasting over fires of Hell,
Roast meat for dogs in street,

Etc., etc.

Renate:
And what of wily Adalbert, apostate priest, enemy of God?

Walther:
Why, wife, verily, miracle on battlefield,
False priest renounced the evil one,
Returned to True Faith! But sharp-eyed enemy archer,
Moved by malice, loosed fatal shaft
And holy blood anointed the ground all round, O woe!

Renate:
Miracle indeed, his repentance and death secured victory,
Adalbert saint for sure, petition we pope at once.

Walther:
Yea, verily, fair wife, here's my mark on paper,
You fill in the details, despatch it soonest to Avignon.
But carry me to yon fenster that I may gaze again
Upon the fields golden neath setting sun
Fructuous land in Dämmerung,
I also in Dämmerung of my brief day, etc., etc.,

Noble sentiments, noble sentiments,
Weeping and wailing of women, but not too many of them, always
bloody distracting, Death of Walther, no, first:

111

Chorus of noble cohorts, alte kameraden:
Dedicate we ourselves to memory of Graf Walther,
Greatness of bürgerliche Freiheit, good for all,
Dedicated to Walther II,

(lad with such great legs in green hose and mighty chest deserves to
succeed, must remain serious)
 Not Abenddämmerung, but Morgendämmerung
(best friend, lieutenant as it were, the baritone, mounts steps to
window):
 Hear the lark in the clear air, ascending:
(flute? piccolo? violin?)
 As our souls do to heaven when we are in state of grace
(make sure I get the theology right! Can't afford blunder on this one.)

 So do our hearts rise now in the clear air,
 Waltherrottner Luft.

Graf Walther:
(voice ascending in quavering solo)
Yea, verily, ye fine people of Waltherrott,
I loved you as well as I could, etc. whatever.

Renate:
Husband gone to reward, I remain and dedicate
My life to his fair city, and fair people herein,
Fairest folk in Christendom, Flower of Creation, etc.

Elegiac but triumphant curtain, perhaps chorus, curtain calls for
cast, music director called to stage, takes bows, even egregious
Wurmlein gets to simper, bouquets for all, then:

Audience:
Von Stumpf! Von Stumpf!
Exultate in jubilo!

(Perhaps I could write a piece for the orchestra to play as I am born in triumph from the hall? If I have time. 'March of the Champagne bottles!')

Done: now straighten that up, do a fair copy and lay it upon Egregious Wurmlein's desk.
>But first, a few groschen for a tankard!
>To Die Drei Grafen!

12 MAY: Well, Herr Wurmlein has his wretched outline, his musical sketches, his bureaucratic outline of my immortal art, as it were. I have distilled the life of the great Walther and into three acts and eleven scenes. I threw in a professorial prologue which explained the 'universal significance' of our founder and hero, how he embodied all the great virtues of Ur-Teutschen, Light of the Civilized, Hammer of the Barbarians.

So Herr Wurmlein has his outline, and I have the second instalment of my fee.

Which means Frau Schweinehaxe is wallowing in the unexpected heap of riches which represents last February's rent.

And Herr Kellner Römer has come to an agreement about advances in my salary, arrears in my bar bill, and my duties at the dread klangerbox. So I am back at my Stammtisch in Die Drei Grafen and I only have to play Thursday, Friday and Saturday evenings.

Fräulein Prima Donna Sängerin Gisela Klatschmeyer, that empty-headed strumpet, that monument to bourgeois envy and acquisitiveness, has a new hat which the furrier swears is sable, which, consequently, I swear is sable, but which she suspects is dyed rabbit. Which at that price may even be sewer rat. But she is moderately happy and went sashaying off to Süßmayer's Chocolate and Coffee House where the ladies of the chorus gather to sip and nibble when they are in funds. And to gossip.

And I? What do I, your humble servant, Herr Komponist Carl Maria von Stumpf, genius, what do I have? I have a large glass of beer before me at my Stammtisch; I have a stack of stave paper, blank; I have the afternoon to get on with my opera. So I shall do just that.

17 MAY: Working like mad this last week. Scenes blocked out fairly well, musical sketches for a dozen sections – but not to be called arias! I have inklings, gropings toward a new organization of an opera; something more unified; get rid of the set piece numbers which stop the flow, the momentum, break the Italian aria-recitative-chorus progression. Of course, the singers are going to hate me! Ha! What do a few warblers count when we're talking about Art? Truth? Life? Eternity?

There is something on paper! Material! Substance!

> *O, pleasure creeps most strangely in,*
> *Suffusing my five senses as I stare:*
> *Sacred joy of youth leaps at the sight,*
> *Fires all my branching veins.*
> *What god set out this mystery,*
> *Which calms my soul's upheaval,*
> *And floods my heavy heart with joy,*
> *Reveals the hidden world,*
> *Nature's secret power?*
> *And I a god? – With a sudden vision*
> *I plumb the enigma of the signs,*
> *Hear Nature's mighty spinning wheel*
> *Divine the wisdom of the sage . . .*

And I a god? When the spirit soars, when the world turns to pin-wheels, galaxies, all light alive in my eyes; in short, when the drink is in me, yes, I feel myself, *know* myself a god, yes, I admit it.

And when I am working, or rather at the end of a hard day's work, then too I know it.

In my soul, deep within, I know that what I am creating is *True*. I can see the work in my mind: I see the scenes as they *should* be set upon the stage, I see the characters, their costumes (could we only

114

afford the materials to do them right), I see light flashing and changing (could we only manage that!), I see movement with the rhythm of rippling brooks, of clouds on a blustery spring day or a placid summer day, of the rolling hills of the Bergwald, movement of the Universe wheeling across the great vault of Heaven on high, and I hear the orchestra and the voices woven together like a carpet, dense, yet discrete like an oak in leaf, but also like the voices of a hundred different trees in a forest: I see and hear it as a symphony in sight and sound, and I compare it with what I sense, feel, know is the world about me, the truth, and I know that what I have is a distillation of all of that.

Is this not the point of art?

So that when I look at the streets, the buildings, the people, the hills and rivers of this town, I see my own creation moving before me. Were I not an artist, it would surely all be chaos, a random jumble of things and creatures wandering aimlessly, bumping into one another, but as I am an artist it all coheres, it dances, vibrates, with meaning, sense which I can comprehend, which I know, for my soul has encompassed it in my art. And yet . . .

And yet to the world, I am the composer of wretched ditties like 'Trink, Vaterlein, Trink.'

And when I show my real work to others, to Gisela, to Wurmlein, even to Meyerhofer, I can see that they do not see what I see. As for the public: after my vision of the universe has been crudely painted in spavined perspective, in the cheapest colours available this week, the movements played out in disjoined, awkward stumblings about on the thumping stage, *when I hear my music blundered through, butchered like a noble stag brought to earth by woodchoppers wielding dull axes:* then, oh ye gods! then do I grieve for my soul, my art: but even more do I grieve for blind, deaf, dull, lumpen mankind!

Oh landlord, bring me another flowing bowl!

Work tomorrow!

Oblivion tonight!

20 MAY: Fräulein Sängerin Gisela has been particularly attentive since the outline was accepted. Much stroking of nape of neck, ruffling of hair, fluttering of eyelashes, moues, etc. Giggles, 'Oh, you are so amusing, so intelligent, so talented.' But then: 'Did Mozart ever marry?'

As if she didn't know.

'Yes, but his father was against it.'

'Fathers are often inconvenient.'

Not the only ones.

'They don't understand.'

Silence for a while.

'I expect she was some rich aristocrat.'

'Who, Mozart's father?'

'Tsk-tsk, oh you are so funny, giggle-giggle, most amusing man I have ever, etc.'

'Some Italian actors were through here last year, commedia dell'arte. They made a mask of my face. Now I amuse clodhoppers from the Baltic to that Adriatic, and never have to leave Waltherrott.'

Not to be sidetracked:

'What do you know about her?'

'The Baltic or the Adriatic?'

'Mozart's wife!'

'Oh, Constanze.'

'How did they meet?'

'Singer in a band. Big in the lungs, I expect, small in the head, spendthrift. Usual thing.'

From the corner of my eye I could see her reach for something to throw at me, but she thought better of it, swallowed her gall, and tried again:

'Oh, a singer. I expect he wrote a lot of material for her, didn't he?'

'Well, he wrote a juicy part into the C minor mass just for her to perform in Salzburg. The idea was to impress Vati and Susi Mozart.'

'And were they impressed?'

'Of course not, no one was good enough for their dear Wolfgang Gottlieb.'

'How sad for her, I'm sure she tried her very best. Did he write lots of parts for her in his operas?'

'I don't believe he did. They mostly lived in Vienna, you see.'

'Vienna: how enchanting!'

Then she got suspicious.

'What do you mean: "He didn't write for her, they lived in Vienna?" What does that have to do with it?'

'I mean she became typically Viennese: "My what a pretty dress, Wolfgang, I must have that dress, Wolfgang, just as soon as I eat a few more of those pastries with the whipped cream, Wolfgang, do you think I should do my hair more up on this side, Wolfgang? And Lisl Susslippe was telling me about a charming flat which she said would be just right for us, very thick walls, only a little more than we were thinking of paying, and it's just a short walk from the opera house . . . in Nußbaumgasse . . ."'

That settled it.

I expected a lamp, at least a book. Tears instead.

'Oh, boo-hoo, you're so cruel, Carli, why are you so cruel?'

'I was only suggesting she was too decadent to be married to Mozart. A composer's life is an austere one. As you can see.'

'A singer's life isn't easy either, boo-hoo, especially when she has sacrificed herself to a composer who won't . . . who won't . . . oh, boo-hoo!'

'I can't afford the Nußbaumstraße or the Nußbaumgasse or any other bon ton street. Even Frau Schweinehaxe is a bit steep for my income.'

'Idiot, I wasn't talking about the flat! We could afford a flat if I could earn more money too, but how can I earn more if I can't get out of the chorus, and how can I get out of the chorus if even my own man will not write in a part especially for me, will not even discuss his latest opera, will not do as any reasonable, decent, human composer would, which is to ask: "Gisela, Liebchen, how can I help you, what sort of part would you like, can I not write some trills for you, a little solo aria, or perhaps a few verses smack in the middle of the ensemble scene at the end Act II or wherever it is, some lovely melody, not too, too difficult, just something to show off the virtues your voice, so that you can stand downstage centre and demonstrate your real talent in front of the whole company with just, let us say, flute accompaniment, no, better make it cello, keep it in the background, the sort of melody which will be on everyone's lips the next day, the sort of part which obliges you, dearest Gisela, to wear a pretty costume with a low neckline to show off the charms I can't keep my hands off at least when I'm sober, and I'm sure I can get Herr Intendant Wurmlein to accept my proposal, it's such a little thing I am offering to do for you, Liebchen, the sort of thing all composers do for their favourites, not to mention being rather closer than that, how would you like to discuss it, dear Gisela, at least we can discuss it, surely that's normal, to be expected?" Oh boo-hoo!'

'I suppose I could always try.'

'Oh, Carli, will you? Oh, mein Schatz!'

'If I can remember it. Let me see; as I recall, I'm supposed to say: "Oh Gisela, Liebchen, can I not write a pretty melody for you? . . ." No, something came earlier . . . was it: "Oh, Gisela, Liebchen, can I not write some trills for you . . ." or was it . . .'

Do I need to point out that the great chancelleries of Europe have not been sending round to Frau Schweinehaxe's rooming house searching for recruits to their diplomatic services?

28 MAY: Tragedy. There must be more a sense of tragedy, of impending doom, of . . . not of failure, but of noble efforts wasted, betrayed. (The papers are all full of the Rights of Man, Freedom and Democracy, the New Order in Society, Unification of Germany, but I keep wondering about the Hohenzollerns, Habsburgs, Wittelsbachs and such trash: they've got the habit of power, and they're not likely to give up as easily as people seem to think.) But there was no tragedy as such in the career of the first Graf Walther: did not dare too much, did not challenge Heaven in an excess of pride: he risked,

118

dared only what was possible, what had to be done. He was a success. No tragedy there.

In tragedy, there must be the dream.

He dreamt of Waltherrott becoming a great city? So it's a tragedy for politicians looking for statues of themselves; tragedy of family which began with great Walther and has produced, these many centuries later, Waltzing Walther; tragedy for innkeepers who did not fill all their rooms, build another wing behind the stables; tragedy for shopkeepers who didn't get to fill their mattresses with gold coins, their wives with children, their mistresses with pastries; tragedy for young louts who didn't have a great army to join so they could travel around Europe thumping other louts and raping milkmaids.

Tragedy of a false Renaissance? Dream not of prosperity, but of flowering, dream of art, of life not just lived but lived gloriously in art?

That would be a big draw at the box office! All of echt bürgerlich Waltherrott rushing in to be told in song and story how their medieval ancestors had the chance to be more than echt bürgerlich and missed their chance, so they've had 600-odd years of stupid, acquisitive, narrow-minded, envious, hypocritical, sanctimonious, sentimental, tasteless, trashy, beer-soaked second-rate Waltherrott; and so they themselves continue.

Make my fortune singing that sort of song.

The Dream of Waltherrott? 'Frülingstraum im Bergwald' is the noblest dream in these parts, noblest ever:

> When April comes I'll blithely wander
> The flowering oaks and pine trees under,
> In Bergwald's air so warm and sweet,
> And there my blushing Irmtraud meet –
> We'll sing and dance away the day,
> Why all the month, until it's May.
> But now in icy dark December,
> I can only just remember,

119

Through the winter's deepest cold,
Mein Frülingstraum im Bergwald . . .

Just repeating the words makes me want to vomit.

Perhaps a personal tragedy? Great Walther in his public ambitions misunderstood first by long-suffering Irmtraud who can't see past the kitchen door, then by pretentious Renate who can't see past her lute lessons?

'Well dear, here it is, April again. Time to be off on this year's campaign, smite the foe.'

'Smiting the foe again? Why couldst not thou stay home just one summer? Leaking roof in the west wing, crumbling parapets, chimney needs repointing . . .'

'I'm the Hammer of the Barbarians, thou silly woman, not the Hammer of the ten-penny nail!'

Tragedy? If this be tragedy, I could write the *Iliad* five times over from the domestic squabbles I overhear in Die Drei Grafen.

If this be tragedy, then a naval battle could be fought in a mill pond.

Tragedy? I need Walther to dare great risks, to brave great foes, to rise above other men, to soar.

What I need is the fist clenched at the thundercloud, hurling defiance at the tempest, challenging the world.

What I have is an exemplary life, an exalted Bürgermeister.

Tragedy of truth betrayed by history? In a primitive age, feudal age, Graf Walther had a dream of a city rising strong under his guidance, *but guided only until the citizens became strong enough to guide themselves, take governance into their own hands.* So: tragedy of the dream lost? Possibly the only road through. There's the Frankfurt idea. But is it valid? Can I hang that story, that theme on this clothesline?

More research. When I find some time.

3 JUNE: Prologue fully written, partly orchestrated, Act I fully sketched through opening, battle, victory celebration – glasses,

wooden mugs, whatever, raised in song, a moneymaker of a theme here, anthem of Waltherrott come next fall, glasses raised in all the taverns! – then on to wonderful, flowing, soaring melodies in Walther-Irmtraud duet scene, birdsong, cows lowing, wind in trees, veritable Pastoral Symphony with aubade motives again, woven in, Peaceable Kingdom, loom and spinning wheel motive from Irmtraud von Linnen's clothmaking family background. Well into the throne room debate with wily Adalbert, complex play of orchestral voices, not discord, but contention. Also making notes for Keilerfelsen vision scene (Sc.4) to be done with spooky winds, tempo changes for percussion bizarre enough to invoke the spirits, little old ladies fainting in fear, children covering their eyes, strong men quailing, etc., wonderful, truly: von Stumpf, Genius.

How sweet life is!

6 JUNE: If she does not stop this venereal fuss soon, I shall throttle her. Drown her. Off the Neuebrücke in the small hours, in a sack with some bricks like a litter of kittens, slipped quietly into the depths, gone, and good riddance.

It is very simple: it is she, Fräulein Sängerin Gisela Klatschmeyer, who has visited the pox upon me, Herr Komponist von Stumpf, and not vice versa. I have pointed this out to her. I have shown her, by the iron laws of logic, the clear proofs of my assertion: *viz.* that the very name 'venereal' means that the disease is transmitted in one way and one way only; and that in the past three years it would not have been possible for me to have contracted the disease from anyone but her; and the disease must have been contracted in the last year; therefore I must have contracted it from her, and not her from me. *Q.E.D.*

It is all quite simple: she is not a virgin, is indeed a lady of some experience, which is to say, she is a singer in the chorus. And I knew what I was getting, I am not naive, I am not complaining despite the considerable discomfort I suffer from the wretched clap; but it is she, and not I, who brought it in from the streets.

Or rather, from the carpenter's storeroom of the Waltherrottner Hofoper, if I know anything about the goings-on inside that den of iniquity. Half-dressed dancers showing off their bodies all the time – actually, showing off their bruises, bandages, palpitating muscles and twitching tendons, more like; crying their aches, moans, and groans like costermongers; dancers? Who could be aroused by those small, sweaty nettle bushes of obsession and complaint? But I mean that the bodies are always about. Then the chorus: dressing room doors open, half off their hinges, singers stepping from behind their dressing screens – 'just hand me that hairpin, Hedi, there's a dear, oh, tee-hee, I seem to pop out of this costume every time I bend over!' Herr Wurmlein's nancy-boys covering all with a general air of decadence. Stage door Johnnies sniffing after the scent of bodily secretions, marking the doorposts. And then the boys in the band, let us not forget them! Has there ever been a more indolent, sly, useless, gossiping, conniving, horny bunch than musicians? Ten minutes in the hour they play (badly, of course) and the other fifty minutes they sit about, wisecracking, whispering, eyeing the girls (or the boys, each according to his wont) and planning, plotting how they shall get the blondie or the one with the cute mole on her cheek to lift her skirts in . . . yes! the carpenter's store room!

And do I object to all this Zigeunerische Stimmung? Not at all! Why, I am the first to approve of anti-bourgeois behaviour. But I do object to her pretence that she works in a convent, eyes cast down, everyone called to prayer on the half hour, yes, Mother Superior, no, Mother Superior.

In the meantime, where am I supposed to be finding the opportunity? In the foul trench room of Die Drei Grafen? In the cellar, up against the kegs? And with whom? Fat Sophie, she suggests to me: 'gross as a Gräfin, dim as a Graf,' to use the common expression. Fat Sophie? No, thank you, I'll take my dumplings from the kitchen, they're not so greasy.

10 JUNE: The moon is rising between the chimneys across the way, and the evening air is thick and sweet. Why do people complain of

the heat? I remember January and smile like the cat by the cream pitcher. Glorious evening! The air is hot and heavy upon the town, but the famous scent of the Bergwald perfumes the air: Waltherrottner Luft. Surely an evening such as this is one of the unadulterated rewards humble people find in this world.

And am I humble? Faced with the miracle of the art which rises somehow from me, yes, I am humble. Act I done, and I wonder that I could have executed it. The bright lines of melody, the weave of orchestration, the skeins of idea . . . but this fails to describe it: the work is a thing itself, cannot be described; I have not the words, there are no words to name the things I see before me on the page: the work must bloom alive on a stage. Yes, I know what false hopes lie in that direction: meddling, incompetence, makeshift sets, lines changed to suit the prima donna, or the stage manager . . . but not to talk of it, not now, not while I feel this peace.

Peace in isolation. There is a small clarinet line in the aubade which, I suppose, suggests the awakening of smaller creatures – some of the birds, perhaps, cicadas – which reappears during the battle, but so lightly that not three people in a thousand will hear it: don't suppose even the clarinettist will think beyond the notes he's playing. It comes back again during the celebration of the villagers, again nearly inaudible, but there, and then it swells through the love scene between Walther and Irmtraud, here obvious, but unrecognizable in modulation to all but a finely trained ear. I know it is there, and perhaps other musicians will hear it. Yet the audience, I am convinced, also hears it somehow, reminded perhaps by the timbre of the clarinet and the tempi; who can say? I know only that I feel my way through the work, trusting that somehow I am getting to their very nerves, unable to prove a thing.

Yet I must trust that somehow I am succeeding, or will succeed. How well I know the reality of public taste! When I do play in Die Drei Grafen, I know exactly what people wish to hear: the most crude and obvious appeals to tears and laughter. Yet the great artists have succeeded by scaling the heights of the immortals, not by climbing down to the level of the meanest fish peddler, but by keeping their eyes firmly upward. Nor do I mean that this is done without keeping one's feet firmly on the ground: on the contrary, yesterday I made note of a peculiar melody a flower girl used in crying her wares: a ninth, if it can be believed! And yet the important direction of the movement is not so much me down to her, but her melody vaulted to the heights by my skills, a conspiracy between us, secret from her at least. And I wonder what other such conspiracies I engage in. Where do these melodies come from which spatter the pages of the score? Are they also lifted from the milkmaid, the coal seller, the newsboy, the fishwife with her trout and pike? Or am I stealing snatches of melody, rows of tones from other composers, from scores I pored over when Geza sent me to the library? Where does it all come from?

Yet the source matters not a touch when compared with the result, the work, the mountain I climb each day. It is a miracle; I marvel that I can work so hard, drive myself for six, ten, twelve hours with only a few crusts and a glass or two of weak beer, yet I am full, refreshed, happy; and after that, I work again as long as my eyes can bear the candle light, then to a deserved sleep, sleep of a bear in winter; but, miracle of miracles, the score wakes me again at first light to straighten up some transition, add a touch more grace to a legato passage, flesh out some complicated orchestration . . . and before I know it, the sun is high and hot, and I can see that people in the street are going to their midday meals. How can this be, that time has passed so? Yet I am never happier than when I work this hard. Tonight, for example, when that moon surprised me with its brightness, I thought at once that I should walk out toward the Bergwald to absorb something of the scene for the writing of the Keilerfelsen scene which (if the muse stays with me) I'll be starting in a day or so. Yet, I felt so peaceful, so confident, yet so nervous of straying from my table, that I have contented myself with these few jottings on this moonlit page. And when I feel rested, I shall return to the score, perhaps to the throne room scene, perhaps make a beginning on the Keilerfelsen.

And now I feel rested . . . and so filled with joy overflowing, my soul like the moon just there, just beyond my window, filling the night with radiance!

14 JUNE: When I needed ink yesterday afternoon, I put off getting it until late in the afternoon, so that when I did get to the shop, Meyerhofer was preparing to close up for the day. I helped him move the tables of books in from the street, then we strolled over to Die Drei Grafen where our Stammtisch promised refreshment. What with one thing and another, I hadn't been around to the table in the last while, so I was looking forward to the relatively novel stimulus of something other than my own mind and the view out the window. Schober and Spaun were already there, Gogolin came later, while Senn and Wayss are out of town, it seems. How wonderful that first stein tasted to my parched throat! What music in those dear voices of my old friends! I was looking forward to a vigorous and cultured discussion of the world in general, of opera in particular, of one specific opera-in-progress. Yet when I began to explain what I have been trying to do in the work, it was as if friendship were just a personal version of revolutionary political theory and music a branch of propaganda.

'What has happened to you all?' I demanded. 'Have you all gone mad?'

'No, we have gone to Frankfurt!'

'Surely others have been to Frankfurt without losing their senses?'

Of course, I know exactly what they meant, but if I admit they are right – as almost certainly they are – I should have to abandon work on the opera and go to Frankfurt myself. I allowed myself to get upset, but they calmed me down and I tried to listen, but to no avail and we argued through the evening. It was particularly distressing to me, because I had come to rest my mind so that I might perhaps attack with more success the scene I was working on. At last Herr Römer threatened to throw us into the street if we didn't stop; as the midnight hour was approaching, we decided to show the discretion of the mature and the sober.

We had not, however, answered any of our questions: whither the Revolution? Whither Art? We were all deeply moved. We tore ourselves apart and, while my friends retired, I was left alone with the night.

And I walked aimlessly through woods, through valleys, and over brooks, and through sleeping villages, to enjoy the great Night, like a Day. I walked, and still looked toward the polestar to strengthen my heart at the gleaming twilight, at this upstretching aurora of a morning beneath my feet. White night-butterflies flitted, white blossoms fluttered, white stars fell, and the white snow-powder of clouds hung silvery in the high Shadow of the Earth, which reaches beyond the Moon, and which is our Night. Then began the Æolian Harp of the Creation to tremble and to sound, blown on from above; and my immortal Soul was a string in the Harp. – The heart of a brother, everlasting Man, swelled under the everlasting heaven, as the seas swell under the sun and under the moon. – The distant village clocks struck midnight, mingling, as it were, with the everpealing tone of ancient Eternity. – I walked silently through little hamlets, and close by their outer churchyards, where crumbled upcast coffin-boards were glimmering, while the once-bright eyes that had lain in them were mouldered into grey ashes. Cold thought! clutch not like a cold spectre at my heart: I look up to the starry sky, and an everlasting chain stretches thither, and over, and below; and all is Life, and Warmth, and Light, and all is Godlike or God. . . .

Towards morning I descried the late lights, little city of my dwelling, which I belong to on this side of the grave (and that deep bed soon enough arrived at, I fear); I returned to the Earth; and in thy steeples, behind the great midnight, it struck half-past two: about this hour, in 1848, Mars went down in the west, and the Moon glowed in the zenith; and my soul desired in grief for the noble warlike blood which is still, in Act III, streaming on the blossoms of Spring: 'Ah, retire, bloody War, like red Mars; and thou, still Peace, come forth like the mild divided Moon.' The very subject for Walther's aria; and so homeward, 'Fleet beyond imagination' through 'scenes of celestial light'; first the words, then the music: – a cornucopia of life onto the page, fingers racing to keep abreast! Ahh, Art! Ahh Life!

15 JUNE: A savage review of my performance on the domestic stage: I am a monster! Not so savage to anyone who knows me well, who has been perusing these pages, but savage nonetheless. And not from the critic you would expect, although she wrote some of the copy. No, the shattering appraisal was delivered in person by Meyer-hofer this morning, this noon hour, whatever. The burden of the problem is that it seems I am not the only one on whom Fräulein Sängerin Gisela Klatschmeyer has bestowed the pox. Except he has swallowed her tale (not the only tale or even tail involved here!) and believes that I bestowed it upon her and not the reverse which, as I know perfectly well, is the correct direction of passage. In vain did I protest this point.

'It is not possible, Carli, for that . . . that angel to have con-tracted this foul affliction other than from a dissolute monster like yourself. She is a lady, a paragon, a delicate flower of rarest purity, a divine soul in flight above this sordid world . . .'

'She was obviously engaged in a bit of the down-to-earth sordid with you.'

Iron logic, I would have thought, but no:

'How dare you! What is between us is . . . is the flesh made spir-itual, a noble thing!'

'I thought the same until I felt the skewer up my wurst.'

'You took advantage of her innocence.'

'As did the first trumpet, the second violin, and the third oboe of the Hofoper Orchestra. That's where she got it, you know. Think, Franz: what other opportunity have I had to catch it? From Fat Sophie?'

Great tears, agonies, gnashings of teeth.

'You might as well face it, she's less Waltherrottner Luft than Lohbachertal Loam.'

'She exhibits more of the spirit of this city than you do: she is a true artist. And you refuse to write anything suited to her talents.'

'Oh, she's been on to you about that, has she?'

'Would it trouble you greatly to do her this favour – a small part in your next opera, something to show off her talents?'

'She is off key.'

'She is dedicated the Revolution!'

'She is dedicated to any revolution which will put her at centre stage in a role that will support her in a Nußbaumstraße flat and win unlimited credit at Süßmayer's Chocolate and Coffee House.'

He had fired all his cannon and had retreated behind his barricade of sullen and frustrated silence. I took pity on him: after all, I knew just how he felt.

'Franz,' I murmured, 'we have been friends these twenty years and more, Stammtisch regulars winter and summer, in poverty and in poverty. Don't let this little misunderstanding come between us. And whatever I have said about her in anger, she is a pleasant enough little thing, doing her best, as we all are, to make her way in this sad world. And I doubt I have brought her much gaiety. Do you think I mind if she fixes her affections upon you, has slept with you, has slept with the brass section, the entire orchestra? She is, as you point out, an artist, so I don't judge her by the hypocritical morality of the petty bourgeoisie she herself is so anxious to join. So she has the pox, so what? If you must blame someone, blame the trumpeter. I have forgiven her this little nuisance, and so should you.'

He struggled to control himself.

'There is nothing to forgive her for.'

'And me?'

He put on his philosopher's face, political theorist's face.

'I am not sure yet. Your potential is greater, I admit, but greater for evil as well as for good.'

'You mean if I write a revolutionary opera all is forgiven, welcome back to the table, drinks this night for the noble Carl Maria?'

'We all have our roles to play in this great drama of national life.'

'And if I decide to sit in the audience? To attend a different play?'

'You'll be a traitor to the cause.'

'A heavy judgment, Franz. And you with my biography filled with hosannas, comparisons with Goethe, Schiller, Beethoven and not to their advantage, at least not in what I have read of it.'

'I can change it.'

'Throw out three years of work? Such profligacy with time!'

'No . . . you're right, I can't afford to discard it. Besides, I have already set the type for most of what I have finished. But I still have four or five chapters to write. They'll tell the true story.'

'So you have already decided to pan me.'

'No, I have not decided. Not yet.'

With that implied threat he stood up to leave. We talked a few minutes more, setting out the conditions of armed peace, I suppose. After all, if we can't drink with one another, with whom can we drink? Not, pray God, with Fräulein Sängerin Gisela Klatschmeyer whose conversation would take the bubbles out of the liveliest beer.

16 JUNE: This morning, a curt summons from Herr Wurmlein to appear in his office before midday bearing Act I score and libretto, Acts II and III sketches. Further instalment of fee promised in return? Yes, and the moon as well, I don't believe; harem of houris; champagne; velvet suits; band playing in tune. I thought of protesting that I was too busy; I considered writing a reasoned note, telling him the truth; but the more I thought about it, the more I was enraged: I would appear in his office, yes, but shaking my fist at his tyranny, at his arrogance, *at his presumption*: that alone, *his presumption*. The creature has asked for an opera and he is getting one. And on schedule: what have I to be ashamed of? Hard work, lots of it, stacks of words, music, letters from Paris, Vienna, Berlin begging first refusal, (have Meyerhofer forge them in half an hour if need be), all more than Herr Wurmlein's wormish brain can digest, everything he requested and more. I could have dumped the lot on his polished desk, played some tunes on his office piano, explained the

motives, the development, the themes, the references, the layering of consequence, the symphonic textures . . .

That's not the point.

Not the point at all.

The point is I do not want to submit work in progress. The lines of development, the sinews, the strands of the web which are tacked tentatively into the scenes of Act I stretch, unwind, unfurl through the sketches and into a misty future, into possibility, *into potential,* and I do not want Herr Intendant Wurmlein poking his silver-headed walking stick through this tapestry.

So I rolled the note into a ball and threw it in the corner.

Then went back to work.

Except that I could no longer work. Distressed by the possibility, the hint, the threat of this interference, judgment, observation, attempted observation, I decided to go for a walk to clear my brain, taking notebook along in case of inspiration while seated under spreading oak tree, whispers of inspiration from the breezes, sun, created great universe inspiring creation of smaller universe, possibly sight of complaisant milkmaid, whatever. Got no further than the next street when a thin rain began to mist in from the Bergwald, obvious dearth of sun, dearth of milkmaids, all of whom would have sense enough to stay in cowsheds, so I took the opportunity of ducking into Die Drei Grafen in the hope that inspiration might strike here. End of working day, obviously. End of life. Such a waste.

17 JUNE: Of course, Herr Intendant Wurmlein has had his way with me. I wouldn't say he sent the bruisers from the percussion section for me; nor a squad of the beefier stagehands. But he might as well have. What he did send was another note:

> Stumpf: If I have not seen Act I and some further sketches by noon today, I shall have you served with a writ of breach of contract and you will be required to return your advances or, if that is impossible, to sit in jail until you have discharged your contractual obligations.

Which struck me as overdoing it a bit. Rather like summoning Frederick Barbarossa from his long sleep in Kyffhäuser Mountain to settle a bar room brawl. However.

As it turns out, little damage was done. I think Wurmlein thought yesterday's refusal to attend, scrape, grovel, genuflect, whatever, arose from an embarrassing scarcity of work done, abundance of alcohol done, consequently he was pleasantly surprised – in fact, stunned – when I dumped the great sprawling stack of paper on his desk. He leafed through it suspiciously, figuring it was largely padded with extraneous material. So after some spluttering and coughing and hemming and hawing, he settled down to a fast read-through, got me to play some of the bits, asked a number of questions, made a number of suggestions – not by any means stupid ones, I admit – and after an hour and a half I left. He wants the completed score and libretto by mid-August at the latest so there'll be time for revisions, 'if deemed necessary,' with casting to take place in early September and rehearsals to begin end of September for opening night Wednesday the first or eighth of November.

All very satisfactory, one might think. And indeed it was. Except that I got no work done again today. So if you happen, gentle reader, to be the Intendant of an opera house, or anyone else of power in opera – or any of the arts, come to that – pray, leave the poor drudge to do it himself.

I did, however, have my revenge. In the few minutes during which Herr Intendant Wurmlein was looking upon me and my efforts with less than his accustomed irritation, I managed to screw another 100 thalers from him and can thus report that while the sun is still high, I am cooling myself at the Stammtisch in Die Drei Grafen. And I intend to remain here until the doors close. Ars longa, vita brevis.

19 JUNE: Herr Intendant Wurmlein wishes me to be a conscientious craftsman, work as ordered, on time, no complaints, no ambiguities, no artistic longueurs, box office guaranteed, all very business-like.

Meyerhofer and the others at the Stammtisch wish me to be the Hammer of the Aristocracy, Bourgeois, whatever, Light of the Revolution, pen made into sword glinting in sun of radiant uplands, storm the fortress of tyranny, bright victory, then over the ridge to a better world for all. Fräulein Sängerin Gisela Klatschmeyer envisions me in velvet smoking jacket lounging in music room of elegant (clean, well-lighted, no aroma of kraut, wurst, feet, farts, etc.) flat in Nußbaumstraße and churning out regular operas featuring large (starring but not too onerous, impressive but not too difficult) parts for weak-voiced soprano along with stacks of appealing lieder for same; churning out bank draughts to pay for clothes, furs, maids, trips to Baden-Baden, etc. Frau Schweinehaxe *usually* thinks of me as a leech upon her body, a wasted beggar living upon her saintly charity; but today, with my rent in arrears by only two months, she thinks of me as a noble gentleman, a knight sent by Saint Amand, patron saint of rooming-house keepers, to protect devout old ladies who have nothing but love for humanity which in turn (in the form of tenants, butcher, fishmonger, etc.) cheats them of the prosperity which is their due as proved by various verses from the Bible, she could look them up for you if she weren't so busy just now, etc. Herr Kellner Römer is perhaps the most practical, most honest: sees me as lazy, drunken, talented piano player who knows how to get his clients singing – and not so coincidentally drinking more beer, fair enough.

All of these von Stumpfs are ghosts, doppelgängers which look and sound and move a bit like me, in something like the same space in the air as I do, but which are never me, never more than a shimmer near me, visible only when I stand in moonlight with darkness behind me. And are true enough, I suppose. As true as the ghost I scribe for myself in the moonlight: von Stumpf, genius. Misunderstood, unappreciated, underpaid, prophet not without honour except in all lands, etc. When the work goes well, when the melodies trill through my brain and down my arm and onto the paper, why all of this moonlight nonsense is but that, like moonbeams at noon, and I am filled with the substantial good cheer which is called Waltherrottner Luft.

But when the work is not going well, when the stack of blank sheets of paper lies there like a watchful wolf about to attack, when my hand is as heavy as a piano, needs two movers to lift it off the bed (aim it toward Die Drei Grafen and it is off like a greyhound), when my lungs rebel at my attempts to breathe, when the weather, the wind, the smell of the city hang oppressively in the air: why, then the melancholy descends upon me like a great weight and I am not a genius, not a craftsman, gentleman, hero, leader, lover, whatever; not a human; a lump, rather, animal, cringing thing, garbage.

I read the above and see that I seem to confuse cause and effect. I *seem* to saying that the weather, whatever, causes the melancholy, but I don't mean that. Rather, when the air seems oppressive as I have described, then I know the melancholy is upon me even before I open my eyes in the morning, know I'll have a titanic struggle merely to get out of bed. The melancholy doesn't come from outside, but from inside. It is as if another creature lives upon my back, hiding in the small of my back and crawls up into my brain, reaching out with grasping fingers to squeeze any Luft from this Waltherrottner. Heaviness, oppressive downward pull, revulsion for the work, premonitions of disaster, the opera is air, nonsense, lies, myself a fraud, fool, hatred of myself, loathing of myself, look upon myself as if I had leprosy, covered in pustulant, running sores, 'Unclean! Unclean!' Ding-dong, ominous intervals in Phrygian mode, whatever.

21 JUNE: I have been invited to participate in the ultimate betrayal: an evening with Waltzing Walther. And I shall go: a matter of research, said von Stumpf disingenuously.

I was sitting with Meyerhofer and the others about five this evening when a chinless creature of ambiguous gender poked his head in the door, fastened upon Fat Sophie as a personage of authority and information, then followed her pointing finger in my direction. Frankly, I thought he was a bailiff; a composer should always expect a bailiff because no matter how scrupulous he has been about paying his debts, there is sure to be someone out there with a resentment, grudge, whatever. In any case:

'Herr Komponist von Stumpf?' it asked.

'You are surely in the wrong jurisdiction; your powers here were abrogated by Emperor Frederick the Prognathous, a decision confirmed in the Golden Bull and further affirmed in the Peace of Westphalia, Council of Worms, whatever. Begone, whelp of tyranny.'

Which said it well enough, I thought.

'A m-message, m-maestro, from the Ruh-ruh-Residenz.'

'The Ruh-Residenz?' sneered Meyerhofer. 'Is anyone there literate?'

'M-maestro?' sneered von Stumpf. 'Does Waltzing Walther think so to insinuate himself into my affections with base flattery? Disgraceful. Begone, wretch, from my sight. But you might as well leave the envelope as a curiosity.'

'I'm to w-wait for an answer,' it replied, 's-should you wish to send one.'

'I expect I'll have my secretary deal with the matter in the morning, but let me just glance at the missive . . .'

'Don't touch it!' cried Meyerhofer, 'It's probably poisoned.'

'My virtue is proof against all poisons, potions, elixirs, whatever.'

'What virtue?'

'My virtue as a genius. Now, let me just . . .' and I pulled the card from the envelope. Rather nice card stock, an embossed coat of arms.

Herr Komponist von Stumpf,

I understand from Herr Intendant Wurmlein that you are at work on an opera which takes as its subject the life of the first Graf Walther vom Faß. I consider it an interesting idea and for obvious reasons think I might be in a position to assist you – but only to the degree that you think you need assistance, let me assure you. To that end, would you be kind enough, my dear sir, to accept my hospitality for dinner tomorrow evening? At, say, five. Don't bother to

134

dress: we shall be alone and 'en famille' as lovers of music. Simply give your decision to the messenger – or send me a note at your convenience. I am, be assured,

Your admiring servant
[signed] Walther

I was stunned. So stunned that I simply handed the card to the others and sat with jaw open. What did it mean? What did I have to do with such a person?

in a position to assist you

Assist how? Money?

My dear von Stumpf, such a gesture of respect and interest in my family deserves to be richly rewarded: do be kind enough to let me press upon you this banker's draught along with a draught of champagne . . .

A subtle case of censorship?

Be assured, Herr Komponist, I only wish to help you avoid the unpleasantness and expense of the law courts . . .

A naked threat?

When I tell you that some of my less sophisticated relatives and retainers are intrigued by crude violence and brutal torture, you'll appreciate the gentle security of the oubliette . . . it's for your own good!

Senn had been reading the note over Meyerhofer's shoulder; now, with an exclamation of anger, he tore it from his hands and crushed it into a ball, threw it into the corner.

'There is your answer; tell your master that Herr Komponist von Stumpf rejects his invitation with disgust and outrage; he is a man, a composer of the people, he glorifies the Revolution and the Constituent National Assembly; he abhors and detests your master and all his spawn!'

Cheers, applause, back-slapping, laughter.

Messenger boy trembling, verge of tears, about to bolt.

I grasp his wrist (thin, bony, don't they eat in the Residenz?):

'Tell your master that Herr Komponist von Stumpf is most interested in the possibilities of some assistance and that he accepts the kind invitation. The Herr Komponist will present himself at the front door of the Residenz at five tomorrow. Do you think he meant me to use the front door?'

'I w-wouldn't know, Herr Komponist . . . I b-believe so . . . it is the usual one . . . the one guests u-usually u-u-u-uh . . . come in.'

'Then the front door it shall be. Tell him I'll be there, and that I thank him most kindly. Away you go then.'

It will be understood that something of a silence fell over the table.

'What?' asked Meyerhofer presently, 'You sent him off without a few groschen for his trouble?'

'Groschen? Do you think me a such piker? You didn't see the golden thalers I slipped him? And be sure you enter the transaction in your biography. As you pointed out last week, you must tell the truth.'

'I am trying to tell the truth, Carli, but it is difficult.'

'Yes. And your readers must have the whole truth.'

'You're betraying your class, your art, your friends, and your . . .' He meant to say 'lady-friend, ex-lover,' whatever, for he eyed me dourly; but we both realized in a moment that Fräulein Sängerin Klatschmeyer, if she heard of the invitation, would be writhing, exploding with envy.

'I'm only going for a meal and . . . curiosity. Franz, you know how much time I have for research.'

Meyerhofer nodded, but the others were more enthusiastic for vitriol.

'Graf von Stumpf.'

'Herzog von Stumpf.'

'Kurfürst von Stumpf.'

'The first.'

'And definitely the last.'

They were ready to throttle me, garotte me, head on a pike at the Kasselertor, crow meat . . . but what are friends for?

Tomorrow another . . . layer, density to my tale?

Part Four

The Journal of Carl Maria von Stumpf
Genius. Failure.
Volume IV [Continued]

24 JUNE: How different the rich must feel with their bellies full every day. It was not just that the food served up by Walther's kitchen was the finest I have ever tasted, food fit for the gods, but rather that there was so much of it. There was a reason for this which I expect will come out in due course. I am used to occasional gorging. Every now and then, when Herr Kellner Römer has a good night and can be jollied into believing that some of his profits have come from my lusty playing, and when by accident there are lots of potatoes, noodles, whatever, left over, I get to stuff myself with a weekly fill in a few minutes.

But at the Residenz, I was served enough for a month. I wish I could remember it all and in the order in which it was served, but certain factors impair my memory of the details. I recall tiny pastries with exotic stuffings, a clear golden soup with tiny noodles floating in it, very light and fluffy (very difficult to keep in the spoon, I noticed), then . . . what? The pot of game stew covered with a pastry shaped like a pheasant and adorned with feathers? Or was that later? The eel in dill sauce and vegetables cut in fans and hats? Never mind the order. The breast of duck with a sauce of wild strawberries, the roast of lamb shaped like a crown with little paper tassels on the ends of bone. The serving lady (yes, lady, as will be explained) kept appearing with more dishes which she uncovered and held for the master's approval; this the dish invariably received and it was then served to me. Meats light and dark, from fur and fowl, hoof and wing and fin. Vegetable dishes, things I had never tasted before, never will again, of which I don't even know the names. Hot dishes were followed by cold, sour by sweet, heavy by light. From time to time, my host drew my attention to the contrasts in taste, colour, texture, and weight.

And then there was the drink. I have been known to bend my elbow, raise my wrist, tip my chin, water my tonsils, God knows; I may claim, to my chagrin, to be less a composer of music than of drunken revelling, composer of a debauched life, but this was drinking of a different order altogether. Waltherrott is known for its beer, of course, but the grape does not fare well in the Lohbachertal, save for the Sylvaner grau, fit only for making sekt. Fine wine can be had in the fancy provisioning shops in the streets between the Opera and the Borse, but if I were to enter such a shop, I would be neatly wrapped in a brown paper parcel and delivered to the Fleischmarkt with instructions as to butchering. But it was neither the expense nor the taste nor the immediate potency of the drinks which was the most stunning. It was rather the variations in drunkenness, a very symphony of sensation: I was by turns light-headed, giggly, profound, diffident, epigrammatic, enraged, sensitive, morose, bellicose, logical, polemical, amusing, confusing, dark, stark, musical, confusical, and finally . . . incoherent, oblivious, comatose. Indeed, had I not had the foresight to spend the night at the Residenz, I have no idea how I would have got back to my room at The Sign of the Pig's Trotter.

Frankly, a few glasses of beer, two or three bowls of the soup with a few pieces of bread would have been more than enough, more than I am used to, but an artist must try to live through varied experiences, must launch himself out like Odysseus onto the wine dark sea of sensations, all for the sake of his art; so I forced myself to sit at the table for the three hours, four, whatever it took to eat through the meal.

All for the sake of the art, as I say.

Beethoven would have approved.

Mozart would have smiled.

Old Bach would have lifted an eyebrow.

Posterity will thank me for this sacrifice.

The result of this feast was that I spent yesterday in bed recovering from all I had eaten. I expect all I drank might have had some small effect as well.

But what did in truth put me on my back was my conversation with Walther. It was, I must say, not just a surprise, but an education. Pax Amici Stammtischorum, whatever.

But enough: I must get down on paper an account of the evening, or I'll forget it. Or have I already forgotten?

The small garden, as any Waltherrottner can see from Opernplatz, has gone to jungle; it prepares the visitor for the decay within. When we bürgers think of Waltzing Walther at all, I believe we imagine him inside with an army of servants to minister to him, fawn over him, sweep, dust, polish, mend, cook, wash, iron, whatever. I suppose the butcher, greengrocer, and the people who live in the Marstallgasse which runs behind the Residenz and who can watch the comings and goings through the rear entrance will have divined the truth: the establishment consists of the woman who served us last night, another who does housekeeping and cooking, the stammering boy who brought me the invitation, and a butler. This latter ancient was yesterday stricken with a liver ailment, it seems, so that it was Graf Walther himself who pulled open the great door in answer to my knock.

'Herr von Stumpf? . . . A very warm welcome, such as it may be.' After explaining about his butler's indisposition, he added: 'I'm afraid Irmtraud the cook's rheumatism has laid her low – as it has done six days out of seven this score of years – so that Renate is rather too busy with our meal and her own to be able to answer the door, while Hanschen, whom you have met, lacks one of the major qualities needed in a doorman: that is, the ability to say clearly and perhaps even with a touch of good taste: "Welcome to the Residenz vom Faß, Herr Komponist von Stumpf."'

I found myself looking about in some awe. Although not as grand as the Hofoper, it was so grand in scale, decoration, and luxury that it seemed more a public than a private building. And, of course, that is the point of a palace, isn't it: it should overawe the visitor with the power and wealth of the owner. The central hall opened to left and right into handsome rooms, a drawing room in cream and gold on one side and what seemed to be a library or more informal room on the other. To the rear, a wide staircase went half-way up in a single flight, then turned to either side and continued to the next floor. Directly above the stairwell vaulted a dome lit by the setting sun through a row of clerestory windows. The dome had been painted in the style of the last century, baroque, rococo, what-ever, with flights of gods and goddesses among clouds glowing, as it seemed, in the same setting sun, and with a chariot, oak leaf crown, sceptre, flowing robes, bared breasts, cherubs, and all the parapher-nalia of someone's heaven, though not, I suspect, of mine. Sadly, perhaps a quarter of it seemed to be flaking off; water seeping through, I assume.

'The apotheosis of my ancestor and, as I understand, your hero. A scene somewhat imaginary, I fear, because done in a style appro-priate to the time of its execution, rather than of the fourteenth cen-tury.'

'Well,' I replied, 'I suppose the painter was doing the job he was hired to do. As we tavern performers say, don't kick the piano player if you don't like the tune.'

He chuckled.

'But let me offer you something to drink. As we are just two, I think the library is more congenial, don't you?'

Without waiting for my reply – what was there to say? – he led me through the archway and into the library. Tall windows were open to the soft breeze and to the light which gave the room a warm glow: I, who was writing of the morning twilight of the first Graf Walther vom Faß was sitting in the late afternoon glow of the cur-rent holder of the name and title. A bit later than late afternoon, actually.

'I'm afraid I don't do as much entertaining as the building was designed for, consequently I have a very limited cabinet from which to offer you something. May I recommend a glass of sherry? It is a practice I learned from the English. Or if you would prefer schnapps? Magenbitterer Urbansky? No, I share your dislike of that medicinal fluid. Sherry it shall be . . .'

As he talked about drinks, the English, the French, the Italians, I glanced about the library. But a library it no longer was. The book shelves were certainly there, but they were empty of everything except spider webs and a few curled up scraps of paper, newspapers, whatever. The sight was forlorn. Then I noticed that above the bookcases, the fabric was stained and discoloured, panels peeling from the walls, mouldings on the cornices dusty and chipped.

'Yes, the room is a ruin, a ghost. Even the bookcases themselves are to go – to join their books, fortunately. I have donated the collection and the bookcases to the new Stadtbibliothek as the beginning of an accumulation of fine editions, incunabula, and manuscripts. Most of the volumes are of indifferent value, but for the rarities a room has been set aside in the bowels of the earth, the idea being that they'll be more secure there; I suspect they'll simply be more in danger of mildew and neglect. But the issue is out of my hands. Do take that chair; it is reasonably comfortable and I asked Renate to dust it today; there is an even chance that she did . . .'

We toasted one another. He took a sip and babbled on about books, rooms, maids, drinks, whatever. He is a slight man in his forties, I'd judge, and rather fussy in his movements. I was surprised to realize that he was at least as nervous as I was. This relaxed me considerably, so that I sat back and began to enjoy myself. Walther, by contrast, was pacing back and forth, now in the light, now in the shadow, his voice rising and falling in an incantatory tone which I didn't think possible in the language. The matter of it was not easy to discern, but certain streams of it took colour, like wisps of smoke in a twilight sky:

He and I represented the two predominant strains of meaning in history.

This was a new notion to me. Sometimes I think of myself as the composer of operas, the highest of all art forms, operas which are indeed the embodiment of all that is best in German Culture, in Western Civilization. Most of the time, however, I agree with my neighbours in thinking of myself as an impoverished drudge of slight competence and general irrelevance, a composer of ditties for the garrulous drunks and maudlin adulterers who gather in Die Drei Grafen. This Graf had other ideas:

'. . . forests and swamps obscure in the medieval mists . . . dark warriors creeping through the pine trees . . . parting the boughs . . . their minds dim as the forests, terrifying in the darkness . . . the Roman world a light unimaginable . . . ruined roads . . . a hill fort at the bend of a river . . . rumours of great buildings crumbling, overgrown . . . Colonia Aggripina, Lauriacum, Borbetomagnus, names unknown to *them*, rumours only . . . while from the south, tales of brigands returning with the spoils of Italy . . . condottieri preying on towns, marching brazenly along crumbling roads which Caesar's legions once trod . . . Caesar's, great Julius's? . . . Germanicus's as well, for we have read our Tacitus, though the condottieri perhaps have not, much less my ancestor . . . and the Roman roads cross France as well, the garden of Europe, but still only a pale shadow of that past, and indeed in those days a broken kingdom, broken by plague and by war . . . scavenged by brigands, hardened captains, freebooters, freelances . . . civilization held to ransom there . . . awaiting the Maid of Orleans, a fantastic world, all too strange for the dwellers of the deep forests here . . . their reality, the world of their days is the reality of the dripping forest . . . reality honour, *honour!* . . . reality brute death of sword, spear, knife . . . muscle and sinew hacked apart rudely, blood dark upon the moss, spoor calling the wolf, the bear, the crow to the spoils of steaming bowels, an eyeball, sightless now, plucked out by a flashing beak in the deepening gloom . . . howls and grunts . . . wet snow grey in the sky . . . wisps of smoke drifting across the horizon . . . dying sun red above a blackened horizon, lurid red through the smoke . . . distant smoke of burning hamlets . . . peasants scattering . . . cries of children surprised by terror, by the grasp of hairy arms, rancid smell of sweat and blood . . . the women pulled to the ground . . . mounted . . .

Oh! God in Heaven, spare me these visions of that world and of this! . . .'

With this he threw his glass into the corner, clapped his hands over his eyes and stood shivering a long minute.

I dearly wanted to throw down my own drink – the English are mad if they esteem that stuff – and go foraging in the cellar for a lager, a schnapps.

But I sat rigid, waiting.

Walther rubbed his eye, shook his head and gave me a wan smile.

'Perhaps you will indulge a man who has . . . not *seen* too much in his life, but . . . *imagined* too much. I hope I do not offend you if I say that your clothes suggest your days and years have not been heavy with the luxury of leisure time.'

'The truth does not offend me.'

'No, time is the luxury of the rich or of the very poor. You have not had it, I have. When one also has imagination . . . well, you have imagination and the talent to use it. I have a measure of imagination and the time to indulge it, but without the talent to make anything of it . . . except these phantasms. Possibly you envy me what you fancy is time and security, and indeed, had you my circumstances, I have no doubt your work would spring up about you like the finest and most elaborate of palace gardens. What style, I wonder? A French garden with parterres of flowers in formal designs, straight avenues lined with marble statues of Athene, Pan, Odysseus? I think not. An Italian garden with falling waters, cool grottos, Lombardy poplars? Possibly. A secret Spanish garden, palms and vines enclosed within the walls of Spanish suspicion and pride? Never! No, I think an English garden with broad sunny lawns, asymmetrically placed copper beeches, an irregular lake, a waterfall, glimpses of distant spires and – of course! – a folly in a wilderness. I confess to an affection for the English – as the sherry will have suggested to you – but perhaps this is not your garden, perhaps I am imposing on you. Perhaps yours is still a German imagination, back in those . . . damp and misty forests. . . . But I am again in danger of offending you. And of starving you. I expect Renate is well into her preparations and we had best go along to the dining room and our first course, or we shall be offending her, and that would never do.'

With a fatherly hand on my shoulder, Walther ushered me out into the hall where he asked me to wait a moment.

'I'm afraid the bell system has not been working for some years; I must tell her we are ready.'

He disappeared through a door behind the stairs. I heard briefly some raised voices, muffled by the distance. Presently he reappeared and led me up the stairs, across the upper hall and into the room in the centre of the upper storey.

'Here is the dining room. We shall still have the glow of evening for some hours and the small table is a congenial size. The large table seated twenty-four, but it and the chairs have been gone these three years and more. Gone with most of the silver and the buffets, with the carpets, the paintings and tapestries, the chandeliers and sconces. Gone the way of all the sublunary world in time.'

Again he had to make an effort to keep himself in control, and succeeded this time without any sighing or moaning. As we walked over to the table, our footsteps echoed in the emptiness. Seated at the 'small' table – large enough for ten, as a matter of fact – I glanced about and saw that the room had indeed been stripped bare, save for our table and chairs, and a cabinet bearing several bottles of wine. Silk panels covered the walls, but they were stained, worn, dusty, tattered, and coming loose, while the great velvet curtains would now have little use beyond horse blankets – or perhaps a swatch could be made up into a new frock coat for me to wear at the premiere of *Waltherrotterdämmerung*.

'It was an architectural whim of the last century to have the dining room on the first floor and commanding a view. I rather suspect it was adapted from the Venetian practice of situating the receiving rooms on the piano nobile. The result is pleasant, especially if the view is toward the setting sun. It warms the room both physically and spiritually; I fear it also chills the food which must travel a considerable distance from the kitchen. I thought of having a table set

144

in one of the small rooms to the rear – we usually eat there – but for a guest of such honour, I thought the house itself should be shown to best advantage. And after six centuries of continuous hospitality of one sort and another, you are, sadly, the last dinner guest of the vom Faß family in Waltherrott.'

He observed me closely and I expect he was not disappointed by my reaction.

'The last . . . in Waltherrott? I don't . . . are you . . . leaving? Is that why the books . . .'

'You have grasped the point of the books. Yes, I am leaving. From tomorrow, the Graf vom Faß will no longer be in residence, in view, in power. Tomorrow I shall be going . . . elsewhere.'

This dampened the tone a mite; and into the silence came the maid, cook, whatever, woman of the house, Renate, all scowls and elbows, carrying a tray. We seated ourselves hastily and in no time found plates of the little pastries before us, along with glasses of wine. As she bustled about I tried to gauge her age – much as mine is – and her lineaments – tall and bony, perfectly in harmony with what I had seen of her character. With a last flourish of glances at the master, all full of secret messages I have no doubt, she strode from the room.

'East,' he muttered, 'let us say . . .'

These matters have never been of much interest to me – what had the comings and goings of aristocrats to do with me? – but if the vom Faß family really was vacating the county, I asked myself, who would rule? Did this have anything to do with the Frankfurt Assembly? What would happen to the city? *What would happen to the Hofoper?* I saw that a main reason for eating in this room was that there was no need to light the candle; and saw at once the reason: Walther, fifty-eighth Graf vom Faß, was as financially embarrassed as I was. Well, not quite: he had the palace, and some land, I supposed, and enough ready cash for the food, but only by dint of the strictest economies. And he had insight:

'You have divined my predicament, I see. Yes, the truth is that my father Augustus, my grandfather Walther, and my great-grandfather Maximilian, were tremendous profligates. Their wives were nearly as bad, would have been worse had not every dress-maker, milliner, furrier, jeweller and wainwright in every known city of Europe been warned that were they to extend credit to the ladies they would be doing so at their own risk. Those unfortunate consorts were thus reduced to frittering away the wealth of the county on food and drink. You may perhaps have heard of their prodigious size.'

As gross as a Gräfin, as dim as a Graf.

'They were monstrous. In any case, the damage was done by the men, not the women. At least my great-grandfather with his archi-tectural projects returned to the city some of the wealth he har-vested from it. And we can all be grateful he was not seduced into trying to imitate Louis XIV in expansiveness. This building is re-markably restrained by the standards of the time, when a number of other rulers across Germany reduced their subjects to beggary in their attempts to shine as brilliantly as the Sun King. No, my great-grandfather was at least somewhat restrained in his enthusi-asms for domestic architecture; he had spent several of his young years in Vienna where many noblemen of his rank, and many much grander, were content with palaces within the city walls and thus traded the vast solitude of gardens for the bustle and sociability of city streets. Of course, he also began the building of the opera house, and that is as lavish as the Residenz is restrained. I have for some time been toying with the notion of opera as an exemplar of certain exaggerated aspects of the human condition; in a sense that is why I have invited you here this evening; perhaps we can discuss it. But whether or not opera has any general significance in matters of extremity, it was, for my great-grandfather, a consuming passion.

'For my grandfather, as for so many of his peers who tasted la douceur de la vie during the last century, it was women. I am con-founded by such an appetite. In my youth I enjoyed dancing, though hardly enough to warrant the nickname which has long been a misnomer. As to more unbridled grapplings with the ladies: well, I admit to you, in the spirit of frankness which I hope exists

146

between us, that I am myself incapable of amorousness, even had I the desire: a certain malformation of the male parts renders me hors de combat in those silken lists. No such disability hindered my grandfather in his obsession: from Sorrento to Stockholm, from Moscow to Madrid, he braved blazing suns and blinding snows, trackless wastes and tumultuous seas for, as he once confided to me with a chuckle: "Forests of legs, mountains of bubbies, and lakes of . . ." Well, you can guess. He was a friend and rival of Augustus the Strong, but without the resources of that worthy's two kingdoms. Of course, he was also far less solicitous of his progeny and, indeed, kept on the move not just in pursuit of women, but in flight from bastards, a luxury not open to the merry Augustus.

'With my father it was the gaming tables. Unlike my grandfather, who was radiant and jovial in his victories, my father was, not surprisingly, grim in his constant defeats. I understand the appeal of gambling even less than I do that of lubricity, but it is obviously an opiate. I have watched gamblers at the spas; they are men – and women – possessed. Au fond, it seems to me gamblers are at war with God, locked in a bitter struggle with the Supreme Being, for surely if anyone can determine the fall of the cards or dice, it is He. So it is a form of worship: in an increasingly godless age, at least among members of my class, gamblers remain devotees. For them, the Universe has a meaning which they see, as through a glass darkly, but then, when they win, face to face; now they know in part; but then shall they know even as also they are known. They are fervent for the liturgy, for the perfections of its movements, obsessed that all procedures be repeated as before – as before when their worship was efficacious, when He vouchsafed His benison in winnings – and obsessed that the priests dispense the sacrament in approved fashion, mumbling the proper versicles in a foreign tongue: "Mesdames et messieurs, faites vos jeux!" to which the congregation offers up the proper, fervent responses: "Rouge . . . Impair . . . Suivi . . . Banco!" Madness, of course. The rational man examines the arithmetic and, if he is not repelled by making a profit from the weaknesses of his fellow man, takes a partnership in a casino. Not the gambler; for him it is not a matter of lucrative investment but a struggle between the Powers of Light and the Powers of Darkness. Such was my father.

'The result of this century of profligacy may be seen around you: the bankers of Frankfurt and Hamburg have long since been harvesting the income of the patrimony; the title to the county will pass, upon my death, to one of several dozen personages or legal bodies ranging from such obscure claimants as the Count of Ost Friesland, the Duke-Presumptive of Jülich, and the Bishop of Wuppertal, all the way up to the King of Prussia and the Emperor Ferdinand . . . or whatever person or body is ruling Prussia or Austria when this year is out . . . and doubtless the Pope is casting eyes in this direction. It is in the nature of such disputes that the lawyers will keep the business circulating through their chambers for a century and more if possible. I have no idea who has the right in the case; I expect that if the Frankfurt Assembly does not find a way of asserting itself more than it has, the good bürgers of Waltherrott will see Prussian blue uniforms before too many months have passed.'

'But Prussia is well on its way to a constitutional democracy,' I said.

'Admittedly, in Friedrich Wilhelm IV Prussia has but a shadow of the Der Grosse Kurfürst or Der Alte Fritz, but he is still a Hohenzollern, and events have not yet . . . Well, ho-ho, you had me waltzing, I must say. But you were right to pin that butterfly. How difficult it is not to make unwarranted assumptions, don't you find? Especially when the speaker is . . . not so much different from oneself, but . . . surprisingly different? And you *do* surprise me, sir. Are not all of young men of your age and class rallying to the black, red and gold?'

'Yes, most are. But may I not make some unwarranted assumptions: that you, as an aristocrat, must be the enemy of revolution, the champion of the red, white, and black?'

He chuckled: 'So we have both erred.'

'Perhaps.'

'Are you suggesting that you, the young composer, are actually a reactionary and that I, the aristocrat, am actually a revolutionary?'

'No, I mean we are both more complicated than the press and the speakers and enthusiasts would like to admit people can be.'

'Ahh . . .'

'For enthusiasm has returned to Germany,' I said. 'I am fervent for liberty and democracy, yet . . . I am confused. I embrace many of the hopes and ideals which animated the American and French Revolutions, and which even now lead people through the streets of Paris, Vienna, Munich, Berlin, and Frankfurt. If the barricades were here in the Bahnhofstraße or the Alte Markt, then I . . . I would have to be there. But as to travelling to Frankfurt . . . what should I do when I got there? I read in the newspapers of debates, clubs, committees, factions, cabals, speeches . . . I have friends whose seeming talents are smaller than mine – small tradesmen, clerks – and yet they have been to Frankfurt and have been of some use. I have always been a solitary man in what is essentially a solitary profession. I declare to you that as long as I am before my paper and with a piano nearby on which to run through my themes, I am a happy man, and perhaps a useful one to mankind and the German nation. But put me in the opera house with singers and musicians complaining of my lumpen melodies, my spavined plots, my dull scenes, why, I am in perdition. And I have not mentioned the omnipotent Intendant for whom a composer is less important than a member of the stage crew, for he has not even their nuisance value of being able to ruin the performance at the last minute. No, everyone can heap abuse upon the composer. In such a chaos of conflicting voices, I am a child again, hiding in a corner from the wrath of his elders. Is this not a fair analogy for the world of politics? What use should I be there? I should be worse than useless.'

'But surely an artist is exactly the man a revolution needs! Why, what of Rouget de Lisle, of the painter David, of Thomas Paine?'

'What of André Chenier?'

He threw back his head and chuckled, for him a violent gesture.

'Touché! So we may cease our fencing: for I think that, against all expectation, we agree on many things. Such an irony! I am of the old order, yet I have moderate hopes for a better world arising out of the Frankfurt Assembly, while you, who should be rabid for Revolution, seem reluctant.'

For a time we talked of the latest despatches from the various capitals, from Frankfurt. Clearly I was not the only one with a sense of bewilderment.

'Being in the middle of history seems to be more confusing than looking back upon it,' I concluded.

'But that's exactly your problem: you are too reasonable. A revolutionary must not be reasonable, but passionate.'

'I have trained myself to be passionate in front of my stack of stave paper; it is a slow passion, a dismally disciplined passion.'

'At least you have an object for your passion.'

'For the composer, passion most often amounts to trying to find a satisfactory modulation from one key to another.'

Renate entered and changed the soup for the eel. He was very solicitous of her, fussing about trying to help and complimenting her on the service. She largely ignored him except for a sour glance as she closed the door on her way out.

'Renate is, of course, not happy about her prospects from tomorrow. I am . . . hoping to arrange something for her.'

As the eel is the cheapest fish the Lohbach affords, I know it well, but this was the finest I had ever tasted, and I said so.

'I think you might easily succumb to the delights of the palate,' Walther replied. 'Ahh, to watch Signor Rossini in the days of his glory as he sat down at the Baron Rothschild's table before a feast prepared by Carême: those meals were operas in themselves!'

'I don't believe Signor Rossini has written much recently.'

Walther put down his knife and fork and gazed sadly at his plate. Then he rose and walked to window where he stood looking toward the twilight.

'Not these twenty years, no. I saw a report in a newspaper the other day that students have been throwing stones at his windows; it seems he once composed some entertainments for a Congress organized by that cold hand, that . . . embalmer, Prince Metternich.

Such is the fate, perhaps, of composers who dabble in politics, although I doubt Signor Rossini thought it a political act.' He turned to face me. 'I have insulted you, my friend. I apologize. I am sure you work as hard as Signor Rossini and you may well have his genius. But that is no guarantee that you will ever dine at the tables of the great; nor have you suggested you would wish to do so.'

Despite the fall of light from behind him, which kept his face in shadow, I could sense the agitation on his features.

'You have not insulted me. On the contrary: I would gladly exchange my stammtisch in Die Drei Grafen for the lavish tables of Paris. To enjoy such feasts as Signor Rossini was accustomed to, I would accept commissions from Prince Metternich, from the King of Prussia, from the Pope, from the Devil himself!' – I rose from my chair and joined him by the window, careful not to scrutinize his face too carefully – 'But what I would especially like is a small pension, from the Tsar, or the Sultan, the Cham of Tartary perhaps, some monarch far away enough that I wouldn't be in danger of offending him, and perhaps I could include some Janitscharmusik, Kosakmusik, whatever, but with my affairs on a sound financial footing, perhaps five hundred thalers a year and a warm, well-lighted room, I would be free of worries long enough to write an opera which would hymn the Revolution, attack the myriad abuses of the *ancien régime*, and in my efforts to reassure you, I have, like the inquisitive cat, walked into a bag and cannot get out because you must now think I mean you as a surrogate source of this emolument, while I was . . .'

'While you are here at the window, let us enjoy the view of the Square. See how the light lingers: we are but a few days past Midsummer Eve and some of the grace of that night is with us still. I admit I prefer the square when a performance is scheduled for the opera house, when the lights are aglow and the bustle of the crowd gladdens the air.'

I now brought up the thought which had struck me earlier.

'But wait: if you are in financial straits, a worshipper at the balls of St. Nicholas as they say in the Alte Markt, then who will support the Hofoper, will it now close? Surely the banks will not . . .'

As he was now in a position of reassuring me, we strolled back to the table and resumed eating.

'The Hofoper will become the Stadtoper, and the city will be its chief patron. In fact, for some years now the city has been taking the part once performed by this family. It was only a matter of time before it gained control in name as well as fact, and a good thing too, for the days of aristocratic patronage are drawing to a close. I have no doubt that the Bürgermeister and the Stadtrat will be anxious to prove that bürgerlich pride in the city is as great as Grafinical pride. What they most need,' he said, suddenly finding something fascinating about his piece of eel, 'What they most need, is a new opera on some subject which flatters the city, which exalts it above the station of its rivals.'

Perhaps the wine was inflaming my brain, or perhaps we were becoming more comfortable with one another:

'You are not, my friend, making a veiled reference to my work in progress, are you? . . . As I thought. And do you mean to suggest that Herr Intendant Wurmlein is under more compulsion than he admits to accept my new work? . . . But no, I divine your message: the compulsion was even greater and the commission came not just from his interest in my fortunately timed proposal, but from a suggestion, perhaps a directive from the Bürgermeister himself? . . . Then I am relieved, for I shall not have to pander to his debased tastes, and the supposed demands of the crowd, but can proceed as I wish, crafting the work to the ideals of a just rendering. Ahh, Signor Rossini, where are your riches now compared with my freedom!'

Walther smiled benignly.

'And if he ate better than this in Paris, what is that to me? A feast such as this one has been is more than enough for a lustrum of Lucullan luxury.'

I laid the cutlery on the plate.

'Does it not tempt you more than you admit?'

'As I said, my needs are modest.'

'You yearn for a pension.'

'Not even behind my jesting am I such a fool that I yearn for the impossible. Every small town in Germany and Italy has its opera house along with no end of similarly obscure composers. To get a pension, I should have to be brought to the notice of the great, but what likelihood is there of that? The great pass through Waltherrott as often as I pass through Vienna or Milan.

'Another path is for my work to be presented in the capitals, and so secure notice for me, but that needs luck and certainly some help from powerful friends within the musical world, friends I do not have. I know that there always exists the possibility that one of my works will capture the hearts of the crowd, although such a success would to some degree make a pension redundant. As contracts are now arranged for composers such as myself, my return from a first success would be a pittance, for the Hofoper would own the work and would reap all the profits. But I could command a princely commission for the work which comes after a great success, sight unseen; that would establish me for life in my room at the Sign of the Pig's Trotter; and if that second one were a popular success as well, my fortune would be made.

'So do I yearn for a pension? Not at all: a man with a skill has a pension in his fingers. Three evenings a week, I play piano at Die Drei Grafen. I am paid my pittance, I gorge myself on Herr Kellner Römer's noodles and even sometimes a plate of Walthers Versuchung, while Fat Sophie brings me a glasses of lager on demand – as long as the demand isn't more than once every hour or two – and I take pleasure in the company of the beating intellectual heart of Waltherrott. What more could I ask of life? Surely nothing.'

In the thoughtful silence which followed, Renate returned with another tray. After the dishes were shuffled and arranged, I found myself facing (I think it came at this point) the duck with strawberry sauce along with vegetables beyond memory. I tried to keep the dismay from my face, and consoled myself that the helping was small enough that I might get through it.

'It is a curious thing,' Walther said at last, 'That while generalizations about mankind may have validity in regard to the mass of people, they fail in regard to the individual. And I think that at the node where the failure occurs we find humour. Your notion of winning a pension from the loathsome Tsar Nicholas so that you could write revolutionary operas is droll. I realize you were, if you wish, performing an opera buffa for me, dropping flats of fantastic scenes, hurrying absurd and ridiculous characters onto the stage to sing their nonsense songs. But like the best of comedies, it was obviously meant as at least a simulacrum of truth. That is, I take it that you do indeed prefer that the great epic of change, the strife and turmoil of alarums by night should rage only in your work, while the streets of your town are quiet, cheerful, and lit by the warm sun of noon.'

'I cannot deny it,' I agreed in desperation. 'How am I to do any work if I live in the middle of a drama? If I preferred turmoil and strife, there are battles enough to be found. And in the midst of a battle, one must fight, one picks up the nearest weapon and flails away at the enemy; that is no time to sit down to elaborate a little cavatina.'

'But if you are to spend your life in your little room, what will you have to write about?'

'Did Beethoven go to prison to write *Fidelio*? Did Mozart become a philanderer to write *Don Giovanni*?'

'They did not write their own libretti as I believe you do.'

This was grotesque, but in courtesy to my host, I thought I should offer some reply.

'It is certain that any artist – painter, poet, sculptor, composer, whatever – who spends his entire life in an ivory tower, a prison cell, or a cave, will produce work of a very peculiar sort, although if he is a genius, the work will doubtless shine accordingly. By contrast, it seems likely that an artist who has lived a life of great adventure, who has braved battle, who has moved in the company of all classes and kinds of men and women, who has perhaps travelled to exotic lands, wandered through trackless forests, over desolate mountains, or across the restless oceans – why such a man, again, be he a genius, will surely produce work of great value, teeming with the lives of memorable people and the vivid events of the great world. I find myself between these extremes. You can see from my body that I am not made for battles, and have not the money to travel like Byron, nor the ingenuity to travel like a gypsy; I can assure you that by temperament and experience I am not adept at the arts of love; and I am incapable of governing myself, never mind a county or an empire. Yet I must, I *have* written words and music for these and many other scenes.'

'Your argument is compelling,' he agreed. 'These last fifteen years, I have lived a quiet life of contemplation, taking what spiritual nourishment I can from books. Without companions against whom I can test my ideas, the only stays to an unbridled imagination are the ideas I encounter in the next book. A man in my position is likely to forget that others may be thinking on the same questions and reaching different conclusions. I am humbled by your arguments and by the passion with which you assert them.'

I bowed my head but kept my silence.

'And yet . . . yet passion is at the heart of the problem at Frankfurt. For history, it seems to me, is the interplay of diverse passions which resolve themselves to a resultant direction, toward an end. Have you ever considered . . . not just the notable peaks of history, the battles, dates, and dynasties . . . but the reality of history, the whole unity of events, people, tendencies, oppositions? Consider: how does history progress? The Orient has long possessed a single essential idea: that *one* man, the despot, is free. The Greek and Roman world knew that *some* are free, some are slaves. The German world knows that *all* are free. This progress of the Spirit comes into being through the opposition of contradictions, and their resolution into a unity, a synthesis, an altogether new idea which, however, combines and includes all that has gone before. Understood in this light, the Frankfurt Assembly is obviously crucial to Civilization: for the aristocratic order of which I am a part, and which has been represented by Metternich, the Emperor and other such antediluvian monsters, is doomed. It matters little whether the new order arrives this year or next, whether the new capital is in Frankfurt or Berlin or Vienna: in this light, it follows that the stronger the Frankfurt Assembly, the more effective it will be in advancing the historical progression; it also follows that the finest spirits opposed to aristocracy should be there; and it further follows that such an assembly must include all artists such as you.'

'But this implies a glorification of the will acting in history!' I burst out.

'Exactly!' he replied, and his eyes glittered as I had not yet seen them do. 'For the State is the actually existing realized moral life: man's spiritual reality consists in this, that his own essence – Reason – is objectively present to him, that it possesses objective immediate existence for him. For truth is the unity of the universal and subjective Will, and the universal is to be found in the State, in its laws, its universal and rational arrangements.'

'You seem to be suggesting that the State is the Divine Idea as it exists on earth, the embodiment of rational freedom, realizing and recognizing itself in objective form.'

'Exactly: the State is the Idea of Spirit in the External manifestation of Human Will and its freedom.'

At such moments, in the midst of such conversations, I find myself saying: Thank God I'm not an Englishman in love with common sense, or a Frenchman in love with wit, or an Italian in love with high spirits, but a German in love with the Abstract!

Oh, yes, indeed.

I decided to bring things back to the world I lived in.

'In that case, I find it difficult to understand your assertion that the German world is so superior: the unity of the universal and subjective Will has not been markedly successful in forming itself into a German state, has it?'

'But that is what is in process of happening at Frankfurt just now!'

'Or in Berlin next year . . . or in Waltherrott the following year?'

A look of pain spread slowly over his features.

'Are you finally a cynic?'

'Perhaps a sceptic.'

'No, I cannot believe you are, for you are an artist.'

'As skilled at making operas as Germans are at making states: I have made a number of small and unsuccessful ones.'

'In a mocking bitterness, you belittle your abilities. But you must not, for I have seen your operas and I know you are a genius. If the critics and the people cannot yet see this, it is of no account. And, indeed, it is through your passion, your self-discipline, and your genius that you embody the aspirations of your fellow man. And that is precisely why you should be in Frankfurt!'

'But if I should be there to voice the claims of democracy, surely you should also be there for the aristocracy, in that your philosophy argues that the Idea, as unity of the Subjective and the Objective, is the notion of the Idea – a notion whose object is the Idea as such, and for which the objective is Idea – an Object which embraces all characteristics in its unity. In that case, surely you also have your part to play . . .'

'No,' he said in resignation, 'My part is played out, and in any case others are there to represent the aristocratic thesis.'

'But not aristocrats who understand their role in the logical development. Surely any aristocrats in Frankfurt are dilettantes at best and most are manipulators hoping to protect their positions. You are a philosopher who understands . . .'

He smiled sadly.

'That is the irony, my young friend. When philosophy paints its grey on grey, then has a shape of life grown old. And by this grey on grey it can only be understood, not rejuvenated. The owl of Minerva spreads its wings only with the falling of the twilight.'

'*Waltherrotterdämmerung.*'

'I beg your pardon?'

'*Waltherrotterdämmerung* is the title of my new opera, although I was thinking of the tentative beginnings of civilization, not of an advanced state of decadence of one stage, to which you are referring.'

He brightened at once: clearly the evening would be more congenial if we stayed with art and avoided history and philosophy.

'Ahh,' he said, 'Ahh, yes. As I mentioned in my note, I have heard of this new work, and I'm most interested in it. I hasten to assure you that mine is not the obvious interest: I am not trying to protect the good names of my ancestors from the libels of a revolutionary. Far from it: you have seen that I am more in the revolutionary camp than you are. My ancestors, especially the earliest ones, have long since stood before the throne of the final Judge of all souls, so that the proceedings of living men are of no account to them. And as I am the last of the line, judgement on the entire dynasty will soon be in His hands and complete.

'I am interested rather in the process whereby you transform the past into action, spectacle, and music. Before we go further, however, let me state without equivocation that I realize the creation of works of art is accomplished through the activities of divinely inspired Genius. For me to interfere would be . . . odious. As Schiller remarks: "Wholly unconfiding, the poet hides himself from the heart that seeks him, and from the desire that wishes to embrace him." Thus the conversation need proceed no further should that be your desire. I admit I am curious about the new opera, curious about your approach to my distant forefather, but all shall be as you wish, and I await its première with interest.'

The unfamiliar fumes of the wine were beginning to fog my mind, and to loosen my tongue beyond what might have been prudent. I do not know. In any case, I shrugged and said:

'You may ask what you wish. At worst, I shall only refuse to answer.'

'Then . . . can you summarize the action? Of what period do you treat?'

I told him I was working solely with the life of the original Walther and briefly passed through the various episodes. Throughout my tale, he sat peering at me with unswerving gaze, intent upon my words, but as I approached the final battle and Graf Walther's death, he rose from his chair and went again to the window. When I stopped talking, he remained where he was, his figure dark now against the last of the light. Having got through it – and I admit it was something of a struggle to talk of the tentative – I breathed a sigh of relief and refilled my glass. Unless the opera is a greater success than I fear it will be, I'll not soon be drinking wine again. What am I saying?! It *shall* be a miracle:

Light of the Nation!

Inspiration of the Century!

and a regiment of wine merchants from Burgundy trailing up the stairs of Frau Schweinehaxe's rooming house: 'Five crates of this one, monsieur, and ten of that and . . .' and, heavens! wherever shall I store it all?

Graf Walther turned and walked to the door. After a minute or so, he returned and sat down again.

'A small sweet and coffee are on their way. The poor woman, I fear, is in some distress. It is the end of an era.' He looked at me. 'The end of . . . well, we'll see.'

Renate, closer to anger than distress I thought, brought in strawberries and coffee along with a bottle of what proved to be French cognac. Much more of this life, I reflected, and I'll be signing this man on as my collaborator. 'You have lived all your life in the city, I believe? You attended school here?'

I nodded.

'So what knowledge you have of Graf Walther you gained from your schoolbooks? . . . Yes, I have seen the tomes in use. The excesses of past historians leave much to be desired: they have been more passionate to please than to instruct, more in search of tales than of truth. There are signs that better history is being written today, so perhaps the future promises more accuracy, more truth, and no one will be happier than I shall be to see the fanciful nonsense of these earlier writers, these dreamers, thrown into the Lohbach. Falsehood is egregious. . . . Hah! Why didn't I simply say: "Lies are bad?" But that is a digression. Now that we have our cognac, and now that we understand one another rather better, allow me to present you with a small gift.'

He arose and took from the cabinet a pair of slim, leather-bound volumes, along with a large dossier envelope. He put them on the table between us, smiled at them, but sat without opening them or offering them to me.

'You will not be surprised,' he began, 'to hear that the first Graf Walther was illiterate, as were most of his subjects. When you spend your life wresting territory from your neighbours, or wresting your survival from the soil, you have no time for the delicate arts. But in late medieval Waltherrott, in Waltherrott of the mid-fourteenth century to be precise, a few people could indeed read and write. Who do you suppose that might be?'

'His wives, perhaps?'

'Storied Irmtraud and Renate. Certainly Renate could. St. Irmtraud was not lettered. Who else?'

'St. Adalbert, I expect.'

'The very man. And not only could he write, he did write. And his writing has survived.'

He directed his gaze pointedly at the dossier envelope. I understood that I was to be impressed.

'What? . . . You mean . . . !'

He beamed and slowly, reverently opened the cover to reveal a number of brownish sheets closely covered with tiny black marks.

'Behold: the annals of St. Adalbert!'

'The popish snake left records?'

'Let me venture to suggest that the only sinuosities he was interested in were the ones he made with his quill.'

'And this is parchment?'

'Yes, but only in fair condition. I expect he prepared it himself, and was not greatly skilled in the trade. In any case, the best pieces he would have used for such parish records as he kept, while the worst he probably set aside for his private writings. And those he was parsimonious with, for you see how tiny is his writing, and how squeezed together.'

He slipped the top sheet from the envelope and slid it carefully to my side of the table. I leaned forward to scrutinize it, but the marks made no sense at all.

'No, my friend, these pages would mean nothing to you. Medieval manuscripts at their best are a trial to read and Father Adalbert's penmanship was not good, he used his quills long past their prime and without proper sharpening, he tried to squeeze too much into too small a space, and . . . he wrote in cypher. No, it is not what you think – a sophisticated espionage device invented by canny operatives of the curia and meant to protect popish schemes from the prying eyes of secular authorities. It is rather a simple substitution cypher such as schoolboys employ in the vain hope of hiding their schemes from parents and teachers. B is A, C is B and so on. The medieval mind was curious in its combination of naiveté and complexity. Do you know the philosophy of Scotus, the doctor subtilis? Ockham, venerabilis inceptor? Profound thinkers. But perhaps Meister Eckhart or Jacob Böhme are more to your taste?'

My own profound thinking went more along these lines: *this man is mad.* My face must have betrayed me, for he stopped abruptly.

'I must ask you once again to forgive me, my friend. Relegated as I have been to a life of contemplation, I have sometimes followed my own paths, far from the practical concerns of men whose lives are spent working for their daily bread.'

'Daily stein, more like. But you needn't apologize, for several of my friends read deeply. I'm afraid I have neither talent nor taste for philosophy, so that I doubt the annals of St. Adalbert could interest me.'

'On the contrary, and that is just the point I was trying to make: that while the middle ages boasted many great thinkers, they also boasted men of astonishing naiveté and simplicity. Such a man was our St. Adalbert.'

'Naive and simple?'

'Yes, indeed. Of course, you know him as the world does, as the conniving agent of the papacy who conspired with Albrecht the

Wolf and Hugo the Bear against the good Graf Walther. The reality is . . . rather different.'

I leaned over the parchment and looked doubtfully at the writing. Walther anticipated me:

'Yes, not only is the calligraphy impossible, the orthography chancy, and part of it ineptly enciphered, but its language is a marriage of archaic and local Low German crossed with the priest's private dog Latin. And you will have noticed that this corner was lost to fire at some time; the same is true of other sheets as well, although I have usually been able to guess the lacunæ. In addition, an unknown number of full sheets seem to have been lost, for the story begins in mid-sentence. To make sense of such a mishmash, the translator would need great knowledge, skill and determination.'

'Indeed yes.'

'And yet this is a miracle of Waltherrottner history lying here on the table before us, so that unlocking its secrets would add immeasurably to our knowledge of the history of our city.'

'I can see that.'

'Because the story St. Adalbert tells is a remarkable one.'

'You have read it?'

He set the parchments aside, then placed a leather-bound volume before each of us.

'I have translated it!'

We tavern tinklers are experts at pretending surprise.

'Astounding!'

'The rather desultory work of my lifetime. In trying to tease out the strands of meaning I have had to make myself . . . an informed amateur on such subjects as medieval church liturgy, land holding arrangements, taxation, medicine, warfare, architecture and many other subjects; I have almost had to recreate that world, and had certainly to create my own mind. For such a document seems to be without form, and void; it seems to offer nothing but darkness. After great labour, the translator manages to shed some light upon this word, that phrase, then a whole passage. I wish I could say that I have brought it all into the full midday sun, but I hope and trust it is more than twilight. But you shall judge for yourself.'

'No, surely not – you could not allow such a priceless volume out of your house!'

I was frantically trying to avoid this unwelcome source of information. How was I supposed to find the time to read it? And what was I to do if his picture disagreed with mine: rewrite my wretched libretto? I groped for the brandy.

'But what has such a labour been for if not to inform art, a creation perhaps even more glorious than history recreated? No, my friend, I have had only these two copies printed. One I shall take with me when I leave, so that I can muse upon it in my own twilight. Indeed, musing upon it as it is, I rather think I may make a few small emendations in what time remains to me. The other I offer to you, to read, to study, to absorb into your soul, and transmute into your art. For the loathsome feudalism which has enchained my fellow Waltherrottners, my fellow Germans, fellow Europeans is, I hope, coming to an end. Whether or not this year sees the revolution succeed is of no consequence, for the revolution must succeed in the end. Under the old notions, the Graf vom Faß represents the spirit of the grafinate. It is my hope, my belief that after the revolution, you, the artist, the composer of operas, shall represent the new spirit of the land and of the people. Thus are you the appropriate ark for this covenant.'

'You honour me beyond my merit,' I said desperately.

'You honour all mankind with your immortal art.'

Frülingstraum im Bergwald, no doubt. I grasped at another straw: 'If you really do only have two copies, shouldn't the church have one? Give it to the bishop up at St. Adalbert's. Hell, give it to the pope!'

'I certainly thought of that, but as you will see as you read the document, neither the local diocese nor the Vatican would be entirely happy with the contents.'

'Then the Stadtbibliothek? Surely . . .'

'Cease and desist, my friend. All such possibilities I have already considered. No, my copy I shall take with me; what its fate shall be, I shall decide later. The parchments I shall indeed donate to the Stadtbibliothek, but I shall not tell them what the document is; let the staff there find out for themselves, let them be worthy of their positions as curators of the soul of the city. The copy I give to you, you may do with as you wish. You may indeed hand it to the bishop, or post it to the Vatican library, or drop it off at the Stadtbibliothek.'

'But . . .'

'For as I trust your art, I must trust your judgment. Into your hands I give the past, the present, and the future of the city.'

The wise man bows to the inevitable. And I wouldn't be obliged to read the thing. We sloshed out several beakers of brandy and Walther opened the book to show me its various wonders. As the print was sharp, and the spacing so generous that what was a slim book in the hand was even slimmer in the reading.

We passed some considerable time, perhaps an hour, in this manner, I filling my mouth with his brandy and he filling my ears with the delights and rigours of the translator's trade, so that as he became more eloquent in explication, I became more impenetrable in comprehension. At some point, Walther went off to find light, and returned with two candles stuck in wooden holders.

'The silverware, alas . . .' he explained.

'What matters is the light.'

'There, you see, at heart you have the revolutionary spirit!'

'No, I just like to see the bottle.'

'But you also will need it to read the annals.'

'Oh, I shall not read them tonight; tomorrow will be soon enough.'

'You will find, if you look carefully, a distant ancestor of yours, the explanation of your name, and the antiquity of your talent.'

'I accept your gracious and generous gift, and will read it with interest and pleasure.'

'Tonight.'

'But we have been having such a pleasant conversation . . . It would take me hours . . .'

'We have hours, and ample brandy, along with more food if you wish.'

'No, the brandy will do. But . . . this is not the way I prefer to do my research. I need leisure, my own bed, solitary hours.'

He sighed.

'I have explained to you, my friend, that tomorrow I leave this city forever. While my ancestors have left behind this palace, the opera house, the Waltherburg, and an endless line of deflowered maidens and their children, this is my legacy. I do not think I am asking too much when I request that the city's greatest artist read it before I leave.'

He was insane and was quickly becoming boring.

'No. I refuse.'

'You need not comment.'

'No. You have no right to impose upon me.'

'I realize that,' he replied, reaching under the table, 'but I shall impose: you shall read the annals.'

His hand reappeared and in it was an antiquated duelling pistol. He cocked it and pointed it at me.

I read.

Part Five

Surviving Fragment
from the Annals of the priest Adalbert,
later Saint Adalbert of Waltherrott
translated by Walther, Graf vom Faß

[Here begins the fragment in mid-sentence.] save only that the beets were blighted by an attack of the blotches. But the orchards bore sweet and plentiful fruit and on the feast day of St. Baldur the sun shone brightly, an infallible sign that the cold, the snow, and the winter winds will be moderate; as was proved, and by the grace of Our Lady, the winter has been born with patience and good cheer.

In humble obedience to Our Lord and Saviour, so ended the winter and the sixth year of the Lord's servant in this parish.

IN THIS YEAR was the wall behind the altar painted with a fine representation of the crucifixion of Our Lord which did much to make the people firm in their faith, for it does most lavishly show the scene as bright as the day: here is Our Lord and on each side the thieves; here Our Lady with St. Anne, the tears coursing from their eyes most pathetically, and St. Joseph staunch in manly resignation, here the twelve apostles with St. Peter and his cock, here Judas counts his thirty pieces of silver, here Pontius Pilate washes his hands with Herod, soldiers, and the Pharisees beside, here our first father, Adam, while Eve in her shame takes the apple from the serpent, here the three kings from the east, here Pharaoh in his vainglory, with Ezekiel and his wheel, Jacob and his ladder, Joseph and his coat of many colours, and Jonah and the Leviathan swallowing him, while above all sing innumerable of the heavenly host with Our Father in his glory on a cloud in the midst, with just above him the Holy Ghost in the form of a wood pigeon. Gathered at the bottom, round an open cavern, the damned in their terror are dragged to their punishment by devils most frightening to gaze upon. But what is finest is that the picture also does most precisely depict the spikes through the hands and feet of our Lord whereby He was nailed to the cross for our sins and Cardinals below collecting the precious liquor in golden bowls, and the wounds of the crown of thorns from which His precious Blood pours down in rivulets over his face and shoulders, and the spear cut in His side with the layers of His flesh peeled open which the painter has most justly rendered for that we went together into the market place on the feast day of St. Wynbald to see the disembowelling of a sheep stealer and the painter did take most particular note of the various layers of flesh and the colour of the organs thereunder so that it is withal a most wonderful sight to see.

This picture so amazed the souls of the parish that they flocked to see it and so was the majesty of the Lord promoted. In return, in His beneficence, did He grant a fine harvest and a mild winter so that there is joy in the streets and a fine lambing in addition to the tastiest Salvatorbier in many years, thus is the celebration of His Glorious Resurrection this year being carried on with great enthusiasm and thanks for the year ending and in and great hopes for the year beginning. So ends the winter and the seventh year in this parish of the Lord's humble servant.

IN THE TIME of the feast day of St. Gulyas, there came ominous signs by which the people were sore troubled. At night was the sky coloured with lights so bright that the cocks began to crow and birds to sing so that folk rushed from their cottages amazed. Hailstones as big as a child's head were reported, and fierce lightning scorched the earth and the great Thor-oak in the Bergwald was felled and naught but a blackened stump remains. Prodigies began to appear. A two-headed calf was born and a raven alighted on a gable on market day and said the Paternoster backwards. Travellers from the south brought tales of war and pestilence, of strange cries

168

from the depths of the forests and of the hairy creatures in the distant mountains. Yet was seeding time propitious and the Lord in His bounty vouchsafed a fine harvest. Moreover, in the deep midwinter were numerous children born and baptized unto Christ our Saviour, and but few souls returned to their Maker. Yet during the celebration of the mass on the third Sunday of Lent, was Simple Meg possessed. The servant of the Lord attempted to cast out the demon from her but without success, so that she was put to the fire to be released from her torment. In humble obedience to our Lord and Saviour, so ended the winter and the eighth year of service to the Lord in this parish.

THANKS TO OUR LADY and to Her Son Jesus who died for our sins, for the great plague has spared us in this year. And while we waited in fear and trembling, other lesser plagues have afflicted us.

As soon as the forest paths were dry there came the most avaricious horde of pardoners, so that all the inhabitants knew disaster had been visited upon more prosperous places, for that the pardoners pay but scant attention to our poor valley save when the easy pickings elsewhere are denied them for some reason. So we learned that the plague rages over all the lands like a forest fire, and everywhere people flee from it, but in vain, for it travels as swiftly as the birds of passage. But the pardoners found a want of trade in the valley, for that the people have but little coin with which to buy relief from their sins, and closed their doors to these carrion crows. Indeed the folk admit but little to being sinful, enjoying the pleasures of their loins and of their bellies with enthusiasm and good cheer and without shame, so that the pardoners were filled with ire and threats. There came one of them with hair as yellow as wax and the glaring eyes of a hare, and offered to save the Lord's servant from damnation for that Sister Irmtraud is great with child again, but I ordered him from our door with the reminder that Our Lord Himself said: 'Suffer the little children to come unto Me.'

'Ignorant bumpkin, do not throw scripture into my face, for I have been to Avignon and there had my authority of great cardinals, yea, even from the Holy Father himself. Your soul is in mortal peril.'

'We are not so deep into the forests that we do not hear news of the great world, and if a priest getting a woman with child be a sin, then by all accounts are the souls of most of the great prelates in Christendom in mortal peril as well.'

'I add the sins of slander, blasphemy, and envy to your fornications,' he hissed.

'How fornication?' I replied, 'Can it be a sin for a vicar of Christ to lie with a nun who is the avowed bride of Christ? You are indeed pissing in the wrong pot, Herr Pardoner, for there is not a priest in the lands between the swamps to the north and the mountains to the south but would laugh at you.'

Confounded by the simple truth, he uttered a foul oath and went his way, and soon enough he and his confederates were gone from the valley.

The pardoners were followed by another human plague, the scourgers or flagellants, who flail and torment their own bodies until their garments are soaked in their blood. In this way do they hope to assuage the wrath of the Lord and to deliver the world from the punishment visited upon it. The people made welcome to the first few companies of them which came into our midst, and great was the moaning in sympathy for these wretches who imitate the way of Our Lord to Calvary. But their arrogance grew and the later companies demanded tithes of coin and food and cloth, so that the people turned their faces from them. Stories came in of thefts from farms along the way, of lambs and calves slaughtered and eaten raw in the fields, of milkmaids violated, so that by the time of the feast of St. Willibald were the people out of patience with the flagellants and did drive them away with cudgels, billhooks, and sickles. So passed the ninth year of the service of the Lord's servant in this parish, and may He forgive our sins and spare His servant and the people in the year to come.

THE LORD FORGIVE US, for that our tribulations this year were many, yet others are more sorely afflicted, even unto death, for the great plague washes over the lands even as Noah's flood did inundate the world in the ancient days. Yet are we in this valley spared, although I am sore afraid that our time is nigh, for tales of its horrors come from places as near as a six days' walk. Rumour from all parts speaks of untold numbers of deaths in foreign lands so that the people are sore afraid and there is much wailing and gnashing of teeth. Travellers passing through at the time of the apple blossoms brought the first news, so that later travellers were stoned and kept from the valley. Yet rumour still sweeps the land, for not all could be kept out, thus many are the tales we hear: that the contagion bursts upon towns like a tempest, or issues from the underworld in times of great earthquakes, or is spread by great sheets of flame across the sky, or by ethers from the marshes, by the birds, by the föhn, by the breath of the afflicted, by the gases emanating from the bodies of the dying, by the plots of heathens and Jews in league with the evil one, by unclean women. Of causes, there are but three which the authority of holy scripture approves: that the plague comes of a most malignant alignment of the stars, of which I cannot judge, for that the study of the heavenly bodies is a most arcane philosophy; that it is a punishment of the Lord visited upon a sinful world, which is certainly very possible, but unlikely for that he has spared this valley; but the most likely is that it is done by the hand of the evil one as proved by the frequent tales of great tremblings of the earth whereby are foul eructions released from the bowels of the earth, for what is the earth but the body of the evil one, and what are these gases but the farts issuing therefrom?

The plague is but the fourth horseman who was prophesied, he upon the pale horse, and I fear that the third, he upon the black horse, has cast his eyes upon our poor valley, for the harvest was but meagre, for that a rust attacked the rye, the carrots and beets were shrivelled and soft, the legumes small and hard, and the fruits fell from the trees before the sun could ripen them, so that the winter has been a hard one and many souls succumbed to the hunger and the cold and only Jens the gravedigger prospered. So it was that harvest time came, and the winter, and yet, through the mercy of Our Lady, and of the Christ our Saviour, was the valley spared the plague which raged across the face of the earth; and the Feast days of the Crucifixion and the Resurrection are upon us and we are yet saved. So endeth the tenth year of the service to this parish of the servant of our Lord, who does pray most fervently that we shall be spared again through the mercy of our Lord.

IN THIS YEAR did the mercy of the Lord, and the benison of Our Lady fall like rain upon the valley. For the plague which has stricken all manner of mortals, men, women, and children, great prelates, princes and their grand ladies, captains proud upon their chargers, rich burgers in their counting houses, peasants in the field, even the most wretched beggar by the wayside, this death which cuts down the folk as the farmer cuts the sheaves of rye in the summer, this scourge beyond the imagining of man, has spared the servant of the Lord and most of his flock, while beyond the forests on all sides are those in the nearest villages stricken, laid low upon the earth, and so great is the stench of their rotting and putrefaction that even the mongrels run away in fear, yea and the very worms of the earth do shun the corpses which lie unburied and so spread the contagion further. And the plague leaves behind it burning towns, burning bridges, fertile fields deserted, hamlets and farms as well deserted, and devilish captains leading faceless marauding troops, rabble, burning, looting, raping, leaving all behind them in ruins, scorched earth, wisps of smoke drifting across the horizon, dying sun red above a blackened horizon, lurid red through the smoke. But the reports we hear are but shadows of the shadow of the great death itself, for it comes here not, by the grace of God, save that the bloated corpse of an itinerant tinker was found by the third ford of the river and a family of minstrels in their motley, man and wife and all their children expired on the path through the Bergwald, all save one scrofulous puling waif cowering behind the stump of the great Thor oak. Some said he should be stoned to death, and others that he should be sent away into the forests to feed the wolves that they might leave the flocks alone, but I prevailed upon them to spare him even as our Lord had spared him; and now does he play upon his tabor and drum in the market place, and so earn his meagre crust, and smile most winningly. And because he has not the tongue of the folk and cannot give his name nor any account of himself, he is called the child from the stump.

Certain it is that others of the parish have been taken to the bosom of the Lord in this year, but none from the great death it seems.

What it all betokens we know not, save that by the grace of our blessed Saviour we are the most blessed of souls. For that about the time of the feast of St. Wotan, when the harvest was in and the orchards plucked of their fruit, and the Wiesenbier brewed and drunk, did rise up certain audacious or foolhardy men such as Joshua sent out of Shittim into Jericho and these did creep through the forests in all directions to spy out the fate of other villages and so did return with tales not to be believed but in this time which surely is that time spoken of in the Revelation of St. John when the book of the seven seals shall be opened, and that for the world beyond the forests is the seventh seal opened, for there is a great silence, even as was prophesied, save only the cawing of the carrion crows pecking at the bodies of the fallen, and the baying of the wolves over the feasts they make of the sheep, the swine, and the kine which wander the fields without herdsmen to care for them; for even the poor folk of this valley who saw these beasts bereft of masters durst not approach for fear of the contagion which laid low all. So did these return and bear witness to the desolation which surely comes at the end of things.

And so the winter came and passed, and the servant of the Lord prepares for the celebration of the Feast of the Crucifixion and the Glorious Resurrection of Our Lord at the end of his eleventh year in the parish; and in confident hope of the final battle between the armies of the Archangel Michael and the hordes of the Antichrist which will come at the end of time; for the silence is all about.

GREAT IS THE WOE of the servant of the Lord and great is the woe of his little flock. We have been spared the ravages of the plague which kills, only to suffer the ravages of a greater plague which brings death in life. For out of the silence and desolation there came a Captain with his rabble of soldiers, band of brutes, to threaten and enslave the souls of the valley. The lives of all hereabout have been under the protection of Markgraf Rudolph these many years and at Martinmass do come his bailiff and officers to collect the feu, the ward fees, and such other levies as from time to time are asked of the people. But last year did they not come and there was rejoicing in the village, and folk said Graf Rudolph would hold the taxes in abeyance for that the misery of his people should be alleviated. At haying time did word come from beyond that Markgraf Rudolph and all his family had perished in the plague, and some said all folk of the valley were without obligations for that there were no heirs. Others said folk were also without the shield of a liege lord and so were prey to all manner of depredations of the heathens, of marauders from foreign parts, of whosoever should come into the valley. The first asked: and how should anyone come into the valley, for that all around are taken by the great death, and the forests and the hills will be our shield? But near the time of the harvest moon the Captain calling himself Walther did find his way here and when folk bethought themselves to call out for Graf Rudolph or his heirs or successors, did the Captain laugh, and drain his flagon of beer, saying:

'I am now your Graf, and in honour of this cask of fine beer, I name myself Graf Walther vom Faß, and I claim this valley unto myself and my heirs and successors even unto the final time. Unto myself do I take the souls and the livestock in their pastures, and the corn of the meadows, and the fruit of the orchards, the wild beasts of the field and the forest, the birds of the air, yea, even the fish of the rivers. Over all things do I claim dominion and all feus, fees, taxes, tributes, rents, incomes, duties, and mortmains, and in return I shall protect all these, and the land, and my vassals, serfs, subjects upon my land from such others as may cast covetous eyes this way, for is it not my own, my väterliches Erbteil, appanage, domain, and who is to gainsay me, my sword, and my company?'

The Captain then did claim for his bed and board the inn at the Sign of the Pig's Trotter hard by the market place and loud were the wailings of the innkeeper Schweinehaxe when he learned that the Captain would not pay with anything but the flat of his sword. Then was the servant of the Lord brought before the Captain and rebuked in heathenish and blasphemous curses.

'Hear this, thou cringing little Adalbert of a priest: your God has died in the great death which has swept the land, and you and your folk have been spared for the worship of the old gods and their hero, who is even me. In a month will come the celebration of the death and rebirth of the sun and in the market square shall the ever-green tree be candled and all due ceremonies and sacrifices be carried out and the folk will rejoice again in the worship of the true gods with mead and ale and feasts of fat meats and such songs and dances as serve to welcome the day of renewal. And such other jollities as befit the celebration.'

With this did he pull to him a passing serving wench and handle her in such a gross and lascivious fashion that the servant of the Lord was forced to avert his eyes and gnash his teeth. And was this but a taste of things to come, for the folk of the parish are but simple souls and do harbour memories of the old times from whispered tales at the knees of toothless ancients; and so did heathenish and ungodly practices seduce their credulous souls away from the one true path and back to the worship of demons, and goblins, and the allies of the Antichrist who ever lurk in the dark corners lusting after the purified souls of the saved; and was our poor church defiled, for soon did the Captain desert the inn and claim the rectory as his home and the church as his great hall for drunkenness and lewd revellings with harlots and such simple maids as could be enticed into the clutches of him and his men; and has he taken Sister Irmtraud in her shame to be his consort for that her dimples charmed him and her bosom inflamed his lust so that she is lost to Christ and her soul is in mortal peril; and reports have it that even the altar has been defiled by the lewd couplings of the Captain and his men with their strumpets; and those who serve there say the painting over the altar is defaced with monstrous daubings even of Our Lord in His Suffering and of Our Lady in Her Grief; and has not even the body of Christ been spared for has the host been defiled; so that it were better had the folk of the valley all perished like our neighbours in the great death of last year and been taken to stand in judgement, even to be cast into the purgatory to time out of mind rather suffer these torments.

So endeth in grief and failure the twelfth year of the service of the servant of the Lord, and may His Mercy and Forgiveness be granted unto us, and the Faith of the folk of the valley be restored unto Christ our Redeemer.

O H, WOE IS ME that toil in the service of Christ the Lord and fail so utterly! For in this year has all the labour of my life been undone, as a great tempest does sweep down from the hills and lay low the farmer's corn, and uproot his fruit trees, and drive mad his beasts, and tear the roof from his humble hovel, and throw down the walls, and in an instant reduce him and his poor wife and children to misery and starvation. For if the list of the woes of this parish were written down in a book, that should be so great a book as would take ten scribes a year to copy fair, and yet would it not be complete.

The sanctuary which was last year the Church of St. Fricka is lost to the worship of the Lord, and is now no better than a low tavern or brothel. There through the winter did the wild barbarians keep themselves warm, howling in riots of gluttony, drunkenness and the most lascivious debauchery. But with the coming of the south winds and the first flowers of spring did they emerge, like bears from their winter dens, into the light of day, and then our shame and tribulation did begin in earnest; for that we thought our misery at its deepest, but now did we sink yet lower. Earlier did they send out but one or two of their number to forage for more meat, or hogsheads of beer, or to abduct another maiden come to bloom that they might pluck her flower from her and debauch her; now did they sally forth as a company to bully one and all, and to put numbers to the sword. Earlier may it be that a score of the parishioners who were weak in their faith had gone over to the marauders; now with the blades of their swords and the knots of their cudgels did they drive others to their following, and away from the worship of the Lord God and his Son who is Christ our Saviour; and those that resist have the limbs hacked from their trunks, or their entrails ripped steaming from their bellies, or their heads lopped from their shoulders and mounted on stakes in the market place to warn the others; and the soldiers did even for a time make a game of kicking about the heads, but they did hurt their feet and so did tire of the game. And such were the numbers of apostates that at Whitsuntide there did come but three to be baptized and one of them was called to the Lord presently; and but a meagre score of souls did that day partake of the Holy Sacrament where the year before was it above eight score, and a dozen and more for baptizing. Stout-hearted are the few who cleave to the True Faith, for the backsliders and sinners do mock and revile the faithful, and do persecute them even as the soldiers of Pilate did torment the Son of God. And when His servant does attempt to administer the Holy Sacrament in a stable, then some do wail and moan that the fair church which was so late builded from trees cut from the forest is lost to the service of the Lord. But I reply, saying:

'Lo, was not the Christ child himself born to His Mother Mary in a humble stable, and now in a stable do we eat of his body and drink of his blood; and this is fitting until mayhap an angel of the Lord shall chevy the defilers and fornicators out from the fair church and from the village and kick their arses even unto the distant mountains.' But some whisper and say the Captain comes on a great war horse, but the angel rides a limping nag. And thus are even the few remaining faithful disheartened.

The feast of the midsummer sun was celebrated in the valley for the first time since I was a romping boy, bewitched by heathenish jollities and ignorant of my sins and of Our Lord's sacrifice. As of old, on the hills round about were great bonfires lighted to the service of the powers of the evil one, and it was occasion for the most wicked debaucheries in the woods and fields all about and even in the very market place; however, such licentiousness having become the way of the valley it is scarce worth notice.

But a few days later did the hearts of the faithful leap up, for was the Captain and his band gone from the valley, along with his most fervent allies and a number of their women. And there was rejoicing and singing at our deliverance, and the servant of the Lord did again sanctify the church and the altar and administer the Holy Sacrament and offer up thanks unto the Lord our Deliverer and Protector; and did numbers of the apostates come slinking back in their shame. Yet all was but a trap! For the Captain did but raid a number of neighbouring villages and towns for some weeks, taking booty or ransoms, burning what could not be taken, slaughtering those who refused to pay homage, and then returning to this valley.

'Oh, ye of little faith,' he cried, 'Didst think I would abandon you to the wolves? You may think me fooled by the pig sty look and stench about this place, with its people drooling and rolling their eyes like idiots, but I know Walhal when I see it. No, my little piglets, you may cease feigning lunacy, you may stop trembling in fear, you may rejoice, for Graf Walther will never leave you alone again. In token of the trust you may place in me, and in the puissance of my protection I do name this village Waltherrott.'

So saying, he and his henchmen hauled their booty and their captives into the church again, and sent out, demanding lambs be spitted and roasted for them, and hogsheads of ale brought; and the great part of the folk scurried about to help and to bow down; and did the servant of the Lord and a few of those staunch in their faith trudge from the village and into the refuge of the Bergwald.

So endeth in chill misery and in failure the thirteenth year of the service of the servant of the Lord, and may Our Gracious Lady who weeps for the downtrodden intercede with Her Son, Jesus Christ our Saviour, that he should have mercy on the souls of sinners in this valley.

PRAISE TO OUR LORD Jesus Christ, to His Dear Mother, and to the Holy Ghost and to all the Saints, that the vassalage demanded of us by Captain Walther has been lifted from our shoulders. For, about the time of the feast of St. Sunniva did Our Lady come in a vision in the dark hours to the Servant of the Lord and reveal a cunning subterfuge. And She reminded me that some years past there did come a letter from Bishop Axehelm saying that he had received a bull of the Holy Father or of some great Cardinal or other, that this prelate was preaching a crusade; and she directed that I should preach a crusade to Graf Walther that he would arise and go with all his men so that he should cease fighting Christians and begin fighting infidels. But I protested that Graf Walther was himself an infidel and so unmoved by any bulls of our Holy Father, and more efficacious it would be if the Holy Father preached a crusade against Graf Walther. But Our Lady replied sharply that She would grant my tongue eloquence and cast a spell over Graf Walther so that he would be ensnared and do as I should bid; and also would she grant him a sign, mayhap a vision of the Holy Cross, that he might follow it. And did Our Lady resemble Sister Irmtraud who likewise will not be gainsaid when she is determined. So it was with great trembling and shaking of the knees that I went to the village and preached a crusade at Graf Walther. And did he indeed laugh most heartily at me, and order his lieutenant to toss me into the Lohbach. But Our Lady stirred me with eloquence and now did Graf Walther stay the man and demand of me what was the contract of a crusader. I spoke of great credit stored up in heaven, of the praise sung by minstrels through all of Christendom, of the thanks and prayers of all Christians, of forgiveness of sins committed while on the crusade, of expeditious entry into heaven for the soldiers of Christ.

Graf Walther listened to me but was not convinced:

'I care not for the regard of stinking minstrels, for if I give a minstrel a loaf of bread, will he sing like the lark in my praise; I care not for the thanks and prayers of Christians, for I hold in contempt anything said by a man with bended knee and bowed head. And certainly I care not for your priest-ridden heaven, little man, for I go to a heaven fit for warriors, a heaven of flagons of mead borne into the great hall by troops of great-bosomed and great-arsed maidens, their soft parts wobbling like jellies and their lips sweet-breathed and wet and open with beckoning glee!'

And such-like heathenish prattle that his lieutenants and hangers-on did begin to laugh and cackle and play the ape.

But then did I come to mention the great hoards of gold and jewels which the infidels keep in their coffers and how without fail crusaders ride back to their homelands with great sacks of booty, so great that its glitter shines brighter than the stars or the moon, perhaps even than the sun, and was it all easy pickings for any great Captain who dared grasp it.

'I grasp this and piss on you with it, for there are easy pickings with less travelling, better fighting, and home before the snow flies, priest. And I piss on your crusade, I spit on it, I fart on it, I vomit on it.'

So I tried my last argument, trusting in the promise of the apparition to make my words flower and fruit.

'Would you go if Our Lady vouchsafed you a vision of the Holy Cross on which Our Dear Lord Jesus Christ died for our sins?'

'Is it like that wooden trinket that hangs from your scrawny neck?'

'In shape, yes, but in visions I trow the Cross is gold or silver, and shining like the sun. Such it was when St. Hubert saw it glowing on the forehead of the miraculous stag.'

'Come close to me, little priest, and I'll tell you how I saw a blood red cross on the forehead of a pig.'

Credulous fool that I am, I came nigh unto him. With a quick lunge he grasped my hair in one hand, and with the other slashed a cross into the flesh of my brow, so that the red blood ran down into my eyes.

The mob of soldiers roared with laughter as I stumbled about and cried like a baby.

'Now throw him into the road so that everyone may see Graf

Walther's miraculous cross and we shall have a great army of the faithful for our crusade!'

So that I was soon lying in a mudpuddle, lucky to escape a worse wounding than I got, and reviling the sorceress who had come to me cloaked in the garments and guise of Our Lady, so to enchant me to make a fool of myself. Yet did She appear to me in a dream again that night and comfort me, saying: 'Do you wait, for the worm is into his gullet and soon will the hook be set.' And, lo, the next day did one of Graf Walther's minions come to fetch me to him; and when I was standing before him, he questioned me closely concerning the gold and silver and jewels of the infidels, and the precise conditions in canon law of a crusader, especially in regard to the sanction of the Lord, and the sanction of the Holy Father, and of the Church, and the protection these would give him in civil law against the complaints of such as might claim he had done them a wrong.

'But how could these complain, being infidels?' I replied, 'For they could have no standing before courts ecclesiastical or civil.'

'And how should I know these infidels? Where should I find them?'

Now was the servant of the Lord perplexed, for that I had never seen infidels save those of my neighbours who yet worshipped the old gods. But I ransacked my memory, and it came back to me that the infidels meant for the crusade are called sarcens or mours or turgs; and that they are known by four qualities, viz.: that they wear outlandish garments; that they worship outlandish gods in great heathenish temples like unto the tower of Babel in the pride of their building; and that they speak in outlandish tongues; and that they dwell in southern lands where the sun is as hot even as a blacksmith's forge. Graf Walther listened intently, then said:

'Little priest, moved by the wisdom of your advice, I shall arise now and go and fight a crusade against the infidel; and I shall return in time, richer even than my cousin, Sigismund the Fat, may his bowels knot up in envy. I am glad you smile your agreement, little priest, for if I do not return richer than Sigismund the Fat, your bowels I shall knot up and with them for a rope shall hang you from the top of your church steeple.'

With that he demanded I provide him with a warrant that he might slaughter and subdue and lay waste the infidel in the name of Christ, and that all Christians should help him and none should hinder him; and I did scribe out such a warrant with many large words and in a very pretty hand with but two small blots. With this warrant in the bosom of his jerkin, and with the four qualities of the infidel learned by heart, Graf Walther did indeed ride off with all his men while the apples were yet green. And the servant of the Lord resanctified the church and another painter came and painted over the lewd daubings which defiled it so that it is again pleasing to the eyes of the faithful, although not so splendid as before. And I moved back into the rectory where Sister Irmtraud is again great with child though she knows not the father for that heathenish coupling is promiscuous; yet have I heard her confession and has she done penance and received absolution and is she content. And Our Lady be praised, the Feast of the Crucifixion and Resurrection of Our Lord Jesus Christ is upon us, and Graf Walther has not returned, so that folk are blithe again; we shall build a Lady Chapel onto the church that we may show humble thanks to Our Lady for ridding us of the vexation of Graf Walther. And so endeth the year and the four-teenth year of the service of the servant of the Lord, and great are his praises to Our Saviour, Jesus Christ, and to Our Lady who has saved us.

O H, WHAT A PRODIGIOUS MONSTER have I created! For Graf Walther, having discovered the profits to made from a crusade, is as zealous as a saint for the faith. Our hope that he had been martyred for Christ was dashed when he returned about the time of the Feast of All Souls.

'Rest you easy, little priest,' he said when I came quaking into his presence at the Sign of the Pig's Trotter. 'For I shall not again take your church as my hall; rather I shall build my own castle in the manner of the great lords of other lands. And now that I am a crusader I am a defender of the true faith and must not harm His church but protect it.' So saying, he told me of his great adventure, which I here set down as best I can comprehend it:

He and his band of above sixty men and half a dozen women started off toward the lands of the infidels, ever mindful of the four qualities they should seek. Hot and dusty were the roads, but no hotter and dustier than here, and the tongues of the folk, albeit increasingly difficult to their ears, were yet the tongue of all folk hereabouts, so they knew they had not found infidels. Yet were these crusaders not made welcome by the Christians they met. For the great towns closed their gates to the travellers and demanded tribute for guarantees of safe passage, and the inhabitants of villages ran to hide in the woods; or sometimes called for help from their lord in his castle keep; so that Graf Walther was pressed ever on, and the band had to provision itself by pillaging such villages as were too poor to merit protection or too small to defend themselves. They came at length to the great mountains which, all assured me, wore snow upon their shoulders even in the heat of summer, and here were the people yet more outlandish in their dress, in their language, and in their temples; yet were not infidels for that their tongue could be partly understood and the sun was not fierce; but these mountain folk were themselves fierce and troublesome about tolls, provisions, and lodging, were it only under the pine trees.

'And I did present my warrant that I had from your hand for the crusade, little priest, and they did show no more courtesy to our crusader band than to a pack of stray dogs.'

But about the time of the ripening of the apples, they came to the end of the mountains, and did descend into the land of the infidels.

'For we did number their qualities, little priest, as you had taught us. First, were their clothes outlandish, being of bright colours like the rainbow, and of stuff as soft as a baby's cheek. Second, were their gods and temples outlandish, for the temples were made of stone, and were like mountains, and their gods were graven in stone and stood all about, without and within their temples, so that they were not worshippers of your one true God. Third, was their language entirely outlandish and sounded more like the twittering of birds than like speech. Fourth, were their nights as hot as our days, and the days as hot as a blacksmith's forge, even as you foretold.'

Yet had our crusaders great trials; for the infidels would not fight, but rather locked the gates of their towns and laughed and mocked them from the walls in their singing tongue. And they did wander about, disconsolate, searching in vain for infidels to put to the sword. Food had they in plenty for that the plague had killed many of the former inhabitants and the trees fruited without care for the plague which killed men; and animals and game were plentiful. But at last they came to a castle whose walls seemed not so high or so thick as others, and seemingly not so well defended. And so it proved.

'Indeed, little priest, the castle was inhabited by an army in uniform dress, but 'twas an army of women! By all the gods, I wonder that the great Captains of Christendom have not conquered all the infidels by now, so foolish are they that they have such soldiers defending their castles. But I own they made a spirited defence, for all that they had no weapons save farm tools, and when beaten they refused to submit so that as the sun went down was the ground as blood red as the sky.'

'How submit?' I demanded, for I half guessed at last that the crusade had gone astray.

'Why, to lie on the ground and spread their legs; how else should a woman submit? But these were foolish creatures, so we put the old ones to the sword and the young ones to the plough, and did till their furrows through the night, and gorge ourselves from their larders, and quench our thirst with their drink which is finer on the tongue than mead, and stronger than beer, and is red in colour, and is called by the infidels "fino" or "vino." Ahh, little priest, say what you will, but their gods are wiser than yours or mine for that they order their lands better so that these infidels live the sweet life.'

'What did you with these young women?' I asked him then, for I had heard rumours of captives.

'Why we culled out the rotten and bruised ones, as the orchardman culls his apples, keeping the best for ourselves, and thinking perhaps to sell the others back to their fathers or their brothers or other such as might pay for them. But as we had not the tongue, how were we to do the deal? So we put these culls also to the sword, brought away the picks of the lot, brought away also a great store of gold and jewels, even as you promised us, and set torch to the castle, what parts were of wood.'

'These women, where are they that I may speak with them?'

'How speak, little priest, you that have not the infidel's tongue?'

But I prevailed upon him and at last he had the wretched captives brought before us. Upon seeing them, I uttered an oath, and rushed to them, to comfort and succour them, for surely could I see they were not infidel women soldiers, but nuns from some order unknown to me. They had not our tongue, and had difficulty understanding me when I tried to speak the tongue which Our Lord spake and which is called the Roman, for I have it but limpingly and have used it but little these fifteen years, save in saying of the offices of the day. The women were amazed to see me, a Christian priest, among their captors, for they did make me understand their tale at last: that their land is called Verona, that they belong to the Order of Merchinensians, a very wealthy order, and that they are for the most part highborn ladies as evidenced by their long, pointed shoes, and very devout, and now their convent is sacked and burned and the greater number of their sisters are slaughtered, and these have been ravished and brought away into captivity in the wilderness, virtuous Christian women outraged by heathens. I forbore to tell them that their captors thought themselves crusaders for Christ and their captives the infidels, but promised them I should do my best to rescue them, praying to Our Lady and pleading with Graf Walther.

Then did the most spirited, who is called Sister Renate, speak to me, saying, 'To hear the noble tongue of my ancestors in the craw of a rooster or a pig would be no less amazing than to hear it spoken by

185

you, little vermin of stench, little hairy bag of filth. But as you do seem to understand, pray tell me if you know of any Christians hereabouts in this dark land.'

'Peace be with you, sister: I am myself a priest of Our Lord Jesus Christ.'

'I beg of you, do not blaspheme, for Our Lord would not suffer any souls of the Faith to be so degraded as to accept as their priest such a scabrous and pustulant dung beetle as yourself.'

Her companions giggled nervously and rolled their eyes in disgust, but I began to say the Paternoster and soon enough they were forced to own that my claim was honest.

'In that case,' said Sister Renate, 'Pray send at once to your bishop with news of myself and my sisters. We demand that he, in the name of Our Holy Church – but not, hear you, in the name of the usurpatious Antichrist in Avignon – preach a crusade against this ravening wolf. We further demand that he send Christian champions to rescue us.'

'Nothing would please me more, sister, save that I have not heard from any bishop, nor indeed from any authority in the hierarchy these ten years any more, and such travellers as brave these hills and forests tell tales of many prelates laid waste by the great death.'

She turned to her sisters and spoke in a low voice, but not so low that I did not catch the sense of it: 'What now, sisters? For our honour is besmirched and we are disgraced and brought low and treated like common harlots to be used by any man who passes. Of course, no one can prove it, but who would believe us?'

And one who is called Sister Franzeska wept and said, 'Oh, how are we to return to our own land to be spit upon by our families? For we had been the jewels of the church, and the brides of Christ, and are now worse than manure, the whores of heathens.'

And one called Sister Luthia cried, 'Oh woe, that we were spared by the great plague when it cut down half the folk of our land. Prey, beg of this heathen warrior that he should grant us death today, that we may be spared further outrages to our bodies, further stains to our honour, and further sins to our souls.'

I sought to comfort them, saying, 'Be steadfast in your faith, sisters, for by me shall you be shriven, and your souls will be cleansed as white as snow; after that, what can your other torments be?'

'Be confessed by a stinking peasant barbarian such as you?' cried Sister Renate. 'What salvation could there be in that?'

'Salvation enough for any Christian, I hope.'

Clearly, Sister Renate may have lost her virtue and her rich convent but she had lost none of her highborn manners.

'Nay, for we are beyond the lands where our Lord Jesus Christ casts His gaze. Since the day of our disaster, we have prayed to Him, and to Our Lady that we may be delivered. We have prayed to St. Vitus that the barbarians should be driven mad, to St. Lawrenso that they should be consumed by fire, and to St. Luthia that they should be blinded, yet you see us here in our disgrace, without help or salvation. Indeed it is worse, for in you do we find another barbarian in the garb of a priest of Christ, and yet of their company.'

I told her that we no more welcomed the attentions of Graf Walther than they did.

'We shall address letters to your bishop, to our order, and to our families and friends: who knows but that one will bring help. But we shall not repine; we have our skills to help us.'

'And the Grace of Our Lady and Her Son.'

'Yes, yes. Now, tell me about this brute who has captured us.'

I began to explain the arrival of Graf Walther and some of the sorrows visited upon our poor village, but the talk was cut short by the man himself, who ordered the sisters into the inn, so I went away to my vicarage, my heart bursting with many things, not the least that I was in part guilty of this adventure and its result, but then reflected that Our Lady in the vision vouchsafed me was also guilty, so that I spent some time in pondering the fate of these wretched nuns and what I might do.

In time, Sister Renate learned from me what she could about Graf Walther and about our little village; more, I believe, she learned from her own watchfulness. And in time, Graf Walther learned the truth about his crusade and his infidels, but was not abashed; for he said:

'Either these nuns were hopeless sinners, unworthy of protection from Jesus, or they are sent here for a purpose, to give pleasure to me and to my men while the nights are long. So is your God proved to me to have great power and wisdom, and from the great and beautiful cities and castles that we did see, and from the red fino the folk there drink, and the comeliness of the folk and the fineness of their garments, is it clear to me that he grants great rewards to his faithful followers. So shall we here in my Waltherrott be fierce in the Christian faith, and I do here order for his worship a great church to be built on yon hilltop, and nigh unto it a mighty nuns' castle, and Jesus shall fill the church full with gold and jewels and he shall fill the nuns' castle with many nuns having breath as sweet as honey, skin as white as milk, breasts as firm and fragrant as breadloaves, bottoms as round as cheeses . . .'

In vain have I argued with him, for in his pride is he like a cock upon his dungheap at morning twilight. Yet is all not darkness and gloom, for our little church of St. Fricka is restored to the worship of Christ our Saviour, that we may celebrate His Crucifixion and Glorious Resurrection now at the end of this year, and of the fifteenth year of the service to this parish of His Servant, in the name of Christ and of Our Lady, may They forgive us our sins.

L O, READ THE WORDS of a simple man, who knows not the ways of the Lord and of the great world; for that our little village is all abustle and become a centre of pilgrimage; and how it came to pass is indeed peculiar and may be indeed a miracle, although I know not how.

Many are the hard words I had with Graf Walther over the nature of the church he would build, that it would not be a pagan temple with standing stones to capture the midwinter and midsummer suns in accordance with the old ways; but in time was I successful and the church will be of hewn stone and like the great churches of this land, even of the lands beyond the mountains.

Harder were the words we had over the convent. For I did strive to convince him that it must be closed to men, that so far as possible the nuns should be virgins, saving those that are widows, and all strict to their vows of chastity. He was amazed at this, declaring that only a cruel and lunatic god would tell his most loyal woman disciples not to lie with men.

'Rather should he reward them with many bedfellows, mighty warriors whose ramping loins are engorged with the blood of the conquered!'

In vain did I explain the virginity of Our Lady and the chaste life of Our Lord Jesus.

'I'll cleave to your Christ so long as he grants me great victories over my enemies, and spoils in riches and women, but I'll not believe the Lady was got with child by an angel. By Thor, if a woman of mine tried that story, I'd have her womb out with my bare hands and stuck on a pike in the market place.'

Moreover had he the gall to upbraid me with the matter of Sister Irmtraud, so that I must expound to him the differences between regular and secular clergy; solemn and simple vows; primary, secondary, and tertiary orders.

'Nay, little priest, confute with me as you will, you'll not call that cloggie a coggie and me to quaff from it: she's your whore and there's an end on it!'

I prayed to Our Lady for eloquence, but She did not answer me, and I failed to move him.

But in time Sister Renate learned the tongue of the folk and did contend with him as well, and to more effect, and was Graf Walther tamed and brought to heel in the matter of the convent, and in divers other matters as well. For though she has but two-and-twenty years, is Sister Renate as learned as a Doctor of the Church, as fierce as a crusader, and as proud as a great lord, in the manner of the people of her land where all folk are rich and highborn, and drink the liquor of the angels, and wear shoes with long pointed toes.

'But, alas,' she said, 'I shall never again see that land where bloom the lemon trees, for I am violated and disgraced and must live out my days in this cold, dark land of pines and oaks.' But I chided her that Our Lord and His Lady have dominion over all the earth and even here may she store up treasures in Heaven.

'Console me not, little father,' she replied, 'For as much as Paradise is sweeter than my land, so is my land more Paradise than this one. However, waste no tears on me, for I am not without wiles and strengths.'

And truly did she speak.

So it came to pass after much struggle and earnest prayer, that we have arrived at a scheme that answers all our needs, the ladies', Graf Walther's, and my own. For shall the castle be built on the one hilltop, and a church of stone on the second hilltop, and nearby a convent which Sister Renate's order shall rule, and Sister Renate shall be Mother Superior and from round about shall maidens be brought to be brides of Christ and to purify their souls in the light of Our Lady's grace and in the peace and contentment of the cloister, and the first shall be any girl children born of Sister Renate and her sister nuns, for are they all great with child, save one that is barren. And Graf Walther has pledged great treasure for the church and for the convent which he will wrest from infidels to the east or the north or I wot not where.

So it is that great doings happen hereabouts and the Lord will be glorified beyond imagining. Yet am I troubled, for as the world changes much and quickly, the old verities are cast aside for the fashion of the time. But I am only a simple rustic, as Sister Renate often reminds me; and as Sister Irmtraud also reminded me in the dark hours of this day, for the night was chill when I arose to say lauds, so that I grumbled as I am rarely wont to do: 'Seemingly highborn nuns need only pray to the Lord but twice a day, and that when the sun is shining.'

To this, Sister Irmtraud replied: 'I'm glad you see the truth at last. Perhaps now you'll send them back where they came from.' I tried at once to dam up the flow of her bile.

'Our ways are not theirs, and who knows what may be the Lord's way? We must be content with the country truths we got at our mothers' knees.'

'Those sluts got their truths on their backs.'

'Then come and pray for their souls,' I suggested to her.

'Do you not hear the babe crying that it must have suck?'

So we arose from our bed into the dark of night, she to her duty and I to mine.

So ends the year and the sixteenth year of the service to this parish of the Servant of the Lord, and I pray that Our Lord may forgive us our sins as surely He will, for He died on the cross that we might be without stain of the mark of the evil one who lurks in wait for the unwary.

L O, IS OUR LITTLE VILLAGE become a great town, with seven streets, four inns, many shops, and dwellings beyond number. The convent, the church, and the castle begin to take shape under the direction of a master mason of great skill from Fulda, and several other masons and builders, while helpers from among the people, who do such work as they can, swarm like bees upon the two hills. Graf Walther and his men stay at the Sign of the Pig's Trotter, while the nuns stay at the newest inn, the Sign of the Wimple, and many are their visitors, for the rumours of their piety, and of their excellent beer, have spread to all the lands round about, and there hardly passes a day when some great captain or lord or merchant does not come to seek the blessing of the nuns. Moreover, Sister Renate is become renowned for her learning, and many do seek her advice, instruction, or judgment; and go away marvelling at her wisdom. She had me consecrate a little chapel at the Sign of the Wimple, that her sisters might say their confessions and have mass said for them there.

'Why should the ten of us walk a mile and back when one walking in the opposite direction is as efficacious?'

To this I could give no answer.

But Sister Irmtraud was wrathful, and chided me: 'Why didn't you tell them to walk, for the Lord's mercy is no trial, but a proof of humility?'

'They would say humility suits me better.'

'They would be right on that count.'

'Besides, they better profit the Lord by brewing their beer and collecting donations for the building of their convent.'

'You are a fool if you think those so-called pilgrims come for beer or for wisdom.'

I forbore to answer, for Sister Irmtraud is more disappointed than she should be over the course of events. She yearns for past times, and would have me believe she is speaking of the quiet days when we lived together in simple contentment, before Graf Walther arrived to ravish her; but I suspect she yearns for the time when she was being ravished, before Sister Renate took her place in his bed.

However, even Sister Renate saw but little of the mighty Captain this summer past, for with the drying of the roads in the spring did Graf Walther ride away with his band of men to gather contributions for his great projects and he returned only with the snows. Indeed he brought great treasure, and workmen flock to the town to get the wages he is able to offer, and no one asks after their masters or if they be freed men; and stone is set on stone and the walls will soon tower into the sky, and vie with the Tower of Babel for magnificence.

All these great events confuse me, for I am indeed a simple man. Nor am I alone in my confusion, for the folk of the parish grumble against the foreigners and their outlandish ways, and against the use of coin which is becoming common, for they say coin makes the prices high, while they get no more for the goods they sell. And the old complain of the debauchery and impudence of the young. For the lads eschew the long hours of drudgery on the farms and go with Graf Walther to be soldiers, and so become lazy, drunken, brawling bullies as soldiers commonly are; and the maids stain their lips with berries and tie coloured rags in their hair, and mince about the market place hoping to ensnare the stonecutters whose purses jingle with silver; and ofttimes they succeed, so that they bring shame upon themselves and upon all good Christian folk; and yet there is this good of it, that come Whitsuntide shall I have many babies to baptize.

And so it is that the love of Christ and the charity of Our Lady fortify me in my faith, and my heart overflows with joy at the approaching feast of His Crucifixion and Glorious Resurrection; and I look back with some equanimity upon this, the seventeenth year of the service here of the servant of the Lord, and look forward to the coming year with rather less dread than I might.

IN THIS YEAR OF Our Lord have the Four Horsemen of the Apocalypse come snuffling about the borders of the valley; and yet are we spared their dread presence in the town, save only in the great Battle of the Lohbacher Ford. For the depredations, as it seems, which Graf Walther visited upon the settlements over the hills and beyond the forest so roused the folk of those lands that they gathered together and made common cause against their enemy. And as that enemy dwells in our midst and claims us as his subjects, so are we vilified and attacked by folk with whom in the past we dwelt in peace; and numerous are the graves of the slain, and numerous the weeping widows and the fatherless children. Yet greater in number are the graves of the enemy, for such is the ferocity and such are the wiles of the man that his attackers are confounded, smitten, and ground down so that Graf Walther now mulcts more contributions from them than formerly and the stone walls of the castle, the church, and the convent rear higher than ever, and I am troubled whether they more glorify God or Mammon.

The castle keep is the most nearly complete, grim against the sky, although Graf Walther plans a great bailey enclosing out-buildings and such. In this castle, since about the time of the feast day of St. Bugomil, has Graf Walther dwelt; and surely no battle train of a kaiser of old was greater than the stream of carts bearing goods and booty though the lowering gates; surely the numbers of beasts climbing into the ark of Noah were not greater than those entering the castle; and surely the hogsheads of beer borne from the convent brewery to the castle would unleash again the flood of our father Noah, if broached all at once.

Of the convent, less is complete, for Graf Walther said that Almighty God needs stout walls less than does mortal man, and was thrifty with his contributions. Sister Renate replied that mortal woman needs stout walls even more than does mortal man, and so bent her will to raise money on her own, and withheld contributions from the sisters to the castle, and ordered the abbess's residence to be built first, and stout indeed are its walls and high; and although Sister Renate does dwell within, is her residence not complete, for she is resolved that the beauty of its windows and woodwork and adornments shall be a fit tribute to Our Holy Mother in her Glory, so that numbers of skilled artisans labour each day therein. As the other nuns dwelt at the Sign of the Wimple on rents which galled Sister Renate, so was a dormitory begun, and enough completed that the sisters do occupy their cells and use a part as kitchen and refectory; and a brewhouse of wood was put up to serve until a better one of stone can be built. When I enquired politely when the chapter house and the chapel might commence, Sister Renate turned on me like an adder, hissing out her answer:

'When Our Lord in His wisdom desires other buildings, He will vouchsafe the necessary monies; in the meantime, do I and my sisters labour so long in His service that our shoulders are bent and our hands hardened.'

'And their heels shiny,' added Sister Irmtraud when I told her, but this did not prevent her from enrolling in the order our little Jutta that grew into a comely woman in this year. When I made protest, Sister Irmtraud rebuked me thus:

'You simpleton, would you rather Jutta be debauched in the castle for crusts of bread from the soldiers' table, or debauched in the convent for ten groschen on the thaler and all meals, as her contract stipulates?'

Indeed, I am a simpleton, and fear I should find another, simpler parish, save that neither my letters to the bishop, nor Sister Renate's have garnered a reply and I fear he is dead, and the suffragans, coadjutors, canons, prebendaries, and precentors dead with him from the plague, and I forgotten, although not forgotten by our dear Lord Jesus Christ who died for our sins and whose death and Glorious Resurrection we soon celebrate at the end of this, the eighteenth year of the service of the servant of the Lord.

I HAVE MY JAILER to thank for the parchments, my ink, and the quills which he has smuggled in to me in exchange for a decade each of Paternosters and Aves, but I also thank the mercy of Our Lady that I may set down my thoughts and so brighten this dark dungeon. By scrupulous care in the forming of the letters, I may record much on these few sheets. Oh, woe is me! that I was brought into this life, a miserable sinner among sinners in this dark world! How much better that my mother had strangled me in my cradle or abandoned me in the forest for the wolves to devour. But I have this consolation, that before the sun has many times risen up out of the forbidding forests to the east, my soul shall be free of this decaying and putrescent flesh and become eternal, whether to light or darkness I know not, but trust in the love of my Saviour, our Lord Jesus Christ Who died for the forgiveness of our sins.

And should my sins in this life be forgiven me in the next, and I go to dwell in the house of the Lord, I pray and trust that a humble angel from one of the lower orders might take me in hand and explain the ways of That Place to me, that I may understand them better than I do the ways of this. For have I not been a humble worm, creeping upon the ground, hidden in this obscure valley from the temptations of the great world? But the great world has invaded this valley, and I am in this dungeon awaiting my fate; and strange is it to be.

How it came about I can but guess at from hints dropped to me during my interview. What chanced, so far as I can tell, is as follows. The mighty works of building which Graf Walther and Sister Renate have undertaken have become a sore burden upon their shoulders and upon the shoulders of all who dwell in the valley and roundabout. Nay, even those strangers who dwell as far away as a ten days' ride are groaning under the burden, for Graf Walther and his men have swept all the lands like the most skilled of reapers, their sickles cutting the stems close that no straw be lost, the gatherers avaricious with the stooks that not a grain fall to the ground, and others coming behind that nought be left to the field mice or the sparrows. But even this harvest is not enough to fuel the ambitions of the two. Which of them it was that chanced upon the solution, I know not, although I can well suspect, but the result is that I am in this dungeon awaiting the end of my stay upon this earth.

I learned of the scheme three days ago, upon the feast day of St. Lug, when a group of soldiers came to summon me to the Waltherburg. I protested that I must bedeck the church with oak boughs as is the custom on that day, but they replied that they would bedeck my behind with oak boughs if I did not come at once. So it was that forthwith was I led into the presence of Graf Walther and Sister Renate in a high room of this castle. The two were seated at a table set before a narrow window, and looked more like man and wife than warlord and abbess.

'What do you know of sainthood, little father?' asked Sister Renate.

'I am but an ignorant man, sister,' I replied, 'and know little of the blessed save that they may hear our most earnest prayers and intercede for us in Heaven; as Fat Hans the butcher prayed to St. Peter and was relieved of rocks in his bowels.'

'Spare me the details, and tell me instead what makes a saint.'

I have never been comfortable with such quizzing, for questioners always put questions to which they know the answer, and to which they suspect the questioned does not. At such times I recall my novitiate and the scoldings my ignorance earned me; early or late, the word 'blockhead' was usually uttered. So I stumbled somewhat in answering.

'Our Saviour's apostles are saints, as are His Holy Mother, and St. Joseph and others who met Him during His life among men.'

'Go on.'

'Other saints are venerated because of their sufferings for the faith, martyrs to infidels or lions or dragons.'

'Fascinating.'

196

'We venerate also those who performed miracles, as St. Hildegard who could tell the future, or St. Katherine who had visions of wheels, like the prophet Ezekiel.'

'Your scholarship, little father, is remarkable; pray exhibit more of it.'

'Then there were the fathers of the church, such as . . .' but in my ignorance I could not think of any of them.

'St. Gerolamo, perhaps, or St. Agostino?'

'Yes, of course, I remember them now.'

'And what did they do that made them fathers of the church?'

I did not know, and made the mistake of clutching at notions.

'They made the great church buildings of stone that are found in distant lands?'

'No, you blockhead, they interpreted the Holy Scriptures and wrote books which elaborated the dogma of the Church therefrom and so built rather the hierarchy of the church. And other saints?'

I stared at the floor in silence, so she informed me:

'Certain hermits and ascetics such as St. Antony and St. Simeon the Stylite who dwelt atop a pillar in the desert we venerate also, for they set examples by which the contemplative orders of monks and nuns were inspired. The founders of those orders, such as St. Benedict and St. Dominic, we also venerate, but no doubt you know all about them.'

'No doubt, sister.'

'And this certainty of knowledge established, we pass now, little father, to the matter which has brought us together today. We are building three edifices which will establish Waltherrott as one of the premier cities of these northern lands. But, as you may have observed, work is proceeding at such a slow pace that we'll all be under the roofs of our celestial dwellings before these earthly edifices are done. The jumped-up labourers demand ever higher pay and do ever less work in return. They point out that the great death carried off many of their kind, so that their labour being thus more scarce is worth more. These notions are most pernicious heresy, of course, but there is little one can do to counter them. These vermin will not be preached at and they cannot be persuaded, fooled, or coerced. Force would keep them at the job only until the guard's back was turned; then they would be off like hares to the woods. We are thus obliged to go some way to meet their conditions. Do you follow me thus far?'

'I hope and trust I do, sister.'

'Good. Now, Graf Walther has been a very St. Matthew in his efforts to solicit contributions from the people who live round about, but they are not as charitable as they should be; indeed, they have sent to various great lords who fraudulently claim vassalage in those lands, complaining of Graf Walther's efforts and demanding protection and redress. For the most part, these absurd moans have been little heeded; but they have attracted a small number of free-lances, rough fighting men who rally to the banner of any town that will pay enough. They will be dealt with in due course.'

Graf Walther pounded his fist upon the table.

'By thunder and lightning, they're all brigands, bandits, out-laws, the dunghill wallowing swine. Think they there is no rule of law hereabouts? Seemingly so, but they err grievously, for I have brought law to this valley and soon enough will they learn of their mistake. I'll string my bows with their guts, I'll quaff my ale from their skulls, I'll feed my dogs on their knackers!'

'All in good time, my dear Graf, but dead brigands will not much increase our revenues. As I have tried to make you under-stand, even if we could lay hands upon all the gold in every town and village within practical reach of your cohorts, we would not have sufficient for our projects. No, Graf Walther, we need volun-tary contributions, money from people who give willingly and who do not run weeping to some great lord to come and take it all back.'

'Well, your little nightingales have been attracting as willing a horde of contributors as I've ever seen, but they'll be lifting their knees in their coffins and we'll still be short.'

'Hold your flapping tongue, you crude thumper, and leave the sisters out of it; they are doing the best they can under very trying

circumstances. No, whatever the drawing power of the local ameni-
ties, we need an attraction which will bring contributors like
swarms of midges, yet with fat purses and giving hearts. And that is
how you can help us, little father.'

And as she turned her eyes upon me, I felt a shiver in my
bonecage, for that it seemed a reptile gazed out from her head.

'But sister, I am of no interest to anyone.'

'Not as Father Adalbert, no, but what if you were someone
else?'

I knew not what to say. She spoke for a time, and the subtlety of
her thought in her several languages was as a wind through the forest, evident and effective, but somehow beyond understanding, so
that my attention drifted, and I found myself peering toward the
window, hoping perchance to spy a bird passing, until she concluded: 'What say you to that?'

I stammered some foolish thing.

'I told you – he's a moron,' cried Graf Walther. 'And your plan is
just as moronic as he is. Look at him, he wasn't even listening, the
drivelling simpleton.'

'No, you've just been dreaming, haven't you, little father?'

'I expect so, sister.'

'Or perhaps having a vision?'

'I don't think so, sister.'

'Don't you have visions? Everyone does.'

I bethought me of the visitation of Our Holy Mother; but then
recalled that in consequence Graf Walther undertook his crusade;
and captured Sister Renate; and decided not to mention any of it.

'No, sister.'

'Perhaps we may be able to jog your memory, because if you
could have some visions, everything would be much simpler, much
less complicated. I don't suppose you have ever flown through the
air?'

'No.'

'Caused bushes to explode in flame?'

'No.'

'Are there any weeping statues of the Blessed Virgin in your church? . . . But there are no statues at all. Perhaps your body breaks out in a show of the stigmata every Easter, does it?'

'I sometimes suffer from piles in the cold months.'

'Hardly a holy affliction. You didn't help relieve the butcher of his stones?'

I shook my head.

'Cast out devils?'

'Only a few times.'

'Well that's a start, but a few visions or miracles would have been a great help. And less painful for you.'

'You speak in riddles, Sister Renate.'

'Heavens, even for a country priest you are remarkably obtuse. I see I must list the alternatives. You are barely literate, thus you can by no means become a doctor of the Church; you have neither the ability nor the ambition to found an order; you'll certainly not pass for a holy virgin; and I doubt even you are stupid enough to desire martyrdom while other courses are open to you. Therefore, you must have a few visions and, preferably, perform a few miracles – you'd be surprised what can be arranged with the right powders and a few mirrors. In any case, it's either miracles or martyrdom.'

'But why?'

'My dear little father, how can I be more plain? You are to be canonized as a saint!'

'But I am not a saint! I do not wish to be a saint!'

'What exemplary humility, how very saintly of you to reject sainthood. But to reject your destiny is nonsense: what higher plane of existence could a person seek in this veil of tears?'

'A peaceful life in harmony with God and one's neighbours!'

'How dull, how unambitious.'

'I am dull and unambitious.'

'No, sainthood is the great goal. Insofar as it does not approach the sin of pride, every virtuous soul should aspire at times to sainthood. Do we not all wish to please the Lord, to earn His Thanks, His Forgiveness, His Grace? Do we not wish to advance the Faith?

To look forward to the certainty of a blissful eternal life in the company of the Blessed? Of course we do. However, as Our Saviour said: Many are called, but few are chosen. I know I should like to be a saint, and dear Graf Walther here has fought mightily, nay, continues to fight in the name of the faith, but, alas, we are common clay, mere drudges in the service of Our Lord. You, however, are nominated for canonization, and I can assure you that I and Graf Walther shall spare no expense, to our last sack of gold, in our efforts to provide the documentation and gain the necessary signatures and seals of the necessary authorities, even if we have to apply to His Holiness the Antichrist in Avignon. But even before that, when we proclaim your nomination, and dedicate the new church as the Church of Blessed Adalbert, why the streams of pilgrims to venerate you shall fill the roads like great rivers in spring flood time, so that even if the Holy Father does not deign to notice you, your sainthood will be recognized, de facto, by the congregation of true believers and, no doubt, by the relevant authorities in Heaven. Avignon will come around in time.'

'But I am only a humble parish priest going about my duties. Pilgrims will as likely venerate Fat Hans the butcher.'

'A very good point – and one which I have anticipated. You shall cease your parochial duties; instead, you shall become a hermit and take up residence in a cave. Graf Walther has already assigned a group of quarrymen to the job of excavating one for you in the Bergwald.'

'But I don't want to live in the Bergwald, and I certainly don't want to live in a cave – I have so little flesh on my bones that I'll be dead before midwinter!'

'I am assured it will be a most salubrious cave, free of draughts or dripping water. With a good fire at the mouth – and the magnanimous Graf Walther here has undertaken to provide a constant supply of logs – why, you'll be as snug as ever you were in that wretched stew you now inhabit.'

'I would rather return to my wretched stew, there to remain a mortal and fallible priest.'

'Out of the question, I'm afraid. We can't afford to have you blathering to . . . all and sundry, so it has been decided you'd best remain as a guest in the Waltherburg until your cave is finished. In any case, I shall have to coach you in your responses: you can gull some of the people all of the time, and all of the people some of the time, but you can't gull all of the people all of the time.'

I protested that I had no desire to gull any of the people any of the time, but Sister Renate had turned to Graf Walther and was telling him the roads through the forests must be improved and a bridge thrown across the river so that pilgrims might pass in all weathers and at all times of the year. When I arose and stepped toward them, Graf Walther called for the guards who came at once and brought me to this cell. And I pray to the Lord to deliver me from the evil fate of contrived sainthood.

I N MY PRAYERS I made moan that I was suffering alone, and this prayer at least is answered, but in such a manner as reminds us to frame our wishes carefully in order that they may be clearly understood. For Sister Irmtraud now shares my cell, and blames me for her troubles, and not without reason. For when she discovered that I had been brought to the castle and had not returned, she came to secure my release. When Sister Renate agreed to meet her, sharp words were exchanged, as I could well imagine. The result is that Sister Irmtraud is also nominated to be a saint.

Yet I am much cheered by her presence, for while I am a simple man and without the wit to fox mine enemies, Sister Irmtraud has many strengths and skills and virtues which she prefers to hide under her bushels so that most folk think her dull and stupid, and thus does she confound many.

'If that lout and his foreign slut think they're going to canonize me, they have another think coming,' she remarked this morning; and took from her habit her wool and needles, a certain sign these many years that she is knitting a plan as surely and as steadily as a spider weaves her web. And when I made to ask her a trivial question, she cast a stern glance at me and shook her head; I retired to my pen and parchment; and if I were Graf Walther or Sister Renate, I should step carefully, for the stone floors of this castle, which are so solid to the feet, are like to give way over the yawning pit of Sister Irmtraud's ire.

H ER SCHEMES having been thought through, Sister Irmtraud has set them in motion, though I know not what they may be, for she smiles and calls me a guileless gull who had best be kept in the dark lest I reveal the snares she is setting.

'And be prudent about those scratchings you make, for mayhap the outlandish witch can read them if she comes upon them.'

I explained the cunning subterfuge of my writing, that letters masquerade as one another.

'Why then do you write since none can understand your words?'

'The Lord understands.'

She looked at me with amazement and, I regret to say, contempt.

'The Lord is too busy to notice the goings-on in this little valley, else we should not be in this dungeon.'

I tried to rouse her faith in the Lord Jesus, or at least in Our Lady, but she turned from me and went to the Judas hole whence she called sweetly to the guard and when he came, began to murmur in his ear; and sweetly can she murmur when she chooses, as well I know.

S ISTER IRMTRAUD CONTINUED her murmurings for several days, sometimes with one of the guards, several of whom are local lads; but at last she was murmuring to Graf Walther himself, albeit in the next cell, so that what I learned I had from the little I heard with my own ears, from the little the guard hinted to me, and from the little Sister Irmtraud let slip. For in the small hours did the guard creep into our cell, and did she rise from our bed; but prudence and fear of her wrath cautioned me to feign sleep.

'What of the little father, sister,' whispered the guard. 'Shall I bind and gag him, or . . .'

'Nay, he is as simple awake as he is asleep and certainly he is asleep. Where is your master?'

'He awaits you nearby, Sister.'

'Quick, then, lead me to him.'

What few noises I heard over the next hour are familiar enough to any man who cleaves to woman, though these groans and hoots were so loud I thought they should wake the castle, nay, the town. So that when Sister Irmtraud returned with the dawn, I was not surprised to see her face flushed. Seeing me awake, for I was at my prayers, she started first in confusion, but then her eyes became thoughtful and she came to the corner where I knelt, and took my hands in hers.

'Ask not too many questions of me, little father, ask only how we shall escape from this place.'

'I enquire not into your comings or goings, dear sister, for you are staunch in your faith to Our Saviour and Our Lady and to our Holy Mother the Church, and you use what weapons they have given you.'

Though I blush to admit it, I sometimes speak with less than complete candour.

'Yea, and though I have carried eight children, and six to term, I have but nine-and-twenty years, and a man may still look upon my hips and think himself a great captain before a prancing charger.'

Or a farmer behind a ploughhorse.

'Nay, sister, 'tis your eyes that shine like the morning star, I trow . . .' and so on in this vein until we were back in our cot and I, trying the skillet, found it already well-greased for my bludwurst, so to say.

As SISTER IRMTRAUD'S PLANS MATURE, she spends more nights out of our cell than in it, and so should she, for albeit a cell is an appropriate place for a priest, it is not for an angel; or so I tell myself. And when she returns, she has a thoughtful mien. This morning I, in pretence of sleep but peeking through my fingers, saw her glance sharply at me, then toward the door. The look she wore was such as when she goes to find a chicken to kill, but whether it was meant for Graf Walther, Sister Renate, or me, I could not tell. But I keep my faith in her as I do in Our Lady.

I N THE HOURS of this morning between matins and lauds, there came to our ears a sudden hue and cry, and all about the castle, within and without, so it seemed, there echoed the alarums of battle. Sister Irmtraud leapt up from our mattress at once, and whispered with excitement: 'They are come, they are come!' It was only later that I wondered why she did not say rather: 'We are attacked, we are attacked!' but then thought better of it, and held my tongue. The window is but small, and high in the wall, so that I had to stand on Sister Irmtraud's shoulders to look out, and then saw nothing, there being dark all about.

'Do you see the light of any fires?' she asked.

'Nay, sister.'

'So we know at least the town is not being torched.'

'Our Lady grant us mercy.'

'If Our Lady is paying attention, perhaps she can have them burn that outlandish whore's brothel.'

To this I deigned no reply, and Sister Irmtraud paced our cell as excited as a caged bear and did not notice my silence.

After what seemed an age, the first light of dawn appeared and I climbed to my perch again; and still saw nothing, for that our cell is on the cliff side and largely gives a view of the distant Bergwald, and of a small part of the town by the river.

Yet did the noise increase, and the confusion, the ringing of steel, the clattering of arrows and the shouts and screams of men, and I was sore afraid, but Sister Irmtraud stood with her ear to the door and hissed at me: 'Hush you, you gabbling goose, for what I have not yet worked in the quiet nights I may yet work in this confusion.' Thinking she was no doubt right, but in any case would box my ears if I did not heed her, I commenced to pray to St. Barbara.

In time the sun came up upon our little world and the din of battle resolved itself. The cries of pain and panic grew without the window, while the cries of confidence and triumph grew within. Then was Sister Irmtraud most intent, and most gloomy. And when, after a space of quiet, we heard a great hallooballoo from the defenders, we understood that they were sallying forth to put the attackers to rout; and such was the case, for the castle became still and from the window came of a sudden a great wailing and fear, as Graf Walther's forces fell upon them. Then did all noises fade swiftly into the distance and we might have been alone in the world, such was the quiet of that fortress.

Sister Irmtraud turned to me and said: 'So the first plan has failed and we must pray the second one succeeds.' Then she stroked the scar of the cross on my forehead.

TODAY WAS OUR FATE SEALED, and we are to face the judgment of Our Lord. For I was in the midst of nones when the guard opened the door of our cell and Sister Irmtraud and I were called to attend Graf Walther. We found him with Sister Renate on a high parapet, with the village below looking very small in its loop of the river, and the fields and forests stretching off to the Bergwald, all glowing in the summer haze. Graf Walther's first words brought me quickly back to my situation:

'It is too soft a punishment for traitorous priests and nuns to be heaved from this parapet to have their bodies broken on the rocks below, but by all the gods I will do it in an eyeblink if you cross me now, you pustulent offal of diseased swine.'

I trembled, but Sister Irmtraud poked an elbow into my ribs. She fixed him with her eye, then looked to Sister Renate.

'I do not well understand this accusation,' she remarked. 'Surely you do not suggest that two prisoners locked in a dungeon could threaten a great lord in his castle keep?'

When Graf Walther turned from us without reply, I realized the subtlety of this sally: for Sister Irmtraud in her nighttime excursions was far from powerless, but Graf Walther could not admit to these trysts in front of Sister Renate.

But Sister Renate had a counter:

'That might have been a convincing defence, sister, had we not captured your ally, the brigand Albrecht the Wolf. Look not about, sister, for he is no longer with us in the vale of tears. Indeed, if you would see him, you must look to the portcullis where you will find his corpse, impaled from fundament to craw upon a great stake. But before that merciful timber silenced his howls, he admitted your complicity in his criminal ravages, that you did by your wiles, your schemes, your enchantments seduce him from afar, coming as a succubus to his bed in the small hours, so to beguile him to take up the sword against his lawful lord, Graf Walther, and even against Our Holy Mother the Church as represented by myself. What say you to these condemnations? Why should you not be burned at the stake as witch?'

'As I am but a wretched prisoner without allies, why should I not indeed be burned . . . or suffer any such punishments as you decide upon? I am not such a gull that I put my trust in the justice of this world, but rather look only to the mercy of Our Lord and to judgement in the World Hereafter.'

In my long experience of her, Sister Irmtraud never calls upon the powers of Heaven save when she wishes to divert prying eyes away from such powers as she commands in this world. Evidently Sister Renate was also aware of this tactic, for she replied:

'This pretence of helplessness prettily becomes your guise as a nun, but the mercy of Our Lord will be unavailing in this case; rather shall his wrath cast you down into the pit of Inferno, and it is a nice question whether, in the description of that place in the work of our divine poet, Dante Alighieri, you shall await the doom of the Last Trump in the Second, the Third, or the Fourth Round of the Ninth Circle of Inferno. What think you, my dear Graf? Shall she be put with traitors to their country, traitors to their hosts, or traitors to their masters?'

'What need I of the warbling of outlandish bards to know of traitors and their just punishment? And what care I about punishment in the next world? I punish in this world. With these hands . . .'

Holding his hands up as if to wrest the sun from heaven, he shouted: 'With these hands, I'll pull her guts out from her cleft and strangle her with them.'

But his glance was caught by Sister Irmtraud, and he mastered his tongue:

'Or perhaps I'll just confine her to her quarters.'

'So she can continue her mischief, her treachery? So she can continue to tempt you in the dark hours?' Both Graf Walther and Sister Irmtraud blanched at this revelation, but Sister Renate went on. 'No, my dear Graf, I think you and the world will be well rid of this witch.'

Meaning she herself would be well rid of her rival.

'But the burning of a witch will not make Waltherrott a destination for pilgrims. That is the point, you see. We now benefit from the passage of divers travellers who stay but a night and pass on to other places. We must establish the town, the church, the convent as a final *destination*, so that people come here and stay a week or a month, dispensing as much of their gold as we can conveniently convince them to part with. So will the prosperity of the town, of its inhabitants be assured.'

'And the prosperity of the line of vom Faß!'

'Indeed, yes, my dear Graf. And of the parish and the convent and, by extension, our Holy Mother the Church.'

'A pox on your Avaricious Mother the Church: the gold stays in Waltherrott.'

'Of course: I meant only that the *reputation* of the Church will be increased. But what matters now is that the means must be decided upon, and witches do not attract travellers; rather, they drive them elsewhere. Thus, whatever the truth of the matter may be, Sister Irmtraud here must not be a witch.'

'I am gratified to hear my innocence admitted, sister.'

'On the contrary, you are condemned as a witch and a rebel against the established order, both ecclesiastical and secular. So you must die; you'll simply not die as a witch. It is a matter of definition, of perception.'

Now Sister Renate's eyes did fall upon me, cowering by the wall.

'Come forward, St. Adalbert, and let us look upon you.'

I had hoped perhaps that as she seemed to have found another saint, she might have forgotten this one, but as Sister Renate smiled at me were her teeth like knifes and her eyes like augers.

'I hope your several days of contemplation have reconciled you to immortality in the service of your town, your master, and your Church, little priest.'

'Like Sister Irmtraud, I entrust my fate to Our Lord.'

'Very provident of you, I'm sure, and I'm sure He'll welcome you as the shepherd does the lost sheep when you join Him ere the sun sets this day.'

'This day?' I stammered. 'But you said I was to live in a cave and perform miracles.'

'*Conditionally*, yes. But on further consideration it has been decided that the sage-in-the-cave strategy is too time-consuming; and in any case, the excavators came upon a great flow of hot water issuing from the earth, so we have decided instead to make the cave into a mineral bath for the cure of ailments. That settled, so is your fate decided. But there is the added question of Sister Irmtraud, here. Obviously, she could not have joined you in your hermitage or you wouldn't be a hermit, would you? No, martyrdom is more efficient. Besides, martyred saints perform as many miracles as do live ones – more, perhaps. At any rate, the weeping statues and walking cripples will no doubt appear when appropriate. What is important, nay, crucial, is that your martyrdom be arranged at once, while circumstances are ripe.

'Here is what has happened: Albrecht the Wolf is a heathen, an adherent of the old ways. Enraged by the success of Graf Walther and of myself at propagating the faith up and down the Lohbachertal, Albrecht rises in bloody insurrection against the legions of Christ. But finding the Waltherburg impregnable, and himself near death, he instructs his lieutenant, one Gunther the Goat, to escape with a small band and return by stealth to fall upon your little church, meaning for them to desecrate the paraphernalia of the Holy Eucharist, even the sacred Host itself. Bursting through the doors, this Gunther and his rabble find the two of you standing stalwart in your Faith before the altar:

'"Avaunt, infidel!" you cry. "Get thee gone from this place which is sacred to the Lord Mighty in Battle, who shall smite you ere you advance another pace!" Then, holding your crucifixes before you, the two of you advance toward the blood-crazed monster. For a moment it seems you have succeeded in your ruse, for he and his mob are stunned by your audacity. But then a rooster crows in the distance – yes, a nice touch, a reminder of St. Peter's denial of Our Lord – and Gunther comes to himself: "Tear them to shreds!" he cries. "Hack and hew, bludgeon and cudgel!" They fall upon Father Adalbert and begin the hacking and hewing, and soon he is indeed a martyr to the Faith. They are about to do the same with Sister Irmtraud, when one dunghill knave suggests they violate her first. They leap at the idea, and drag her screaming to the altar, where . . .'

Graf Walther interrupted her: 'Yes, well, I don't think we have to go into detail, do we, Sister Renate? Let's just get the dirty work out of the way, then we can fix the story later.'

Sister Renate, who had been pacing about the parapet and waving her hands to suggest the various actions, glared at Graf Walther, then at us.

'Very well, then, but see that you don't botch the job. And make certain there are no witnesses!'

While Sister Renate swept away to her convent, Graf Walther returned us to our cell, explaining that while the sun was yet up, he must keep us from sight. With the darkness, he will return and see to things. He had some quiet words with Sister Irmtraud, then was gone.

I expected her to be despondent, but she smiled gently and told me to attend to my 'chicken scratchings,' as she calls them, and she will see to our welfare.

'Set down all that has happened, as it happened, then put the sheet with the others in a safe place. We may yet have our witnesses.'

Indeed, we have, as do all Christians, the witness of Our Lord Jesus Christ.

S HORTLY AFTER THE HOUR of vespers, a lieutenant of Graf Walther, one Wurmlein, came with two guards and took us from the castle, and by moonlight down the hill to my dear church of St. Fricka. Here he told us we must await his master, and keep ourselves from notice. So we bided our time, Sister Irmtraud first going to her old room in the rectory, then returning with her knitting, and I with my prayers and my scratchings, all by the light of the candle before the altar in the Lady Chapel. Well before the hour of matins, Graf Walther returned and laid his plan before us:

That in the small hours, we are to slip down to the river and across, and then make our way through the Bergwald. We must avoid such villages as Oberdorf and Waldental, for we are both well known to the folk there. Then, with such store of coin as Graf Walther may give us, and with such charity as we may hope for from good Christians along the way, we must make our way to the land of the great mountains to the south, for there will we find many convents and churches in the valleys and folk who speak a language near enough to ours. Meanwhile, Graf Walther and his men will torch the church and be sure it is burned to the ground, claiming that a remnant of Albrecht the Bear's force returned by stealth to have their revenge upon Christ, as Sister Renate explained. And so would the town have its saints and the saints have their lives.

'A wonderful plan,' said Sister Irmtraud. 'But what about the children? Are they to stay as hostages to that witch on the hill? And what protection are we to have past Waldental? And what is to convince her that we are dead? I know her suspicious mind: she will want relics.'

'I will guard the children from her as my own, but so long as she thinks you dead she will pay them no heed, and may even favour them should our plans for this saint business bear golden fruit, for surely the children of two saints must share some of their glow. There is little need of protection beyond Waldental, for the roads and villages are mainly peaceful. Coin will see you through well enough, but if you are frightened, you may well join a company of pilgrims; when we were on our crusade, my men and I tried taking contributions from a number of them, but they resisted fiercely. As for the relics, I have two goats tethered by the door, and will slaughter them presently. Their bones will make relics enough for any great church.'

'And what of the horns? She is not such a fool as that.'

'Why, Gunther the Goat beheaded you and took the skulls away with him as talismans.'

Sister Irmtraud pursed her lips and considered these replies, and much else, no doubt. At last she said:

'It might work, I grant you, but I think you had better find two corpses from among the dead and use them instead. And be sure to knock out the teeth so that the witch will not recognize them. The best lies are simple ones and closest to the truth.'

'By St. Logi, you are a shrewd one, Irmtraud. I'm glad I never tried to fool you, because I never could have done it.'

'May all the women of this town be so canny,' she replied.

'And may all the men be so witless,' he said.

'If your wishes are granted,' I added, 'Waltherrott will indeed be blessed, but bizarre.'

They both stared at me as if I were a simpleton, a fool, or a clown. Doubtless they are right.

She then questioned him closely about exact amounts of money and particulars of our route. Something in the picture they made as they sat with their heads bent together and their hands carving the air touched my memory, so that I left the Lady Chapel and went a little way off and held my candle before the great picture behind the high altar. I remember what suspense held all the parish as the painter worked upon it; the joyful hosannas we sang when the scaffolding came down and the sheets were removed so that we beheld the finished work; and remember also the dismay among the faithful when we beheld the desecrations visited upon the picture by Graf Walther and his men, and again the pleasure when it was repaired. Soon this masterwork of Our Lord will suffer its last, dying for us, as Our Lord himself did; so I looked upon it as closely as I could in the moonlight. Yes, there I found what I sought, by a rock just behind Our Lady and St. Anne in their grief: the soldiers casting lots for Our Lord's robe, and in their poses did they look like Sister Irmtraud and Graf Walther haggling over their coins. I prayed for their souls.

And I prayed for all the souls of this place, and was overcome by love for all who dwell here in this little valley which I shall never see again.

But thinking upon these weird events, I went through to my own old cell and retrieved all the previous parchments I could find – some are mislaid, Heaven knows where – and brought them to join the most recent sheets. And as I sit before the high altar to tell the end of the tale, I hear sounds from the direction of the Lady Chapel and know that Sister Irmtraud and Graf Walther are taking leave of one another with more enthusiasm than discretion.

SISTER IRMTRAUD DIRECTS ME to be quiet but ready to run at her signal, so do I take the minutes to record briefly what befell us, and Graf Walther.

Their dalliances at an end, Sister Irmtraud and Graf Walther sought me out where I sat.

'All is settled then, little priest, and you are to see Sister Irmtraud safely to the far land of the mountains, is it not so?'

'Yea, verily,' I said, 'And many thanks I am sure for your help.'

'And mine as well,' added Sister Irmtraud. 'But let us drink to this parting. Bring you the sacramental liquor, little father, and three coggies that we may praise His Name for our deliverance.'

'Yea, by God,' said Graf Walther, 'I'm that thirsty I could drink from a swineherd's breeks.'

I brought a flagon of the berry liquor and was about to pour when Sister Irmtraud took the vessel from me.

'Nay, little father, it is the task of a woman to be submissive and serve her two lords.'

I should have guessed she meant some mischief, for Sister Irmtraud must swallow her gall even when bowing submission to Our One Lord that is in Heaven.

In a moment we raised the wooden bowls and vowed faith and goodwill; then quaffed the full measures down. Living as I had been on prison gruel these many days, I was not prepared for strong drink and coughed and gasped for air. But my spluttering was as nothing to the paroxisms and contortions of Graf Walther. He dashed the cup to the floor, clutched his throat, gagged, and tried to vomit, but to no avail. In a moment he sank to his knees and began to thrash about like a stuck pig, and clutching his guts and tearing his hair. Great farts rent his bowels, and foul wind rushed from his throat. His eyes bulged so that they popped from their sockets and swung by the strings that held them, and his face turned black in the dim light.

'However foul, the smell of revenge is sweet to the nostrils, is it not, little father?'

'Revenge how, sister?'

'Know you his promises were like snow to melt in our hands. He meant to kill us as the slut demanded, but I marked his treachery and forestalled him. So we have escaped for the moment. Be you ready to leave upon the signal; I have allies among the guard and will return when the time is ripe, then we shall be away to work our further wrath upon the foreign witch. For if the town needs martyrs, then martyrs it shall have.'

'Do we not escape to the mountains?'

'Foolish little father, did you think a mother ever meant to leave her children?'

'But how shall we stay with enemies all about who wish us dead?'

'Sister Irmtraud and Father Adalbert will indeed be martyrs, and the others shall rule on as they planned.'

'But . . .'

214

'With a false beard you shall be Graf Walther and lead his army, while I take the other's place to rule the convent for the profit of the Lord.'

'I shall be Graf Walther? But I am a small man and too timid to lead an army.'

She considered this.

'You are right. I had best wear the false beard and be Graf Walther. You shall trade your cassock for a habit and make a winsome Sister Renate.'

'But I shall be a fool, a clown, a laughing stock!'

'It need not be for long – only until I have done away with the foreign slut and have taken control of the rabble of soldiery. In the meantime, we shall have our martyrs, and the pilgrims shall hear of them, and soon enough the town will be prosperous, and no one will care to reveal the truth to the gullible who come flocking from far and wide. Finish your scratchings and hide them, for our plans must never be revealed. Indeed, it were best you should destroy them. Leave them here, for the church must be burned as they planned just as soon as I procure another corpse.'

She went silently toward the side door of the Lady Chapel, while I sat here to watch the death agonies of our captor, and soon did they come and were most horrible to witness. For with a last great arching of his body did Graf Walther beat his brains out on the flagstones and die. And wondrous and horrible to witness were the worms and maggots which crawled from his nose, mouth, ears and other openings and fled into the ground between the flags; and vile and loathsome was the putrid bile which soon followed, and the stench was like unto the corpse of a beast dead a week in the forest. But recalling my profession, I made the sign of the cross over the body as hastily as I could, regretting that I had not been quick enough for more of the rites for the dying that Our Father in his mercy might have saved this soul from damnation. Then I did run and vomit, and from fear and revulsion will not return there, but cower here in the Lady Chapel.

But I sense that Sister Irmtraud's plans are ripe.

So does this entry to my annals end, and so does the service of the servant of the Lord, in the nineteenth year in this parish. I am to be a busy Mother Superior, so it seems, and will have little time for these chicken scratchings save perhaps as in other times, at the end of the year just before the Feast of Our Lord's Crucifixion and Glorious Resurrection. In accordance with Sister Irmtraud's orders, these sheets I shall leave here in the church, but I shall secret them under a flagstone behind the altar here in the Lady Chapel in the hope that they may survive the fire, and that one day some good soul may ponder them and read herein this account of these wondrous years in this curious town.

[Here end the annals of Father Adalbert.]

Part Six

The Journal of
Carl Maria von Stumpf
Genius. Failure.
Volume IV [Concluded]

WHEN AT LAST I closed the cover, I poured myself another brandy – I had lost track of the number – and looked at my expectant host.

'A remarkable work,' I said. 'A remarkable translation.'

'I am gratified that you think so.'

He was beaming; he had long since put the pistol into discreet retirement.

'How could I think otherwise? But you promised that I need not comment?'

'Yes. I think that reasonable. If you have comments, you will make them in your opera.'

'Yes.'

No.

Unfortunately, Walther had another gift for me; and if the annals of Saint Adalbert were an unwelcome nuisance, the other was positively dangerous; and all the more so for being entirely, impossibly unexpected.

'You pretend to cynicism, my friend,' he said, pouring more brandy, 'but you are of the angels' party and do not know it.'

'You mean angels are also impoverished, consumptive, alcoholic failures?'

'There is nothing wrong with you that some recognition will not repair. These trivial matters of health and wealth can be solved. The world will recognize your genius soon enough, for there burns within you the spirit of truth, the spirit of the age: I sense it, I know it. The revolution is poetry, music, spectacle, drama: it is, in short, politics as opera, and you are the composer for the age. As the noble Schiller put it: "Dare to be wise! Like Athene, the energy of spirit which is wisdom must be warlike against sloth and cowardice."'

'I am surprised you quote Schiller at me.'

'Because I can see you revere him.'

'But he was not an unqualified admirer of revolution. He also said: "Truth in poetry is universal, and so is not identical with reality."'

'He also said: "The mind shrinks in a shrunken sphere. Man grows great with great purposes."'

'He also said: "Real art has nothing to do with the passing scene. The artist isn't trying to give his audience a vision of freedom for a few hours, but aims to give him real freedom."'

'He also said: "Any man who places himself at the centre of society and can raise his individuality to the level of the race, becomes an arbiter of the highest judgments of reason just as he is also a citizen of the world and immersed in it."'

'He also said: "This bottle is empty."'

'Heavens, it is. Let me bring us another one.'

Away he went again and I burst into my best tavern howl of one of F. von Schiller's better known ditties, setting by L. van Beethoven, a great stein-clunking rouser down at Die Drei Grafen:

> Freude, schöner Götterfunken,
> Tochter aus Elysium,
> Wir betreten Feuertrunken,
> Himmlische, dein Heiligtum.
> Deine Zauber bunden weider,
> Was die Mode streng geteilt,
> Alle Menschen werden Brüder
> Wo dein sanfter Flügel weilt.

Although it is usually sung in the local variation which begins like this:

Lager, schöner Brauerfunken

Yes, a disgrace, I know, but Schiller's soul is too great to be besmirched by such nonsense.

Ein Maß aus Elysium, usf.

Walther returned filled with enthusiasm for my wretched voice: 'A tribute to the marriage of two great souls. Do you admire Beethoven as much as you admire Schiller?'

'Fine musician, but he could have used a better librettist for *Fidelio*.'

'You always insist upon practicality.'

'Or perhaps a wife, so he'd have had some idea of conjugal love.'

'Perhaps every composer needs a wife to take care of him.'

'You haven't seen what is on offer to such as me from the matrimonial stall in the Fleischmarkt.'

In my drunken state it took me a few moments to sense the change in the atmosphere as he said quietly:

'Perhaps there are wives on offer from other quarters.'

I was about to say: 'Yes, from the chorus of the Hofoper,' but got out only the first word or two, when Walther interrupted:

'Why look in the market place? A great artist can look where he wishes, even in a palace.'

Silence seemed the only response: in any case, what words could express the confusion and turmoil in my brain? Walther opened the new bottle of brandy and poured himself a measure. He walked to the window and raised the glass to his lips, but did not sip.

'How peaceful the city looks in the moonlight; in such a glow, how unlimited the possibilities of human happiness seem. But we know only too well how narrow are the limits. Poverty and snobbery bar you from the eminence you deserve. Oddly enough, poverty and snobbery also limit me. I am not, of course, as poor as you are. When the solicitors, the insurance company, and the bankers settle matters, I and my sister will have enough to live comfortable, if severely reduced, bourgeois lives. Such a fate will be as humiliating to me as it would be to you. The snobbery which keeps you out conspires to keep me in, so that only by abandoning my position entirely will I be able to make myself useful to the world.

'Earlier you joked about a pension from the Tsar. But what if such a pension could be found from another source? What if you were to be raised up from your present state? Not to a palace, but to a bourgeois competence: a pleasant, if modest flat, perhaps in one of the new blocks in the Nußbaumstraße, along with an income sufficient to allow you to retire permanently from your piano stool at Die Drei Grafen; enough to put nourishing food on the table, but not enough, perhaps, to fill your glass with champagne; enough, my humble genius, to ensure that you need worry about nothing but the composition of great operas for the foreseeable future. What do you say to that?'

What would Fräulein Sängerin Gisela say about it, ho-ho? I used his return to the table to cover my silence, to grope for an answer, to grope for the bottle in his hand.

'How rude of me . . . let me leave it here with you, my friend.'

And I decided to pretend ignorance, for I suspected he was planning some sort of donation to the cause of the operatic arts hereabouts, and I was determined not to beg.

'The Nußbaumstraße? Sounds fine to me. I could walk down-hill to the opera house instead of up. Not the least of benefits.'

'You jest because it seems impossible, but it is not.'

'I jest because it is absurd. You need the money yourself. And in any case, a stack of government bonds and a new suit of clothes will not make me acceptable to the boxholders of the Waltherrottner Hofoper, never mind to the great patrons of Vienna or Paris. Money will not make me a gentleman – only my talent will help. In any case, why should I aspire to such status?'

'To be cynical: because respectability would pave a path for your genius. But I have a more complex reason for my suggestion. We have spoken at length of the revolution and the new world we hope for – in our different ways, admittedly. But surely we both agree on one thing: that class differences must be abolished. There are those who propose to rid the world of the aristocracy by lining all of us up against a wall and shooting us. Reactionaries are all for starving the peasants into submission, while the liberal middle classes would level the rich down to their rung and level the poor up . . . to one rung below theirs, shopkeepers trying to ensure customers for themselves. But you and I and the other revolutionaries do aspire to one goal: a classless society. If it is not to be produced by destroying other classes, how is it to be accomplished?'

I shrugged.

Walther answered himself quietly, in grotesque seriousness: 'By a union of the classes, but not in some grandiose plan. Why not, rather, selective unions? Why not do away with class through marriage between the classes? Yes, I see the amazement on your face, my friend, but why should not the best be joined with the best? An aristocracy not of wealth or birth, but of sensitivity, of talent. What do you say to that?'

My humour, sarcasm were roused by the fumes of the brandy – I am never like this sober:

'I'm afraid we don't see many duchesses or princesses pining for love down at Die Drei Grafen. Perhaps Herr Kellner Römer could order in a few cases of French champagne as bait, but . . .'

He raised his hand to silence me, then pulled on the bell cord. Almost at once, the door opened and the serving woman entered with brief, fierce looks for both of us, and stood beside Walther.

'Herr Carl Maria von Stumpf, genius, I offer to you the hand in marriage of my sister, Gräfin Renate vom Faß, lady.'

Well, yes, he did manage to surprise me beyond my wildest prophesies. I began to stammer out syllables, trying desperately to decide what was most important; and concluded I must at all cost avoid further embarrassing, mortifying, humiliating the unfortu-

221

nate woman: '. . . muh . . . muh . . . most honoured, I'm sure, buh . . . buh . . . but . . .'

'My friend, I can well imagine your shock, but do not reject this proposal out of hand. Its advantages for you I have explained, but consider it from my sister's position. Our straitened circumstances these many years have precluded a marriage to anyone in her own class. Tomorrow we must leave this home forever. If I take her with me into my anonymous retirement, she is doomed to a life of obscurity and humiliation far from the only city in the world where her name carries with it the consequence she might expect. Married to you, she would live in greatly reduced circumstances, granted, but an artist may walk with kings or beggars, he is without class, beyond class. Married to you, she has the chance of a life of some dignity when you become better known. And how much sooner might your success come if you are united with her name! The nobility which is yours through your genius bolstered and supported by this last flower of the noble house of vom Faß. The allegedly noble house of vom Faß.'

This madman was in full flight, so I stopped listening to him and looked instead at his sister. What had she to say about this grotesque proposition? For the fierceness she had shown throughout the evening belied the passivity she showed now. What could make her stand silent through his raving? Surely not his power, for like so many of the women of this town, she showed more spunk in her little finger than do any three men together. She was suffering this only from sisterly love or regard or forbearance; she would let him blather out his speech, she would hope that I would reject the idea, then she could go away and forget about it and me and the city and the palace and all. And if I were to accept, she could heft the brandy bottle and brain the two of us.

'. . . revolutionary social changes which are sweeping the continent and which . . .'

Gräfin vom Faß was giving her brother the gorgon stare, so I sneaked an appraisal. She seemed, as she had on first impression, to be about my own age, and wore her years better than I do. I doubt she had ever been a beauty – with those eyes about the house, you'd never want for an awl – but neither was she ugly. How much she had worked about the house or for how long I wasn't told, but she had not surrendered to her state, and bore herself with dignity. She was, so far as I had any way of judging, a woman of character.

Her and an income and a flat in the Nußbaumstraße.

'. . . sweet sister of my flesh, cheated by profligate ancestors, reduced to . . .'

The time had come to sing the final tutti, get off the stage, send the band home, whatever. With a swing of the arm I threw down my remaining brandy and tried to stand. I have had some experience of the inebriated state, but I had never been paralysed in quite this way before. I glanced at my legs and hips: yes, they were still there, but they seemed unconnected with the rest of me. I stared at the bottle in dismay, something my host immediately misunderstood.

'But your glass is empty, let me fill it at once, my dear fellow . . .'

My legs having failed me, I made the supreme effort with my tongue hoping for that bogus eloquence which is the prerogative of drunkards and government functionaries.

'No, thank you . . . really, no . . . I must be going . . . Act III themes to elaborate . . . splendid evening . . . remarkable . . . offer honours me deeply . . . most sincere regards to you, Gräfin vom Faß . . . granting consideration to unworthy self . . . most delicate condescension and propriety . . . your humble servant, my lady . . . beyond expectation or hope . . .'

With what strength I could find in my arms, I levered myself into a half standing position.

'. . . but the hour is late, and I have overstayed my welcome . . . no doubt some last minute packing . . . most gracious lady and most esteemed sir . . .'

'But what can you mean by this, von Stumpf?' cried Walther. 'Surely you do not mean to go before we have solemnized the engagement? Think of the advantages both to . . .'

I had a sudden panic sense of the meal returning, propelled by the brandy, so I sat down again.

'. . . manifold advantages . . . too great to contemplate . . .'

'You want better terms? Of course you do, how thoughtless of me. A guaranteed clothing allowance? Beer allowance? I know! A piano!'

I knew that if I moved, the meal would go vaulting across the room, the sky like a meteor, brief, brilliant, awe-inspiring. A Mozart of vomits.

'. . . piano not necessary . . . have piano at Drei Grafen . . .'

'A mistress? You have a mistress whom you refuse to abandon: how noble of you! Is that not gallant, Renate? But of course the young lady must not be injured, something can be arranged, I'm certain, visiting privileges once a week, twice, unless perhaps she would make a suitable maid, housemaid, lady's maid; what say you? Advantages for everyone!'

The lady interrupted him:

'Don't be a fool, Walther, he thinks rather of the disadvantages. Why should he want a union with an impoverished old maid who has lost what few looks she ever had?'

'On the contrary, Gräfin, I assure you, please, your beauty is . . .'

'Yes, you underestimate your charms, Renate, and we must do all we can to . . .' And reaching around her shoulders, he grasped the bodice of her gown and tore it open.

'You see what beauty, what . . .'

But he had exposed little of his sister, covered as she was by several layers of undergarments.

To my surprise she did not scream mayhem and rape, but rather looked at her brother with a mixture of contempt and pity.

'Sit down, Walther, and be quiet. You dreamed up this spectacle, this opera without music, and you have played your part as incompetently as you usually do. It is now my turn at centre stage.'

He slumped in his seat and lifted the bottle to his lips. He fell silent, and in a few minutes he had slumped back into an aristocratic but well-intentioned stupor and said not another word.

'You must forgive my brother, Herr von Stumpf: you can see how little the man knows of the lives and conditions of women. You, on the other hand, must surely be familiar with chemises and camisoles and such, with their ribbons and bows and hooks and laces . . .'

And as she spoke, her fingers flew and the garments fluttered from her body like a flock of birds, leaves from a tree, whatever. In no time she stood free of all but stockings and the dainty boots with their many buttons which defeated her fingers.

'But this will do, I expect,' she said. 'My brother aimed to display for the buyer the few remaining assets of five hundred years of vom Faß acquisitiveness and profligacy. Are you sufficiently impressed?'

Yes, I was impressed: for although I admit I did glance at her, I tried to bury my face in my hands, but she firmly parted my wrists and murmured, 'No, Herr von Stumpf, as my brother says, you are an artist and thus beyond ordinary mortals. What no man has the right to see is your right, what no man has possessed you may possess. Now say what is your judgment.'

My experience has been much less than they thought. I have shared a bed with a few of the fair and not so fair sex over the years. However, what with cold rooms, feminine modesty, and the high cost of candles, I have rarely had the opportunity to examine the female form at leisure. Fräulein Sängerin Gisela Klatchmeyer, for example, is exceedingly coy about such matters, and has never shown me more than a few inches of ankle and one blushing shoulder, although I have sometimes managed to pull the blanket from a squirming mound or two. On one occasion I feigned sleep while she dressed for an early rehearsal, and glimpsed a few pink curves and a sweep of backbone. I suspect, actually, that because of the many undergarments women wear, the figures we see clothed are very different from the bodies underneath. Such is surely so with Gräfin Renate, for she had seemed a sticklike creature, flat-bosomed and scrawny. She is indeed slim, but by no means scrawny, and the curves of her hips and belly are firmly rounded, while her breasts keep the pear shape of a much younger woman. No doubt she has kept this youthful grace because she has never borne children; and her virginity, so it seemed, hung about her like a glow, an aura, a perfume, a promise unfulfilled, a reproach to men, to a world which has denied her love and marriage, had they been her choice. As I assume they would have been. Her brother may claim he is a drone through some chance of nature, but in character he is a desiccated creature compared with his sister who is as full of life as her namesake ancestor five hundred years ago. And what conqueror, crusader, city builder would come to rescue her from this convent? Not this hunched, smelly, drunken lout, not this wretched, dying inditer of ditties, not Herr Komponist Carl Maria von Stumpf. Again I levered myself upward, and this time, with the help of the chairback, managed to stand more or less erect before her.

'Gräfin vom Faß, you have asked for my judgment. Had the gods added your form to those others Paris judged, I think his difficulties would have been doubled, quadrupled, and Troy would still be standing. I have no others before me for comparison, so my choice is made and my problem rather that of saying truly how beautiful is the vision, how overwhelming is the privilege, how cherished will be the memory.'

'Ahh, but my nudity is beside the point. My brother has offered it to you, along with what little more I have. Are you tempted?'

'Tempted, indeed, as you must know. But, you must also know, I must decline the offer. However the fates may intertwine the threads of our lives, no marriage rings are knotted there. Your brother has argued that because of my art I am above or beyond class. Indeed, I am no believer in class distinctions. But I am not the revolutionary he wishes me to be. While I have nothing but contempt for the pretensions of the mighty or the fallacies of an aristocracy by birth, and while I loathe the system which keeps down such talented commoners as share my evenings at our stammtisch at Die Drei Grafen, yet I am indifferent to class so far as it applies to me.

226

Whether I would marry an Austrian archduchess or Fat Sophie the kellnerin would depend not on honours, wealth, birth, or beauty, but perhaps on sense of humour. I think, Gräfin, you have a marvellous sense of humour. Indeed, I sometimes suspect that all the women of Waltherrott are laughing at all the men and always have been, at least since the time of Saint Adalbert, Saint Irmtraud, and the first Graf Walther. I suspect we are all clowns, and you are our audience, not often amused, but patient enough to let us caper and tumble through our pathetic routines.'

'This is an interesting theory. Do others agree with it?'

'I have never mentioned it to my stammtisch circle, nor can I tell if it is true elsewhere in Germany. Certainly some men aspire to serious greatness: Goethe was no clown, nor was Bach. I know little of other countries.'

'Perhaps one day you will travel and find out.'

'No, Gräfin, I shall stay here in Waltherrott, racing to get done my work before the last page of my calendar is turned. In a few short weeks I must finish the opera I am working on; then I shall begin a new one. Perhaps I can develop this notion of clownish men and forbearing women.'

'With such a theme it will never be produced.'

'I'll hide the theme under a lot of frothy nonsense and several hours of beguiling melody. It will be a secret.'

'To let it out would be a revolution indeed.'

'I shall dedicate it to you; my gift in return for yours.'

'I am enchanted.'

'And a final gift: I assure you the memory of this night will be mine alone: no one shall ever learn the gift you have granted me.'

'Your promise is reassuring.'

'I swear it on my honour as an artist.'

And with that I reached for the brandy, thinking to drink a toast to beauty, honour, art, whatever. As I was still standing, this was a mistake. The world turned upside down and I recall nothing else until I awoke the next day on a sad sofa in another room. The palace, I discovered, was empty, the brother and sister gone. I found my way out into the street with my hazy memories, my copy of the annals of St. Adalbert, and a hangover the size of the opera house.

And because I have wasted a day jotting down my account of that evening, I am behind in my work. Herr Intendant Wurmlein will be sending out to the Fleischmarkt, hiring bully-boys to encourage me.

The annals tell a fascinating story, one which no doubt deserves an opera, but not one I intend to write: I have no time to spend making my art conform to history; let history conform to art. As Schiller put it, 'Das Weltgericht ist die Weltgeschichte.' Or would have put it had he been a full-time playwright, and not a part-time historian as well. Besides, I have not heard the story as told by Graf Walther, Sister Irmtraud, and Sister Renate, much less the chorus of peasants, and Albrecht the Bear.

In any case, I have no idea what it all means. Is it a story of naiveté, of power, of the battle of the sexes, or of medieval Germans? For all it means to me, it might as well be a story of Canada without the snow.

No, I shall finish *Waltherrotterdämmerung* along the lines I have already mapped, and then I shall begin a new opera. I have it all in my head (of course, none of it will change in the composition, and it's merely a question of jotting it down on paper, yes, yes) complete with characters, act and scene divisions, climaxes, musical and intellectual themes, costumes, sets, lighting, whatever. The point of it will be to include all of Waltherrottner life, including the luft.

Especially the luft.

The problem is the message. Everyone expects art to have a message:

Long live the revolution!

Freedom for all the people of the earth!

Cheap bread, beer and rail tickets!

Give me a bi-cameral house with proportional representation, tripartite division of powers, abolition of the aristocracy and of ecclesiastical tax exemptions, and lower subsidies for East Prussian farmers . . . or give me death!

(Long live the Revolution: what a wonderful idea! I can just imagine how popular a long-lived revolution would be:

('Well, Gretel, glad the revolution is alive and well, are you?'

('Oh, tickled pink, Liesl, no pun intended. Of course it's a nuisance not seeing any bread since last December, and the barricades mean I have to walk three miles for a turnip, but it's all in a good cause, isn't it?'

('Yes, long live it, I say. Although I admit it would be nice if the schools were open again – after twelve hours of minding six screaming kids, I sometimes find my revolutionary fervour waning ever so slightly.'

('I know what you mean, dear. Mind you, there are benefits, as my Hans was explaining to me when he got home at three this morning: "The revolution liberated the brewery, Gretel," he said, "so that the meetings of the Revolutionary Constitutional Doctrinal Theory Committee are self-catering."'

('Yes, and they deserve a few barrels, the poor dears, after chanting slogans all day. Their throats must be parched.'

('Yes, may the revolution never end, bring on tighter rationing,' etc., etc.)

Messages? Here is my message: Art has no message!

A lie, of course, but the truth is so complicated that I've never had the time to work out the theory. As I have tried to explain to Meyerhofer, in opera it isn't a matter of stating the thing itself, but of how this thing sits next to that thing. And more: you have to be able to see those two things (and the myriad others) and their relationships to one another and to all together, but you have to be able to see them all *from above*, as it were. *From off to one side.*

The message is not the melody, but the harmonic progression.

Not the aria, but the orchestration of voice and other instruments, of words and melody, melody and story, thematic motif and character trait, movement and stasis, solo and chorus . . .

Sometimes the message is what is left out.

229

What is going to be left out of *Waltherrotterdämmerung* is any commentary or discussion about the question:

How do we live with one another?

How do we make space, time, happiness, health, concern, food, drink, shelter for ourselves and one another? That is what it is about, what all my operas are about, even though what is on stage is love and betrayal, meditations and battles, dances and marches. *Waltherrotterdämmerung* is a pageant of distant history, inaccurate so it seems, but compelling, stirring, and truthful within itself.

And the next one will also be about the same question, but it will be (I know it with complete confidence, yes, yes) a sort of comedy of love, although rather sad in the overtones.

It will make people laugh and cry at the same time.

But it will not be like other comedies I have ever heard about. None of your Beaumarchais, Shakespeare, Schiller, whatever: pure Waltherrott, pure Stumpf.

That is: overstatement, understatement, nothing what it seems, disguise, sleight of hand, audience looking one way and Stumpf scurrying for cover in the other. In fact, as much as *Waltherrotterdämmerung* ignores the annals of St. Adalbert, so much will the next one scour the Middle Ages for material, knight and lady theme, ladies to be rescued but preferring to be left alone, hands off the dumplings, Sir Kavalier, if you please, preference of plate armour between me and that wurst of yours. And because it seems we men are all clowns, a carnival of clowns: fools and grotesques gorging themselves on heaping buckets of Walthers Versuchung (surely the most disgusting dish produced in a nation of deplorable food), swigging beer by the pitcher, the pail, the hogshead, men farting hurricanes, bellowing symphonies of lust . . . and cacophonies of frustration *because the women are not clowns.*

Title:

Der Tosenkavalier, the roaring knight, rampaging in drunken lust, great moustachioed lout from Waldental; has possibilities.

Der Kosenkavalier, the caressing knight; no, Waltherrottner knights too drunk for caressing; groping more likely.

Der Hosenkavalier, knight of trousers which keep falling down in front of the women, big hit with local audience, won't do so well in Vienna.

The women. The women in this opera will be a collection, a gaggle, a battalion, a big battalion favoured of God, of nags, shrews, and teases; they'll be harpies who hold the reins, the purse strings . . . and the family jewels. But their rule will be a secret: the men will prance and snort and caper like warhorses, while in reality they are the drays, the donkeys who pull the carriage in which the women ride in style. (Speaking of which, from the sounds coming through the wall, a certain woman from the chorus of the Hofoper, Stadtoper, seems to have converted her bed to a carriage – not for the first time – and if I recognize the braying of the donkey, it is Meyerhofer; which confirms certain things.) Anyway, fair portrait of the women as presented by St. Adalbert, but reversed image of actual Irmtrauds and Renates of Waltherrott who are all sweet, gentle, loving, obedient, self-sacrificing, etc., etc.; as we all know.

Except heroine: someone special, wife to colonel, major, whatever, of the battalion; no, this is not Vienna or Berlin, lower rank, wife to sergeant, Feldwebelin. But something special, neither very young nor very beautiful – perfectly suit most lead sopranos – but also ambiguous, complicated, contradictory, a mirage, a phantasm, an illusion: that is, a living human being, something rarely seen on the stage of an opera house. Perverse notion: why do I keep producing work certain to baffle, confuse, irritate audiences? Why give them what they neither expect nor want? Why not bow before them with flattering self-portraits, tales of their own glory?

But that is exactly what I do! Yes, here are the nostalgic glories of *Waltherrotterdämmerung*: wallow in them. Tell yourselves that your distant ancestors did great deeds, waved great swords, thumped great thumps on the noggins of their neighbours, and therefore, by a logic which escapes me but which seems compelling for most people, therefore you too are glorious. That is the most transparent of a composer's tricks, obvious to all who pay attention to the niceties, the fine distinctions, the little byways of the trade.

231

But *Hosenkavalier* will be fiendishly more complicated in this sense. It will in fact be (and whatever I plan, I carry through, yes, of course!) a cunning trap for my fellow citizens. And I have a theme:

FIG. 9: Holzschuhtanz theme from *Der Hosenkavalier*, Act II.

I'll give them portraits of themselves, but in such perfect allusiveness, such perfect transparency that they'll never recognize themselves. For would I recognize myself in such a work? Ho-ho: will I recognize myself in Meyerhofer's promised biography with the limbs of widows and orphans clamped in my rapacious jaws, their blood dribbling from my chin? No, I would not, nor will my fellow bürgers recognize themselves in my opera. They'll howl in laughter at the simpletons, clowns, tarts, and drabs on the stage without realizing that the real grotesques are in the audience. And only when they begin to laugh at themselves will the beginning of recognition come. Most likely, they'll pick some honest, hard working, humourless drudge, a paragon of bürgerlich virtue without a stain on his virtuous soul, save that he has made the mistake of taking himself too seriously, of thinking he is not a clown like all the rest of us; and they will humiliate him with their laughter, destroy him with their laughter, and only when they see in him their own clownishness will they approach an understanding of *Der Hosenkavalier*, of opera, of art, of life.

232

All of which is enough nonsense for one day even for me. Meyerhofer may have the earlier volumes of this journal, but he shall not have this one so as to condemn me from my own pen: straight into the Stadtbibliothek it goes today, with orders that it be sealed from all prying eyes until after my death; thus, no more lies from Carl Maria von Stumpf.

Today . . . or tomorrow . . . more important things to do today: To Die Drei Grafen: in lager veritas!

Part Seven

DESPITE VON STUMPF'S PROMISE, there were several more pages
to the journal. But when Herr Einzelturm glanced through
them briefly, he found they were filled with musical notations, and
what writing they contained seemed to be sketches for characters
and scenes from *Waltherrotterdämmerung*; on the final page was a
brown stain which Herr Einzelturm took to be a spill of the consumptive blood which drained the composer of life. He gently
closed the cover and rose to his feet. The librarian had instructed
him to leave everything on the desk; that she would reshelve the
items. Without a further glance, he left the room, locked the door
behind him, and returned to the circulation desk with the key.

'I hope you have found what you wished, Herr Professor
Doktor Gräber?' asked the librarian.

He paused and it appeared that the answer must have been
difficult.

'What I . . . oh, yes, yes, Frau Bibliothekarin . . . everything.'

'Will we expect you to visit again?'

'No. I shall not visit again.'

As before, muted snickers and whispers followed him through
the door.

. . . ucking Franz Josef or something?

a deranged janitor, I'd say.

*a scandal that they let so many of them out on day passes: think of
the children!*

Children? . . . Sows more likely . . . sheep.

But Herr Einzelturm seemed oblivious, and walked with
thoughtful resolution. Once in the street, he paused only to consider his route, then strode off down the sloping streets of the city
which had been his home, his workplace, his life.

Our care, he reflected. *Our care these many centuries.*

And yet . . .

Avoiding the bustling Bahnhofstraße, he took a quicker route through the small streets nearer the river, streets whose charms have been ignored or belittled by the guidebooks. The Michelin Green apparently means to include this quarter under the adjective 'indifferent' which it applies to all but the grandest streets and squares of Waltherrott, while Baedeker's 'insalubrious' is so ambiguous that it might be taken as a warning against dog leavings, air pollution, muggers, or plague. Herr Reiser of the Watherrott Tourist Office can thus surely be forgiven for erring on the side of generosity when in the pamphlet *Gemütlichkeit Hopp!* he compares the area favourably with the less palatial parts of Vienna's Innenstadt.

In less than ten minutes Herr Einzelturm was back in the Geflügelstraße and entering the shop of H. Schnabernack.

'Excellent, sir,' said Herr Schnabernack. 'You wear the whiskers well; no loosening, no fraying, no slipping. The disguise is perfectly convincing.'

'Thank you. It served its purpose. But I find it is not complete.'

'A good disguise allows for a certain amount of elaboration, all within taste and discretion, you understand.'

'Elaboration I want, but you needn't worry about taste and discretion.'

'I am, if I may say so, a master of disguise, an artist.'

Herr Einzelturm looked at him with hooded lids.

'An artist? Somehow I am not surprised.'

FRAU EINZELTURM HAD SPENT her afternoon visiting friends and doing her speciality shopping. 'It is impossible to find decent chocolates in that Sonnfeld mall,' she remarked to Gisela Faulstich, offering the freshly opened box of truffles from Süßmayer, the famous chocolatier in the Bahnhofstraße. 'And we must have our little treats, mustn't we?'

'How ever could we bear it all without them?'

'Indeed. Now you must tell me all about your trip.'

'Well, in Belgium I wasn't baring my bosom, I can tell you, not like some people I could mention who went to the Seychelles.'

'Renate Krankheit has never had any sense of shame.'

'How did you ever guess? Yes, I heard it from . . . saw her at the health club, you see . . . tanned *all over*! . . .'

quite all right for young women, but
be surprised what doctors can
sagging
tucks
drooping
lifts
flopping
implants
cellulite
liposuction
not surprised

'. . . not only that, my dear, it seems there was a very attractive waiter . . .'

'Not the first.'

'There's more . . .'

'A native?'

'Of course!'

'Tell me all about it . . .'

Later, on Greta Stahlmeister's patio, Frau Einzelturm caught up on the office gossip. These worthy matrons were not intimates, but they shared opinions about the men who fussed and prattled through their lives, about the obsessions which kept the men, thank God, out of their houses, out of trouble. And from time to time they collaborated on little schemes.

The big news was that Fräulein Farber has accepted a position with the Munich Transportation Authority.

'And good riddance to her,' said Frau Stahlmeister. 'I've always been suspicious of her and her hemlines.'

'Yes, so innocent behind those big spectacles. Still, I've never heard a hint of gossip . . .'

237

'Except with Wassertor in public relations, surely?'

'Well, yes, but he wouldn't be safe with a bus: he'd be bothering the exhaust pipe!'

They had a little laugh over that picture.

'And how is your stay in the Bergwald?' asked Frau Stahlmeister.

'Restful. *He* takes long walks every day. And I have my amusements.'

'Very pleasant.'

'Yes, but it will soon be time to come home. There is work to do: we can't leave them at loose ends.'

'Exactly. Have you any ideas?'

Frau Stahlmeister had a few of her own, but she knew better than to push them in front of Frau Einzelturm.

'Yes, I have been thinking about opera.'

I am not surprised, thought Frau Stahlmeister, but she held her tongue.

'A number of cities have festivals – Salzburg, Bayreuth, Edinburgh. They must be very difficult to organize.'

'I should think so. And expensive, surely?'

'Yes, but these things always have subsidies. Getting them would be very time-consuming. The organizers would have to spend thousands of hours meeting with state and federal officials to arrange the subsidies. Then there would be travel, accommodations, advertising. And if it becomes a success, there would be new theatres and hotels and a concert hall and all manner of diversions.'

'But – forgive me – this doesn't sound like a job for the WVV.'

'Not directly, no. But I expect, don't you, that, for the first few years at least, much of the work would be by volunteers – city officials experienced in complex administrative projects who would be donating their spare time to the arts.'

'We would have to work through Renate Krankheit.'

'Don't worry: I can handle her.'

'Yes.'

238

Frau Stahlmeister considered the idea: it was brilliant, far better than her weak efforts. Irmtraud Einzelturm was . . . well . . . the only word for her, redoubtable.

'Yes,' she repeated, 'I think you have it. Again.'

THE STAGE DOOR of the Waltherrottner Stadtoper is reached from the laneway behind. This laneway is also used as a garbage deposit by the Stadtoper and by the shops and restuarants in the next street, so that the first impression guest artists receive is often disagreeable.

they don't really expect us to
I mean to say, in Vienna
I'm afraid they do
always tingle during that magical stroll from Sacher's
glad someone can afford Sacher's
admit you have to beware of the fiacres, but
a matter of civic pride as in Frankfurt or Düsseldorf

But such cavilling is specious: opera houses are relative latecomers to cities, and many of Europe's greatest – La Fenice and Covent Garden, for example – have had to be squeezed inconveniently into corners of their cities. If civic pride alone were the determining factor, Waltherott would set the Stadtoper in a paradise of gardens, avenues, fountains, statues, promenades, and plazas. But the Waltherrottners do not waste time on idle dreams: here it stands, here it stays. They are happy enough to have the front of the Stadtoper facing its own square – surely one of the most perfect in Germany, never mind the guide books – and if the pleasure the citizens enjoy from having it in the centre of the city means some displeasure to visiting artists then so be it: 'No wife without warts, no life without farts,' as they say in Waltherrott. For the Waltherrottners above all are realists.

But the clown who made his way along the lane that golden autumn day was touched by a concern, a reality that had little to do with the bins overflowing with vegetable parings and gollops of uneaten Walthers Versuchung. The clown wore a common enough costume: large floppy shoes, a baggy polka dot suit in garnet and gold with a garnet ruff about the neck, and a pointed gold hat.

With a tentative yet dogged push, he tried the large steel doors of the equipment bay (they had to be opened from within), and blinked at the sign on the basement maintenance door:

EINTRITT VERBOTEN!

NUR FÜR

AUTORISIERTE BELEGSCHAFT!

Surely he was authorized? But no, he remembered, he was not authorized, not here.

The stage door was up a few steps in an alcove. Beside it was a small window. The clown pushed the bell button and a face appeared briefly in the window; a buzz indicated the door was unlocked and the clown stepped in. The old doorman peered from his cubby hole and asked through his walrus mustache:

'What do you want?'

'I wish to see the person in charge of hiring performers.'

'Which one – the Intendant or the Chorus Master?'

'What is the difference?'

'If you don't know the difference you want the Chorus Master. He's not here.'

'I shall wait.'

'You'll need a bed, then: he's in Salzburg for the weekend.'

The doorman regarded the clown's turned-down mouth and droopy eyes, the shoulders slumped in dejection.

'Most of them are gone, actually. *Lucia* finished last Saturday and *Wozzeck* doesn't go into rehearsal until Wednesday.'

The clown rubbed his eyes and pushed his spectacles back on his nose.

'Come into my office,' the doorman said, opening the Dutch door. 'Have some coffee.'

The tiny room was so filled with clutter that there seemed barely space for the doorman on his stool, but the clown found a

240

chair between a locker and the door, squeezed himself into it, and tried to tuck his great shoes beneath.

'Cream? Sugar? It's good, I just made it, hope you don't mind the chipped mug. I always have mine in this one, Fräulein Puppel gave it to me after her debut as Fiordiligi in *Così*. A nice girl is Fräulein Puppel, not like some . . .'

He babbled on, fussing with the coffee, letting the clown settle in with a few sips. The doorman lifted himself onto a stool. After a pause he said:

'You're not a regular, are you. Not on the roster.'

'No.'

'Been on the stage, before? The Sonnfeld Light Opera, perhaps? The University Opera?'

'No.'

'Ahh. Well, that makes it a bit of a problem, doesn't it. It's not that it's a closed shop, but there are procedures. Start small, get your name on the roster, work your way up. Where have you sung?'

'I do not sing.'

'A dancer, then?'

'I do not dance.'

'And you aren't a musician, not dressed like that. Though a good many musicians are clowns, you'd be surprised.'

'I thought I might be useful as a spare . . . a supernumerary.'

'A spear carrier. Yes, well . . .'

'I did not think of carrying a spear. I am dressed as . . . I am a clown.'

'No, "spear carrier" is just a way of saying "extra", someone who comes on stage to fill out the ranks in big scenes, spear or no spear.'

A man in coveralls stuck his head in the door.

'Still sitting on it, Stein?' he asked.

'Yes, and I'm going to get Fräulein Kirschen from set design to paint your face on it.'

'You'll get a tickle out of that.'

This was evidently a reference to the workman's beard.

'Or your wife's,' added the doorman.

241

'Wouldn't look like her – your equipment isn't big enough for her nose.'

'It was big enough for the other end of her.'

'Then you got the wrong hole,' quipped the workman as he left. That Waltherrottner Luft!

The doorman made a note on his clipboard and continued:

'Trouble is, the company has its roster of extras, you see. Regulars there too. They have to be careful, don't they? Can't have drunks, they aren't dependable, the curtain comes up on the triumphal return in Act II of *Waltherrotterdämmerung* and half the townsfolk are down at Die Drei Grafen getting a skinful, can't have that.

'And there are the men who think all girls on stage are free with their favours. But I'll tell you the truth: they're just like shopgirls or housewives. Well, not just like, because they're artists, they can sing, they work hard, and they have their dreams of getting to centre stage, but in their lives, I mean, they're like any other girl down the Bahnhofstraße window shopping for a new pair of shoes. When everyone is out there, when the show is on, there's magic on the stage and dreams do come true, I'd be the first to admit it. But in their real lives the girls laugh and work and sweat just like any other girls. Not that they're all girls, either, half a dozen at least are grandmothers. So you see . . .'

'I am not interested in girls.'

The doorman stroked his mustache.

'Ahh. Well now, if it's . . . I mean . . .'

'I am not interested in boys, either. Do I look like a pervert?'

'Of course not, no, I can see you're a respectable man, sir, quite the regular sort of gent, not of the . . . other sort. Though it's not always easy to tell, you'd be surprised. And, speaking frankly, sir, I wouldn't take such a strong line on . . . the boys if I wanted to find a place in the company. There's a lot of that in the opera world, you know. Not like ballet, of course, but they're often sensitive, the boys, artistic. They often go together, sensitivity and . . . the boys.'

'You are right.'

The clown gazed at the wastebasket; it was filled with used coffee filters.

'I apologize,' he said. 'I am not in a position to judge.'

'Very wise, sir. Live and let live, that's the motto around here. As long as they can hold a tune and get to their places without tripping over the diva's gown, who's to question their private inclinations, eh?'

'Live and let live. Yes.'

'It makes things go more smoothly, doesn't it? And that's the point, you see. The show must go on, and you might be surprised at the things that can go wrong. Sets collapse, lights blow, trap doors open when they shouldn't, curtains don't open when they should, and still the show must go on. Now, with that kind of trouble from *things*, the last thing you want is trouble from *people*. And opera does attract some troublesome ones, let me tell you. A few years ago we had a fellow in the chorus, seemed a decent sort, no drink, no wandering hands, with us a few years and everything as regular as my bowels. In time, Herr Wurmlein gave him a few small parts, but the lad thought he had more to give. He had this need, you see, to express himself. So one night he steps forward during a solo – don't remember the show, *Meistersinger* perhaps, I was here in my office – anyway, he pushes the tenor aside and begins to sing the part himself!'

'Shocking.'

'Well, yes, but at least he tried to sing his way to glory. There was the girl who also had a dream to offer, and she tried a different short-cut. This was during a duet with peasants or priestesses, whatever, in the background. I was also back here during this one, wish I'd seen it. At any rate, our young lady is upstage leaning against a temple or something, wearing a long gown. Now picture this, sir: the soprano and the tenor are tootling away downstage centre, lights on them, of course, and a very touching scene. But they begin to sense something is wrong somewhere. They carry on, but begin to glance around, trying to see if the horse is doing his business or a door has opened and there's three stagehands playing cards. It doesn't take them long to see that it's our young lady extra who is slowly pulling up the hem of her gown. Already it's at the knees, now it's creeping up the thighs and heading for heaven – which it gets to at the climax of the duet. They're hitting their high Cs or whatever, and everyone in the house is watching as the young lady jerks the hem the final stretch to her waist. And I'm sure I don't need to tell you what she was wearing next to her skin, do I?'

'Nothing?'

'Not a stitch, sir. Of course, you can see all that and more for the price of a beer in any of those joints down toward the Bahnhof, but you don't expect to see it on stage at the Stadtoper, do you?'

'No.'

'And of course even the immortal Carl Maria could be difficult at times.'

'You don't say.'

'Oh yes, hit the bottle, I hear . . . women, brawls, all-night carousings, the usual things. But the pain they suffer, the obsession – it's like a madness, they say. But genius and madness live up the same stairs, as my old mum used to say.'

'How true . . .'

'Even the audience gets into the act sometimes. Why just this summer some special guest gave a speech one night at the end of *Hosenkavalier*' – he tapped the August block of the schedule taped to the wall – 'and got the audience howling with laughter. I never did make out what it was all about, something about the trams, I never use them, live a few streets off at The Pig's Trotter, I can walk everywhere, but whatever he said it took an extra half hour to get the seats cleared. Cost a fortune in overtime and some people missed their rides home and so on. We have our routines here, you see, and that fellow put everything off balance.'

'Off balance, yes.'

'Yes. So you see, we have to be careful.'

'Of course.'

The clown's shoes had crept out from under his chair; he pushed them back.

244

'Not that I think you . . . well, I'm sure you're sincere. And some shows need clowns. Happy clowns, sad clowns, tumbling clowns, juggling clowns. Can you tumble or juggle?'

'Well . . . no . . . that is, I haven't tried.'

'There you are, then. If I were you, sir, I'd take some time to practise, work up some routines that might come in handy on stage. They're always looking for some business or other for crowd scenes. Though I'd stay away from the tumbling, if I were you, we're not getting any younger, you and I, are we? And we don't want to be riding unicycles or climbing up any stacks of chairs at our age, do we?'

'That is true.'

'But you might try some juggling, sir. Balls or rings, something simple, don't go for spinning plates on sticks, they'd be too distracting on an opera stage, just a bit of a flurry for a few seconds is all they're likely to want.'

'Very sensible.'

'Yes. But your cup is empty, sir. Will you . . .'

'No, no, thank you. I have taken up too much of your valuable time as it is. I must be off. Thank you for the coffee and for the advice. It has been most valuable.'

'My pleasure, sir.'

'I shall heed your suggestions.'

'And perhaps you want to try one of the amateur companies. The Sonnfeld people would probably welcome you. Let me just see . . . it's here somewhere . . .'

The doorman shuffled through a mound of paper on the shelf next to the coffee maker; he found a brochure and offered it.

'It would be a start, sir, a place to discover your talents and then to develop them. I know that Herr Wurmlein always tries to take in a performance of every show they do, looking out for fresh talents, you see.'

The clown opened the brochure then closed it. When he tried to stow it, he found the costume had no pockets.

'This will be very useful. Thank you.'

'And you'd build confidence working with others. That's the important thing, to become a part of the company, to make things all work together as a team, everyone in his place, doing what's proper according to his talents and his training, eh?'

'I can work as part of a team.'

'Just the thing, sir. And of course the work is not all beer and gemütlichkeit. It's hard work, very hard, everyone taking endless pains to get it just right.'

'I can work hard.'

'Well then, you have that to start with, don't you? Of course, it is also hard work being a clown. Folk think it's all head-in-the clouds dreaming, but really the dream is beneath your feet, you jump down into it, splash about it in: you have to live in it, get comfortable enough that the dream holds you up, you make it your everyday work, your life. Then, out of all the planning, the rehearsals, the false starts, the sweat, the arguments, the tears, the new directions, the compromises, the discoveries, the dream comes into being. Folk are in their seats, the lights come up, and the curtain rises, and . . . it's all make-believe . . . all a dream.'

'That is it, the very thing. I have done hard work, I have been part of a team. Now I am here, I am as you see me. I wish to make dreams.'

'Of course you do, sir, people need dreams, don't they, but perhaps they don't dream too well on their own. So they need someone to make dreams for them, they do, or the opera would die. And it is a privilege to be a part of it.'

'Yes.'

The clown stuffed the brochure up his sleeve.

'A privilege even if you're only sitting behind this window as a doorman like me, or dressed as . . .'

The clown arose.

'A clown. I am a clown.'

'Yes.'

THE DELIGHTS of her visits accomplished, Frau Einzelturm treated herself to a pastry on the terrace of the Renatenhof. She had arranged to meet her husband here at five; the snack eaten, and with half an hour to spare, she ordered another coffee and began the crossword puzzle in *Brigitta*. Her skill was so fluent that she gave the puzzle only some of her attention, bending the greater part to scrutinizing the passing scene, and to blocking out the selection of von Stumpf's melodies which the small band was playing from the balcony of the Stadtoper. Buskers of various sorts also offered entertainment around the square – an automaton, a sidewalk chalk artist, a juggler, and a clown.

This was satisfaction. To sit here on this golden day, without a care, in this square in the heart of her home town: what more could she ask?

She exchanged greetings with a couple crossing toward Bahnhofstraße, the Ditschlers who lived along her street. A young woman leaving the inner coffee room smiled and nodded to her – one of the tellers at the bank, she remembered.

Indeed, the scene was so peaceful, so stable, so reassuring, that one sometimes forgot the hidden tensions which . . .

The comptroller of the WVV, Herr Wechsel, and his wife, stopped by for a few words. They were going in to dinner, then to the theatre.

'. . . middle of the second act and you're dreaming of a heaping plate of Walthers Versuchung . . .'

'. . . told them I do not eat "fast chicken!"'

'. . . and our best wishes to Herr Einzelturm.'

'Thank you.'

. . . the hidden tensions which . . .

The clown caught her attention because he seemed different somehow, awkward, inept. He (or was this perhaps a she, a clowness?) stood irresolutely before the fountain. He picked up several small objects, stones perhaps, and tried to juggle them, but they fell at once. He appeared to consider a forward somersault, but thought better of it. At last, as the band swung into the beloved

Holzschuhtanz from *Der Hosenkavalier*, he began an ungainly shuf-
fle, waving his arms, flapping his feet, and heaving his great bulk
about like a bear, a pudding, a quaggy bucket of Walthers
Versuchung. But before the dance was done, the clown stopped to
catch his breath, and Frau Einzelturm might have returned to her
crossword, save for the gesture the clown made of reaching under
his spectacles to rub his eyes, then pushing his spectacles up onto
the bridge of his nose. She hastily threw some coins onto the saucer,
stuffed the magazine into her shopping bag, and strode out into the
Opernplatz.

The late afternoon sun bathed the square in a soft, seductive
glow. Where were the guidebook writers now? Surely, like Herr
Reiser of the Tourist board, they would find words tripping from
their pens as they stepped 'through this light like liquid champagne?' Surely the buildings were 'never more elegant': the lively
Renatenhof with the tall windows of the bar and the restaurant
beckoning passers-by to 'an evening of romance or amusement'; the
Residenz with its 'assurance that Waltherrott built as elegantly as Vienna, Munich, or Dresden'; the Corinthian pillars of the university
with their 'evocation of classical learning and wisdom'; and finally
with the 'exuberant' band playing from 'the Stadtoper, beloved soul
of this sanctuary of artistic high spirits, whimsy, and poignant love
for all that is noblest in the noblest of all Creation's creatures.' Surely
the guidebooks could have phrased it so?

Frau Einzelturm stopped before the clown and peered closely
into his eyes, searching for the face beneath the make-up.

'Well?' she asked when she was sure, 'What sort of nightmare
notion is this?'

The clown shuffled his great floppy shoes.

'I am come to be myself.'

The painted mouth so offended Frau Einzelturm that she was
about to strike it from his face with her shopping bag. But then she
noticed the tear starting from the corner of his eye. She reached up
and, taking care not to smudge his mascara, lifted the tear away. As
she did, she felt a tear in her own eye.

'Yes,' she said softly, 'Yes, I see.'

The clown struggled to find words.

'It is . . . it is a dream . . . I wish to make a dream.'

She took his hand in hers.

'Not this dream,' she said. 'Not here. Not now.'

Gently she pushed his spectacles back up his nose.

'Somewhere? Sometime?'

'We'll see . . .'

All about them the air sparkled with that special tingle, that radiance, that Waltherrottner Luft; and through it floated the music of Carl Maria von Stumpf.

'Well . . .'

Hand in hand, Frau and Herr Einzelturm walked away.

Acknowledgements

Over several years during the writing of this book I received invaluable help from The Canada Council and The Scottish Arts Council; to them I return my sincere thanks.

I should also like to express my gratitude to Anthony Advokaat and Walter Larink of the Canadian Embassy in Bonn for the advice and assistance I received while doing research for the novel in the Federal Republic of Germany.

I must also add thanks and warmest greetings to Frau Bibliotekarin Kristena Kaulbach and her staff at the Waltherrott Stadtbibliotek without whose generous help I could not have assembled this bizarre account.

I alone can be held responsible for the undoubtedly questionable translations from German. As Schiller so aptly puts it: Mit der Dummheit kämpfen Götter selbst vergebens. (The stupid struggle in vain with God.)

Readers knowledgeable in the conventions of typesetting will have noticed that non-English words are not italicized. That is, no languages are emphasized as being outlandish or foreign, let alone illegal. The Waltherrottners are a genial people; Waltherrott is a distinct society.

A native of Mabou, Cape Breton, Ray Smith has lived
in Montreal since 1968, where he teaches English litera-
ture at Dawson college. In addition to *A Night at the
Opera* (winner of the 1992 QSPELL Hugh MacLennan
Prize for Fiction), Smith is the author of *Cape Breton is
the Thought-Control Centre of Canada* and the novels
Lord Nelson Tavern, *Century*, *The Man Who Loved Jane
Austen*, and most recently *The Man Who Hated Emily
Bronte*. A new novel, *The Flush of Victory: Jack Bottomly
Among the Virgins*, will be published in spring 2007 and
is the first in a projected series of Bottomly misadven-
tures. (PHOTO: BURT COVIT)